DUDLEY PUBLIC LIBRARIES

The loan of this book may be renewed if not required by other readers, by contacting the library from which it was borrowed.

Millie vs the Machines

Kiera O'Brien

Quercus

First published in Great Britain in 2015 by

Quercus Publishing Ltd
Carmelite House
50 Victoria Embankment
London EC4Y 0DZ

An Hachette UK company

A CIP catalogue record for this book is available
from the British Library

PB 978 1 84866 9 550
EBOOK 978 1 84866 8 430

10 9 8 7 6 5 4 3 2 1

Printed and bound in Great Britain by Clays Ltd, St Ives plc

*For my grandma, who trusted technology
about as much as Millie does.*

London, 2098

I gaped at the screen above me. The six-second film looped over and over again, and I understood it less each time. The crowd ebbed and flowed around me, but I was frozen to the spot, goggling, until a woman barged into me.

'Oh, sorry—' I started to say, but then I saw her T-shirt. And then suddenly it seemed the same image was everywhere: staring out at me from the sky, winking through the crowd, shoving itself right up into my face.

I needed to find Jake. He'd made me come to the rally – he was the one interested in unit rights, after all; I wasn't particularly bothered if they were free or not – and now he'd abandoned me. He knew all the people involved in the Artificial Intelligence Rights campaign group. I wouldn't be surprised if he was best friends with all the

1

units here too. But I didn't care. I didn't know anyone and I knew Ms Llewellyn was going to work out we weren't with the rest of our history class any minute now. And then we'd be in trouble.

Jake had said we'd stay for the first speech. On the stage in front of me, a stocky man was walking out to the podium. I had to find Jake before he finished speaking, otherwise we'd never leave.

The man threw his arms wide. 'Welcome, everyone—'

A scream and a bang like a gunshot filled the air and deafened me and the ground shook like it was trying to throw me off it. People were screaming and the last thing I saw was the two giant screens falling towards me . . .

One

The sunlight filters into the dormitory and through my closed eyelids. I know it's time to wake up, but I'm still struggling out of a dream involving a maths exam and my shoes turning into fidgety rabbits. I roll over and wrench my eyes open – and suddenly jolt upright, my heart in my throat. There's a unit leaning over me.

It looks back at me as I stare at it – its blank inhuman gaze holds mine, then it slowly goes back to sweeping the floor under my bedside table. *The crowd closing in, the brush of metal against my arm, the screen above me . . .* It's just a cleanbot, I tell myself. They have to come into the dormitories sometimes. The unit clanks along the room away from me, its boxy silver frame glinting in the morning light, but I don't move. I clutch the covers round me.

3

Lu, on the other side of the dormitory, sits up, stretching.

'Morning, Millie,' she says, her eyes half closed, as she gets up, walks past the cleanbot and goes into the bathroom.

Whirring quietly the bot finally sweeps its way out of the room, and I slowly let out a breath I hadn't realised I was holding. I can't see one without those fragments of memory resurfacing in my head – I just don't know what they mean.

I stretch until my joints click, then log on to my Retina-Chip with a flick of my finger. My timeline maps out across my left eye, suddenly full of action now everyone around me is getting up.

Nick Hayes is brushing his teeth.

Riley Thomas tagged you in a brainstream.

Charlie Rowan is heading to the library early today.

Lu Shipley has nearly finished the set text for English lit!

Out of habit I scroll quickly past the nationwide news posts, but the morning update from the Look makes me stop.

'Today's hot colour is *fawn*! Everyone across your network is wearing dresses, tops, shirts, skirts, trousers and jackets in this versatile neutral colour! A selection of outfits based on your previous choices is hanging in your wardrobe.'

By 'fawn' I assume they mean beige. I love the way they always try to sell it to us, as if we would ever choose

4

something else. They say every colour is versatile. I remember one day pink-and-white candy stripes were in; the email claimed they would 'sweeten up your day'. The email lied. But we all wore them anyway.

I hop up from bed and look inside my wardrobe, and sure enough a beige T-shirt dress, a beige striped top, a beige pair of leggings and a choice of beige shoes are inside. Changing out of my temperature-controlled sleep-suit and pulling on the dress, I can see fawn clearly isn't as versatile as the Look seems to think. The mirror-me looks like a corpse.

Although maybe it's not so much the dress and more the bags under my eyes or the greyish tinge to my skin. Even my blonde hair looks pallid. I rub my sore eyes in an attempt to make them look less pink, but it doesn't help. I keep jumping awake in the middle of the night, surfacing from weird dreams, convinced, for a second, that I've remembered everything about what happened last autumn, but it always fades away quickly.

I smooth my hair flat against my skull; I know the stitches don't show any more, but I can always feel them.

'Shell,' I say to the lump under the cover in the bed opposite me. 'Does this dress make me look like I might be about to throw up?'

She pulls the cover off her face but I can see she's still logged on to her RetinaChip. She has that focused-yet-unfocused stare people get when they read something projected on to their left eyeball.

'Oh, Millie,' she says, and just from those two words I can tell we're going to be very late for breakfast. 'Megan Wickham's run more cross-country miles than me! She's going to snatch the long-distance-running prize right from under my nose!'

'What?' I say. 'When?'

'She must have got up early this morning to get her total up,' says Shell as I log back on to the network and scroll through. 'Who *does* that?'

There it is. *Megan Wickham has just run 5 miles. Miles run this school year: 692.*

'Oh, Shell,' I say. 'There's still two weeks to the ball and the prize-giving ceremony and you're only about three miles behind—'

'Two weeks of *revision*! And then exams!' says Shell, slumping down further into her covers. 'Stupid Megan Wickham. With her perfect hair. Why does she have to be the best at everything?'

'Shall we get ready?' I say to distract her. She's become increasingly intense about getting at least one end-of-year prize, ever since lacrosse was cancelled. 'It's beige today; it's supposed to be a versatile neutral.'

Shell can spend ages getting ready for the day. She brushes neon-pink or coral hair powder all over her silvery blonde hair, puts iris drops in her eyes so they turn from greyish green to an intense violet, and applies tiny gems to her collarbone, wrists and sometimes up and down her fingers, if she's particularly hell-bent on being late. (I usually just smooth my hair down so it looks neat, and slick on my eyelash fibres as quickly as possible. Then I spend about ten minutes applying tiny gems to my nails. It's a diversionary tactic. Otherwise I end up with bitten stumps.)

So I know Shell must be really upset when she simply puts on a beige skirt and vest top, pins her hair in a knot and listlessly slaps on some vitamin cream.

'There,' she says grumpily. 'Let's just go to breakfast.'

Before we leave I quickly pull my bedcovers neatly over my bed and plump my pillows, while Shell sighs and taps her foot. Her bedcovers are always left in a crumpled heap in the mornings. Lu, her dark hair still damp from the shower, tries to help Shell see the positive side. 'If you ran, like, a hundred miles in one go, she'd never beat you!' she says brightly.

Riley, who has put beige iris drops in her eyes in honour of today's colour, catches up with us as we leave the dormitory for breakfast. She's annoyed about the end-of-year prizes too.

'Unless I find out what the world-culture exam is going to be on, I'm only going to come top in about six subjects,' she says, as Shell's mouth sets into a line. 'That'll be three less prizes than last year!'

Finn and Nick meet us outside their dormitory on the floor below. Finn, who's gelled his hair into a style I can only assume was inspired by an ocean wave crashing against the surf, says, 'Wow, fawn really isn't your colour, is it, Millie?'

'Good morning to you too, Finn.'

'Oh, leave her alone,' Shell says. 'She can't exactly wear something else, can she?'

'I don't get why you always wear what the Look tells you to, no matter what it is,' Finn says, shaking his head. 'Girls.'

Finn has worn the day's colour every day since we were all babies in the nursery together thirteen years ago. Today he's wearing a beige T-shirt, a beige hoodie, beige trousers, beige trainers with beige laces and even has a beige skin on his tablet.

I look him up and down and laugh. 'Er, excuse me?'

'What? I just happen to like this colour,' he says defensively.

'Nick, are those *jeans*?' asks Shell.

'I think so,' Nick says, sticking one leg out for our consideration. 'They feel like it. Denim-y.'

'You are so lucky with your wardrobe!' says Lu.

Nick started getting natural fibres in his wardrobe about the same time his mum got promoted to creative director of the Woodland River Centre, the Company's biggest mall. I mean, I'm not saying anything. I'm really not.

There's a path from Hawthorn house leading to the courtyard at the centre of the school, and there's a path from the courtyard to the white domed canteen building, but I don't think I've ever walked from one to the other without cutting across the lawn. Our feet naturally follow the furrow in the grass trodden in by hundreds of pupils before us.

'I can't wait for this day to be over,' says Shell, stretching her arms up.

'Why?' says Nick flatly. 'Just one more day of lessons then we get to revise for a week. Woo.'

'No, we're finally getting our dresses for the ball!' says Shell. 'Tomorrow's the appointment at the Look, with the custom pods. It's going to be toxic! Just thinking about it is cheering me up!'

'Why do you need cheering up?' says Finn.

Shell takes a deep breath, about to launch into one of her you'll-never-guess-what-Megan-Wickham-has-done-this-time rants, when Lu cuts across her.

'Look – the babies are here,' she says, pointing across the grounds.

A line of seven-year-olds, every one of them looking around with wide eyes like they're animals trapped in a zoo, snakes across the front of the library. Every summer the children about to start their first year at the school have a special visit day, when the head teacher Dr Cranshaw shows them round.

'Remember our visit day?' says Shell. 'It seems like a thousand years ago now.'

'I was about to say it feels like it was five minutes ago,' I say.

'That shows how awful your memory is!' says Riley.

Then her hand goes to her mouth. 'Sorry . . .' she says, her eyes wide. 'I didn't mean . . . I know your head thing isn't funny . . .'

'Oh, it's OK!' I say quickly. It is funny how I can remember that first visit to Oaktree six years ago perfectly clearly, but I couldn't say what formula we learned in maths the other day or anything about the Industrial Revolution, which we've been studying all term.

Compared to our nursery school, Heathersdown, Oaktree was enormous. The school grounds had seemed to stretch on forever and the buildings towered over us. My heart had started thumping as soon as we trailed into the courtyard. I was so nervous I felt slightly breathless. We had to line up in alphabetical order, and even though Jake was technically before me in the alphabet, we walked together, hands clasped, occupying one space. The Hendrick twins.

We don't really look alike now – Jake's taller than me these days and his hair is darker – but we really did back then. If my hair was pulled back in a ponytail, our own parents could easily get us mixed up. Of course, anyone who actually knew us well was never fooled. Even then I kept my clothes uncreased, my shoes clean and my hair smoothed down, while Jake always seemed uncomfortable if he wasn't caked head to toe in mud or dirt and his hair constantly stood up in tufts, as unruly as mine could have been if I'd let it. Even on that visit day, he had squirmed simply with the effort of wearing clean clothes and standing still.

Shell had been nearer the front of the queue. Her blonde head bobbed along in front as she walked, not swishing back and forth as confidently as usual. I could hear Lu, just behind me, chewing her hair.

Jake kept trying to wrench his hand from mine but I held on. 'It'll be fine, Millie,' he kept saying. 'Cranshaw's not that scary.'

'She scares me,' I said.

Jake was the only one of us who didn't seem to be at all nervous. But there were no teachers like Cranshaw at Heathersdown. With her huge puff of white hair she seemed to be about a hundred years old and, though she smiled at us, it felt as though she could switch to anger in a heartbeat if any of us crossed her.

'I wonder where her unit assistant is?' Jake whispered to me as Cranshaw welcomed us. 'I wanted to see it. Florrie. I've never even heard of a unit with a name before—'

'Shush,' I said.

Jake had bounced up and down on his heels all the way through her talk about the history of the school buildings; I kept tugging on his hand, trying to get him to keep still. I was terrified she'd notice and tell us off.

'Any questions?' she asked, clearly not expecting a response. Jake's hand shot straight up.

'Jake, don't!' I said, but he was already talking.

'Is it true there's an unexploded bomb from World War Two under your office?' he asked.

His voice carried clearly across the heads of all the

11

other pupils, and Cranshaw's face froze. The air stood still. I remember seeing Shell's face along the queue – her eyes widened with a combination of hilarity and horror. Then Cranshaw smiled.

'What's your name, young man?' she said.

'Jake Hendrick,' he replied.

'Well, that's a very honest question, Jake,' Cranshaw said, her voice suddenly warmer. 'Would you like to come and stand up at the front by me?'

Jake pulled his hand out of mine and ran towards the front . . .

'Millie, what do you think?' Riley's saying.

'Oh, sorry,' I say, shaking off the memory. 'What were we talking about?'

Lu points across the ground to the nursery-school pupils. 'Cranshaw's not leading them.'

I focus and she's right; Harrison, the Mandarin teacher, is at the front of the queue of small children, his bald head catching the sunlight.

'Maybe she's just busy,' I say, 'talking to the Company's board or something.'

'Maybe she's choosing *her* dress for the ball,' says Finn.

Lu gets the giggles first, then Shell, then me and Finn and Nick, and even Riley start laughing.

'Cranshaw . . . in a ball dress!' Shell squeaks.

'She could wrap fairy lights around Florrie,' Lu says, which sets everyone off again.

The canteen is always really busy in the mornings, as

it seems everyone leaves the shortest amount of time possible between waking up and getting to lessons.

'I don't know why they don't do hazelnut mudge every day. It's so good,' Shell says as we walk in.

'Oh, I think I'm going for natural food today. There are eggs,' I say.

Shell rolls her eyes. 'Yum, eggs.'

'Oh yeah, because *mudge* is such a delight to the palate!' I say as she moves away, laughing.

There are two queues. One is for the mudge machines, which scan your IndexChip and, based on your height, weight, gender and nutritional deficiencies, produce an edible substance with the correct balance of macronutrients and essential vitamins for your body. The other is for naturally produced food, which is portioned out to contain a good balance of protein, carbohydrate and fat. The mudge machines are much more popular and the queue is at least ten-people long as we walk in. You have the option of taking it in solid cubes or liquid, and it always comes in a sweet flavour and a savoury one. Today it's hazelnut or sage.

The queue for natural food is much shorter. Only Jess Turner is ahead of me, dressed in bright orange so everyone knows what an individual she is. She glares at me, sneers at my beige ballet pumps and then smiles simperingly at the foodbot dishing out poached eggs, asparagus and a wheatgerm cake on to her plate, probably just to prove that she thinks of it as a real person.

13

'Thanks!' she says in a weirdly high voice. The food-bot doesn't react. Jess pauses for a few awkward seconds, clearly waiting for a response. I stifle a laugh and she glares at me again and flounces off.

The foodbot starts loading eggs and asparagus on to my plate. It's designed so its square upper body can turn and scoop with its lower body planted on the floor for maximum efficiency. There's no real reason for it to have a human-like face though. I don't know why the Company builds them like that. They can't form expressions. As I reach out to take the plate, the bot looks right into my eyes and blinks slowly, its eyelids shifting like a doll's. It's so close I can hear the machinery moving around inside it. Automatically I flinch, whipping my hand away from the plate. It bounces on the metal tray and the food spills all over the floor.

'It won't bite you, Millie,' someone behind me says.

I know who it is before I turn round. Jake. He half raises his eyebrows at me.

I look at him very steadily for a long moment. Then I bend down slowly and pick up the plate from the floor, and in one swift movement I smash it over his head.

OK, I don't really. But I can't stop playing the image in my head; my fingers itch with the urge to reach down to the plate. The anger boils up inside me like an overflowing kettle. If only I knew *why*. I curl my hands into fists, glare at him and abruptly spin round.

'Millie?' he calls after me. 'You're going to have to talk to me at some point—'

I don't know why this happens. Ever since I injured my head in London, when I got hit by a car – not that I can remember anything about it – I can't look at or talk to or be near Jake without wanting to throttle him. He wasn't even with me that day. And he's angry with me too for some reason. There are so many gaps in my memory, before and after the accident, that I don't even know who did or said what to whom. And that's not the only weird side effect of my head injury.

I reach Shell, who's waiting for me by the drinks fridge, eating cubed mudge from a box. 'Shall we eat outside today?' I say. 'I don't think there's many spare seats.'

Shell looks towards the eight empty tables on the far side of the canteen, and then looks at me. 'You don't have any food.'

'Oh yeah,' I say, 'I'm not that hungry after all. Let's go and sit outside.'

'All right then,' says Shell. 'I'll message the others and tell them where we're going.' She logs on to her RetinaChip.

'Shell, seriously, they're about five metres away,' I say. 'Can't we just wave and point?'

Shell logs off her chip and rolls her eyes at me. 'It's done now!'

Outside in the courtyard, the sky is a solid blue. If you squint, you can see the weather adapters far above, glinting in the sunlight like stars at night, which disperse rain clouds and manage the temperature. Sunny with a gentle breeze is a classic Friday, after Thursday's rain and before the temperatures increase slightly for the weekend.

The grass has dried out after yesterday's downpour, so we sit under the massive oak tree in the middle of the courtyard. Of the five oak trees left in Britain, it's said to be the oldest and the only one not in an arboretum. The Company actually built the school around the tree, so it must be at least a hundred years old. In one direction from the tree, you can see all the way across the school's grounds to the row of trees in the distance that indicate the border. In the other, you face the three school buildings that make up the courtyard. The Company designed them – and the six dormitory blocks behind them – to look like a proper old-time boarding school, unluckily for us. Apparently some other Company schools have jet packs, travelators and anti-gravity classrooms. We're all very jealous.

We sit on one of the tree's huge roots and Shell offers me a cube of mudge. 'Can you believe the summer holidays are almost here?'

'No,' I say. I really can't. I haven't caught up since last November.

'Yeah, and the ball and the prize-giving ceremony, when I will be receiving exactly no prizes,' Shell says. 'Stupid Megan Wickham.'

'Shell, does it really matter that much?' I say. 'Are the end-of-year prizes really so important?'

Shell looks at me wide-eyed. 'Yes!' she says. 'Of course they are!'

'But they don't actually mean anything,' I say. 'It's just a little statue to put on your bedside table—'

'Well, it's important to me,' says Shell. 'You're fine, you know you'll win the maths prize—'

'Hmmm,' I say. I managed to forget the seven times table the other day; I doubt they'll be giving me anything.

'— and Riley will win all the other academic prizes, but the long-distance prize was something I actually thought I had a shot at.'

'You still do,' I say. 'I just think isn't it more important that everyone makes it through to next year? That everyone's still here after the summer?'

Shell sits up. 'What do you mean?' she says, blinking at me.

'I just mean . . .' I feel a sigh rising up from the very bottom of my lungs. '. . . I think we should focus on actually passing the end-of-year exams before we start worrying about the prizes too, that's all.'

I'm so behind now that something I know coming up in the exam is about as likely as rain on a Saturday. Sometimes the volume of stuff I haven't learned yet seems to be falling in on top of me, crushing me.

Shell rolls her eyes. 'Oh, Millie, you're not going to fail everything,' she says casually. 'Cranshaw wouldn't let you take the exams if she didn't think your head was better.

17

You're only a little bit behind. They're not going to move you to another school.'

'But—'

'And,' says Shell, cutting across me, 'I heard once you're in the sixth year if you win a prize, you get a free trip to the Company's theme park in Beijing.'

'That's just a rumour,' I say. 'There's more chance of there being a World War Two bomb under Cranshaw's office.'

Shell straightens up. 'I thought that was true!'

Lu flops down next to me, followed by Finn and Nick.

'Riley's spotted McNabb in the canteen. She's trying to pump him for information on the world-culture exam,' Lu says.

'Wow,' says Shell. 'Does she actually think that'll work?'

'Well, if it does, she said she'll tell us what he told her,' Lu says. 'I doubt she will though.'

'Mudge never seems as good the day after they serve ice cream for dessert,' says Nick, scraping the bottom of his bowl with a spoon.

'But the ice cream is just frozen mudge,' I say. 'It's exactly the same thing, but cold.'

'I know, I know,' says Nick. 'But it's so delicious!'

'Millie, you haven't got any breakfast,' Lu says.

'I'm OK. I'm not really feeling that hungry,' I say, as my stomach rumbles loudly.

'Just have some of mine,' says Lu, passing her box of mudge over. 'It's hazelnut!'

18

'Urgh, why didn't you go for sage?' says Finn.

I take the box from Lu and pop a mudge cube in my mouth. Hazelnut is far too sweet but Lu's watching my face so I nod and make 'mmmm' noises. Lu raises her eyebrows at Finn, who mutters, 'Sage is better.'

Something glints in the sunlight behind Lu's head. It's a groundbot, planting flowers along the border of the path round the Main Building. All units have the same metallic finish, so they catch the light. But groundbots are bigger and sturdier than foodbots and cleanbots; they're also weatherproof. As I watch, it raises his head and unmistakably locks eyes with me.

I instinctively smooth down my hair again. *The crowd closing in, the brush of metal against my arm, the screen above me.*

'Millie, you're spilling it!' says Lu, as the box slides off my lap.

'Oh! Sorry,' I say, trying to scoop the cubes up.

'It's nearly nine,' says Finn suddenly, sitting up straight. 'We need to get to the debate class.'

'Oh, it's the last lesson,' says Shell, leisurely hauling herself to a stand. 'I'm sure Welbeck won't care that much if we're late.'

'Shell, have you *met* Welbeck?' says Nick, pulling me to my feet.

As we enter the Right Building and hurry down the corridor a message beeps through on my RetinaChip, but when I open it, it's totally blank. There's no sender registered, which is the weirdest thing. I delete it.

We file into the classroom and sit near the back. Welbeck isn't here yet but that doesn't mean he won't storm in soon and demand to know why we aren't reading quietly.

Shell leans over. 'Have you started revising for this exam yet?'

'I don't even know what it's on,' I say. I barely know what anything's on.

'No one knows. All I've heard is that it's going to be a persuasive essay on a topic that's in the news at the moment,' she says. 'Riley is convinced it's going to be on brainstreaming. You know, whether it's ethical or not to use people's thoughts in the justice system.' She waves her hand around airily.

'Pfft,' says Jess, sitting behind us. She leans forward. 'We all know what subject it's going to be on. The one thing that's constantly in the news right now . . .'

Shell and I both turn to face her. 'Which is . . . ?' I say.

Jess looks at me as if I'm five years old. 'Don't you keep up with the news, Millie?'

'Nope,' I say. 'Can't you just tell us what it is?'

'Oh!' says Shell suddenly. 'It's not that thing about units is it? I keep scrolling past those stories . . .'

My stomach clunks with dread. 'What?' I say. 'What thing about units?'

'The government is about to pass a new law,' Jess says. 'If the Company and the other Big Four companies agree to it, units will be granted freedom. They won't be owned

20

by their companies any more and they'll be equal to humans.'

My mouth goes dry. '*What?*' I say. 'Seriously?'

Jess gives me an odd look. 'Yes,' she says. 'It'll become law in a few weeks, as long as the companies vote it through.'

'I thought . . .' I say. 'I thought there was some kind of protest group against it or something?'

'Oh, Humans First?' says Jess, snorting dismissively. 'Yeah, they're all a bunch of crazies though. No one actually listens to *them*. They hate all machines. They didn't even want units working at the World Cup last year.'

'But . . .' I say. 'But surely the companies aren't going to vote this through?' I look at Shell, expecting her to be nodding along with me, but her eyebrows are drawn together. 'Because the companies need the units, don't they? To work for them? They're not just going to set them free!'

I turn round to Lu and Finn on Shell's other side, but they're not even listening.

Jess snorts. 'All the companies will have to do is pay them a salary, like they should have been doing in the first place. And of course they'll vote it through. It'll be a PR disaster for them otherwise.'

I can't think of anything else to say, so I shake my head. Am I the only one who realises this could be danger-ous? It's not like we know what they're capable of. I shiver as I think of *the brush of metal against my arm*. There must be a reason I keep remembering that.

'Anyway,' says Shell quickly, 'maybe we should look at the history of brainstreaming then? Just so—'

'It's *supposed* to be a good thing, Millie!' Jess says to me, cutting across her. She pulls something up on her tablet and shows it to me. 'See?'

It's a news story filmed outside the Houses of Parliament in London. There are crowds of people waving huge banners, all cheering. I quickly turn away but Shell leans over, peering at the screen.

'What's that?' she says.

'It's the pro-units group, Artificial Intelligence Rights, celebrating after the law was agreed on by the politicians,' Jess says. 'They've been campaigning for months.'

'But there are no units there,' says Shell.

'Exactly,' says Jess. 'They don't have the freedom to campaign for their own freedom! Don't you think that's wrong?'

'Yeah, I suppose,' says Shell, watching the screen. 'Will they still have that unit soap on the network if units are granted freedom?'

Jess rolls her eyes. 'I don't know.'

'Because when Loretta finds out Damian is cheating on her—'

'I said, I don't know,' Jess says.

'I hate that show,' I say.

Jess glances up at me again, her nose wrinkled. 'What is your *problem*?'

'Quiet!' says Welbeck, bursting into the room. 'You should all be reading page thirty-two of the document I set *without talking . . .'*

Jess sneers at me quickly before I spin round and try to make it look like I've just been quietly preparing for the lesson this whole time. Welbeck surveys us all and says, 'Beige today, is it?' which is the same 'joke' that he makes every lesson. The teachers don't wear clothes from the Look obviously, but there's definitely a certain way they all dress. Shell has a theory that they need to demonstrate a certain amount of authority. For example, Welbeck has grey temples and wears glasses, even though eyesight problems are cured at birth. Cranshaw has a huge puff of hair the texture of candyfloss and glasses on a string round her neck, which she never puts on, and Harrison's bald spot is carefully cultivated.

The exception to the rule is Llewellyn, who teaches history. As all the teachers have to work for the Company for at least thirty years, and then complete ten years of teacher training, she must be at least sixty. Yet with her blonde hair and baby-plump skin, she sometimes gets mistaken for one of the pupils. Also she will occasionally wear the day's latest colour, which, as you can imagine, is embarrassing for everyone.

'Now,' Welbeck says. 'I know you're all itching to start revising –'

Shell snorts quietly next to me.

'– but we're going to cover some very important points

23

in this last lesson. It's going to be hard and intensive work, so I hope everyone's awake. I want to go back to some of the things we've covered in previous lessons, but we will also be touching on some new topics, which I think will be invaluable to you when you walk into the exam room—'

At that moment an alarm blares through the room. For a second everyone freezes, but then Welbeck jerks into life. 'Oh, for . . . It's the fire alarm! Again! Everyone to the courtyard! Come on!'

Shell pokes me in the ribs as we stand up. 'That was a lucky escape, hey?'

We file out of the Main Building into the courtyard. Llewellyn is standing near the doors, ushering pupils through. 'Girls, line up in your year groups, please,' she calls to us as we pass her.

'Miss, what's going on?' Lu asks.

Llewellyn's hands are shaking. 'Don't worry, everything is fine. No need to worry,' she calls after us.

We line up in the middle of the courtyard, next to the oak tree. From here we can hear the alarms blare out from every building, even the dormitories, which are empty at this time of day. More and more pupils flood into the courtyard in front of us from all directions, a sea of beige. There are enough people that the whole school must be here. I don't think I've ever seen all the school assembled together; we're always divided by year or house or how we did in our end-of-year exams. The twelfth-year pupils, who'll be leaving soon to join the Company, saunter past us, rolling their eyes at each other. A group of nine-year-old boys attempt an impromptu wrestling match, gripping each other in headlocks, as they line up three rows ahead of us. I wonder what happened to the visiting nursery-school pupils.

As a class of kids from the youngest year spill out of the Left Building, faces bright with the prospect of at least ten minutes of freedom, the alarms stop.

Finally. The silence is like balm to my ears. If it is a fire drill, they'll let us go back in a minute or two.

But they don't. The minutes tick by. The swell of conversation among the lines of pupils rises; the teachers, roaming the edges of the courtyard, shush us and silence falls. Then, as inevitable as the tide, the level of noise rises again.

'What is going on?' Shell whispers next to me. 'Do the teachers even know?'

'I don't think they do. They wouldn't be so grumpy otherwise,' I say, just as Harrison yells 'Quiet!' from the end of the courtyard.

He passes behind us, counting quietly, then crosses back behind the row of pupils in front of us.

'Shell, are they *counting* us? To make sure we're all here? Why would they need to do that?'

'I don't know, has something gone wrong with our IndexChips? Maybe there's been some kind of glitch and they're not tracking us any more?' Shell looks at her fingertip. There's still a tiny white line there, from where the chip was inserted when we were ten.

'Wow, does that mean we can just take the rest of the day off? Go shopping?'

Shell laughs and at the same time the doors to the Main Building open. The murmur of conversation immediately stops.

Cranshaw stands in the doorway for a moment, looking over the rows of pupils. Her eyes dart from face to face and her jaw is rigid. Florrie, Cranshaw's unit assistant, lurks behind her in the corridor. She's built from the same model as the other indoor units at the school, squarish and metal with the same blank face stuck on, except she's got piercing blue eyes. She towers over everyone, even Cranshaw, who's pretty tall. But all the units do.

'Pupils,' Cranshaw says. 'I regret to inform you . . .' Her voice, always so stern and strong, cracks on the last word. 'Someone is missing.'

Two

For a second I don't understand what she's said. There's a machine in the library that scans your IndexChip when you need to return a document, but a lot of the time it fails and just flashes up a 'does not compute' message over and over again. I feel exactly like the library machine when Cranshaw speaks. My brain refuses to accept the information. No one's ever gone missing at Oaktree. It's unfathomable.

Around me the crowd hisses with a hundred gasps of shock. Shell, next to me, looks like she's been kicked. Further down the row, I can see Finn's mouth hanging open.

'I'm afraid Daisy Bridgewater's IndexChip has not registered her presence since she entered her dormitory last night,' says Cranshaw. The big puff of hair on her head quivers, as if there's a breeze. I realise she's shaking.

Daisy Bridgewater – I know her. She's Nick's cousin, in the year below us. She always wins the athletics prize. I glance down the line, where Nick is. His face has turned the same shade of pale beige as his T-shirt.

'She entered the dormitory at nine p.m. and spent time chatting with friends, preparing for bed at approximately ten p.m.,' Cranshaw says. 'This morning, her roommates noticed her bed was empty, but thought she must have got up early and left the dormitory before eight. When her IndexChip didn't register her for breakfast or her first lesson, and she was found not to be in her room, we scanned the school grounds for the location of her chip. We found nothing.'

Thoughts are rolling around my head like clothes in a tumble dryer. Has Daisy been kidnapped? Attacked? Or has she run away? But how? The IndexChips in our fingers allow us to control the images in our RetinaChips. They also transmit information to our tablets, the canteen and library machines and the sensors on every door in the school, meaning our movements can always be tracked. The teachers always know exactly where you are if you're not in a lesson. If they don't know where Daisy is, it means something's happened to her chip. My fingers scrape at the gems on my nails.

'What could that mean?' Shell whispers to me.

'I don't know,' I say. 'This is so weird.'

We're not the only ones confused. All around us pupils have huddled into fevered conversations. A girl in the line

28

directly in front of me – the rest of Daisy's year – has burst into tears, sobbing on to a friend's shoulder.

'Quiet, please!' says Cranshaw. The noise level has risen so high she has to almost shout to be heard above it. This in itself is strange – usually when Cranshaw talks everyone listens.

Cranshaw waits for us to be quiet before continuing, her jaw set.

'Company representatives are currently scouring the land outside the school grounds from the air. I have no doubt that within a few hours she will be found safe and well.'

We all know who she means by Company representatives. Last year Adam Reese, who knew he was about to be expelled, locked himself on the roof of the Left Building and held a solo party, blasting out music from his tablet and throwing mudge into the courtyard. None of the teachers could get on to the roof, so after four hours, the Company representatives arrived, strode through the courtyard and battered the door down. It was equal parts thrilling and terrifying.

The Company's official name is a fifty-two-digit serial number. Its 'commercial' name is always changing as it acquires smaller companies every few months. It owns over a thousand different brands now, in all sectors of the market. The Big Four Committee, made up of Britain's four biggest companies, was founded last year to advise the government, and our Company sits on it. I say 'advise',

29

but what actually happens is the companies make all the decisions and the government agrees to them. Most media outlets seem to believe the government had to set up the Committee or risk becoming totally obsolete. The companies make the rules. Everyone obeys their own company's laws. The government's no more than a figurehead really. They don't have any actual power.

We call it the Company, which you'd think would get confusing when talking to people from other companies, but we never mix with them. I've met one person from outside the Company in my whole life – Dr Tavish, who patched my head back together after my accident – and I'm the only person I know who has. We're born into the Company and raised by them so they can mould us into the perfect Company workforce. As our parents are high-ranking employees, mostly board members or heads of departments, we're educated in the Company's best institutions. Other lower-ranked Company employees are working in factories or offices by the time they're our age. Changing the rank you were born into is very rare; I've never heard of anyone, ever, being promoted from a lower-level school to Oaktree, and only a couple of pupils have ever been expelled from the school and demoted in the school's history.

If Daisy is found trying to run away by the Company representatives (which seems pretty inevitable if they're looking from the air) she won't be coming back to Oaktree. We're free to leave the school if we want to, but the moment you pass the border of trees into the wilderness your chip is blocked from the network forever. As soon as the Company representatives track you down, you'll be officially expelled. Even though one of Daisy's parents sits on the Company's board, like my mum does – that won't help her. *If* she's run away.

If she hasn't . . . I don't know what will happen. If someone's taken her . . .

None of this makes sense; if she's just given up her whole family, friends and future . . . for what? What could have been so important? And where did she think she was going to go? The school grounds are surrounded by wilderness, so she would have to walk miles before she could travel anywhere else. There's the shuttle to the Woodland River Centre, but you need a working IndexChip to get on it. And if Daisy's IndexChip hasn't registered her on the system since last night, she won't have been able to.

'I know this is distressing news for you all,' says Cranshaw. 'But I can assure you, Oaktree is the safest place in the world for you. No one unauthorised can enter the school grounds without the Company and the teachers knowing about it immediately. Remember that we have your best interest at heart.'

The level of conversation is slowly rising again. I wonder how many pupils will remember what Cranshaw said when they write a tell-all email to their parents later. She clears her throat. 'We've just conducted a test of your IndexChips. All other chips seem to be working, but this seems to be quite a severe glitch. Further tests may have to be conducted.'

Cranshaw glances at Florrie behind her. Florrie's face is totally expressionless, but Cranshaw seems to take some strength from it, as her voice is strong and clear when she speaks again. 'Thank you for your patience. I trust you all understand how Daisy's friends must be feeling at this time. It's now nearly ten, you may go on to your next lessons.'

The rows of pupils immediately disperse and every-one around me starts talking at once.

'This is so strange,' says Shell straight away.

I keep my eye on Cranshaw for a second. She turns to go inside, but Florrie stays still, eyes sweeping over the crowd. I watch until her eyes drop and she retreats inside too.

'Poor Daisy!' says Lu, joining us. 'What do you think happened?'

'Have you spoken to Nick? Is he OK?' I say, searching the crowd for him.

'I don't know. He just walked off. He must have gone to make a phone call to his family.'

Riley joins us as we walk to our Mandarin lesson in the Right Building. Her beige eyes are wide. 'I can't believe it. What could have happened? Did she run away?'

'Could it have been the end-of-year exams?' Lu says. 'Maybe she thought she was going to fail.'

'No,' says Shell, shaking her head. 'She was super smart, I remember. And she was going to win about eight of the sports prizes . . .'

'You don't think she could have been kidnapped?' I say.

Riley, Lu and Shell look at me.

'Could that even happen?' says Shell after a moment. 'It's impossible. No one unauthorised could break into the school without Cranshaw knowing.'

'It was just what she said about Oaktree being the safest place,' I say. 'I thought it was odd.'

'Oh yeah, well, she has to say that, doesn't she?' Riley says. 'So we don't all freak out.'

'I'm surprised she told us anything,' says Lu. 'You'd think they'd want to keep this quiet.'

'Daisy's dormitory would have all known,' says Riley. 'Probably her whole house.'

'And Cranshaw's so big on honesty,' I say. 'She hates rumours spreading.'

As we enter the classroom, Harrison stares us down. 'So nice of you to join us, ladies,' he says. Harrison is the sort of teacher who would consider an earthquake an 'inadequate excuse'.

We mumble apologies and sit down at the back. Finn is already there, but Nick's seat is empty.

'I want you to copy down these characters, and then write a paragraph on each subject,' Harrison says, flicking through Mandarin characters on the screen. 'And if you could refrain from gossiping at the back, that would be wonderful.'

Harrison puts a block on our chips inside the

classroom, so we can't log on to the network. I lean back on my chair, reach round Shell and poke Finn's side.

'Is Nick OK?' I whisper to him behind Shell's back.

'I don't know,' Finn says. He looks pale. 'He's talking to his parents . . . I don't think he'll be in lessons for the rest of the day.'

'What about her IndexChip?' Shell says. 'Does he have any idea what happened?'

Finn's eyes shift from side to side. 'Well,' he says quietly. 'I might have a theory about that—'

Harrison interrupts. 'Finn, do I have to move you to a different seat? I'm aware the head teacher has given you a lot to talk about, but you have exams in just over a week. I *suggest* you get on with this.'

'Yes, sir. Sorry, sir.'

Finn shrugs at me and we both go back to our tablets. I'm typing down the characters without even seeing them. Daisy's IndexChip failing is something I can't figure out. We've always thought that they're absolutely infallible, especially the tracking device. Wherever we are, the school's system will always know. I mean, it's a bit annoying we can't skip lessons whenever we want to, but it's always made me feel safe too. Did Daisy manage to disable it in some way? I can't really believe that it spontaneously stopped working, as Cranshaw seemed to be suggesting. They *never* break.

Harrison finishes placing characters on the screen, and, after checking that we're all working quietly, slips out of the room to get a coffee-flavoured caffeine drink as he does every morning. As soon as he's gone, I turn to Finn.

'What happened to Daisy's IndexChip?' I say. 'Do you actually know anything, or—'

'It's just something Nick told me ages ago,' Finn says, leaning across Shell. 'And if he knew it, I assume Daisy did too . . .'

'What? What?' says Riley next to me. Typically impatient.

'The only way to get rid of the chip,' Finn says. 'Cut your fingertip off.'

'Urgh, no!' I say. 'She couldn't have done that!'

'What?' says Shell.

'Nick said it's the *only way*,' Finn repeats. 'But no one wanted to try it out.'

'Obviously!' I say.

'Daisy didn't chop off her fingertip,' Riley says. 'She would've had to do it in the dormitory. Not only would someone have noticed, but it would be pretty hard to avoid leaving evidence of it.'

'Like what?' asks Finn.

'Well, like a massive pool of blood, for one,' says Riley, 'or the actual fingertip plus chip, which I'm pretty sure the waste disposal unit would reject.'

'Also, what would she use to cut it?' says Shell.

Finn shrugs. 'Anyway, there are other ways of disabling your chip. They're just not all foolproof.'

'Like chopping your finger off is,' I say.

'It gets rid of the chip, doesn't it?' Finn says, rubbing his chin. 'Maybe Daisy tried the trick where you run an electric charge through a glass of water and then stick your finger in.'

'What does that do?'

'Well, apparently the chip shorts, but I *think* nine times out of ten you get electrocuted.'

'It'd be more like ten times out of ten,' says Riley.

I shake my head. 'She couldn't have done that then,' I say.

'Why not? She *has* somehow become free of her chip. She must have done something.'

'Well, maybe she didn't go through the door,' says Riley.

'What?' says Finn. 'She just flew out of the window? Or a unicorn picked her up and gave her a lift to the ground?'

'No,' says Riley. 'Well, OK, yes. Maybe she climbed down, out of the window? There'd be nothing scanning her chip if she did that.'

Finn looks at Riley for a long second. 'She lives in Birch house. On the sixth floor or something. If she'd tried to climb out of the window, she'd be splattered all over the path below by now.'

Riley screws her face up. 'Thanks for that image.'

Lu's face is also screwed up, but for a different reason. 'Oh,' she says hoarsely. 'Just thinking about her out there . . . all alone in the wilderness . . . with half a finger . . .'

'She didn't chop off her finger, Lu,' says Shell.

36

'Can you imagine though, not having a chip?' Finn says. 'No one would ever know where you were, you could come and go as you pleased, you could sleep in—'

'I don't think Daisy is exactly having the time of her life right now, Finn,' I say.

Finn rolls his eyes. 'No, obviously. But imagine if we could do that – I mean, not the running away part, but if we figure out how she disabled the chip, then we could – argh!'

Harrison is standing over us. I've become so engrossed in the conversation I didn't even notice him come in.

'If you're quite finished,' he says to Finn, his face puce. 'There's a desk at the front for you.'

I don't think anyone does any work for the whole day. Every lesson is just another chance to have a new whispered conversation about *how* she disabled her chip? What did she do? And how can we do the same thing?

Everyone is obsessed with the chip. I don't think it's ever occurred to anyone before that they could be disabled. We're so used to them, so the idea of not having one makes people go a bit giddy. Finn is fixated on the idea of staying in bed for his first lesson (not seeming to realise the first place the teachers would check would be his dormitory) and eating ice cream for every meal, even breakfast (not seeming to realise he wouldn't be able to get any food or drink as he wouldn't have an IndexChip to scan).

'Oh, there'd be ways around that,' he says when we're meant to be making notes on *The Secret Garden* in English literature.

'What ways?' I say.

He shrugs. 'Borrow someone else's or something.'

'But anyone with a working IndexChip wouldn't *be there.*'

'Oh whatever,' he says, leaning back in his chair. 'You think about stuff too much, Millie.'

It's Saturday morning and we're still talking about it, as Riley, Shell and I walk down to the shuttle station. Shell bumped into Nick in the common room last night, but couldn't bring herself to ask about Daisy's chip.

'He just kept saying no one knew why she'd done it,' she says, her mouth pulling down at the corners. 'I couldn't exactly say, "Yeah, yeah, anyway do you know how she disabled her chip? Because everyone really wants to know so we can sleep in instead of going to lessons."'

I laugh but Riley looks stern. 'You should have just asked!' she says.

'Maybe at least wait until she's found safe and well,' I say. 'I didn't think you'd be so interested in skipping lessons anyway, Riley?'

Riley runs a hand through her hair. 'Oh please,' she says. 'If I spent every Mandarin lesson in the library teaching myself, I'd be fluent by now. Harrison couldn't teach a cleanbot how to use a mop.'

We bleep our chips at the entrance to the shuttle station, which is about a mile away from the school buildings.

The shuttle travels underground directly to the shopping complex; it only takes ten minutes.

We sit down on the shuttle and strap ourselves in. Riley messages us a picture of the dress she wants to buy.

'I want that but with a shorter skirt, I think,' she says. 'I might see how it looks.'

'That's so pretty. I want something like that, but in pink,' says Shell.

'What are you thinking, Millie?' says Riley. 'I'm guessing perfectly symmetrical pleats? Sequins only applied in parallel lines?'

'I haven't really thought about it that much.' I shrug. 'I might have to see what they've got.'

I can't really work up the excitement the other two have. All the furore over Daisy going missing briefly distracted me from the holes in my memory, until this morning when I woke up from a nightmare prickly with sweat. *The crowd closing in, the brush of metal against my arm, the screen above me.* It's the screen that bothers me most. What was on there? Why do I remember that and barely anything else?

'Millie's not that excited because she had a dress custom-made when she was ten,' Shell tells Riley.

'I'm still excited! Kind of. I just haven't been planning it since forever like *someone*,' I say, elbowing Shell.

'Was that for winning a maths prize or something? I remember,' says Riley. 'Have you still got it?'

'It's at my parents' holiday home wrapped in tissue paper,' I say.

'Wow,' Riley breathes. 'After three years? That's so toxic.'

That was such a great day. I'd won the maths prize with the highest exam mark ever for someone in the second year and my parents said I could have a custom-made dress as a reward. They were meant to come with me, but at the last minute they had a big meeting or something and couldn't make it. It didn't matter though. I went with Shell instead. The pod made me the most beautiful white lace dress. I still occasionally go and look at it when I'm at my parents' house.

'Just make sure you don't get a pink dress,' says Shell. 'Two blonde girls both in pink dresses – it'll look like we did it deliberately. And that we're really sad.'

'All right, I won't get a pink one,' I say.

'But you have to get ruffles on the sleeves,' says Shell. 'Everyone's getting ruffles on the sleeves.'

'But what if I don't want sleeves—'

'*Everyone's* getting ruffles on the sleeves,' Shell repeats.

'I can't wait for the ball,' says Riley. 'I was talking to Emma this morning—'

'She's on the ball committee, right?'

'Yeah. She said they're going to decorate the marquee with over two million fairy lights! She said it's going to be like being inside a disco ball.'

'I can't even think about the ball until the exams are

over,' I say, my stomach already backflipping about the revision I haven't done.

'I know. I'm so worried about the world-culture exam!' says Riley.

Shell gives me a look; once Riley gets started on revision, she doesn't stop.

'Ah . . . anyway,' I say quickly. 'Where's Lu? I thought she was coming?'

'Lu already has a dress,' says Riley. 'A vintage one handed down from her grandma. She said it's a family tradition.'

Shell and I wince. 'Urgh, poor Lu,' I say.

'Yeah, I couldn't imagine wearing something that had been worn by *someone else*,' says Shell.

'I know,' says Riley. 'And it's old. It could just fall apart at any moment!'

'Her family is weird about clothes though, aren't they?' says Shell. 'Like that striped sleepsuit that she has to wear for luck the night before an exam. That's a hand-me-down.'

'Is it?' I say. 'I suppose you couldn't imagine any of our wardrobes producing a sleepsuit like that. I only ever get grey or blue ones.'

'Yeah, me too,' says Shell. 'Did you know the final-year pupils get silk-lined sleepsuits? To keep their brains functioning at the highest level apparently. One day that'll be us!'

The shuttle pulls up into the Woodland River Centre

and we zoom up the escalator to the entrance. One of the weirdest things about not being at school is all the people from all over the country milling around and pouring into the centre from the other two shuttle stations. Shell always likes to spot how many people are wearing T-shirts printed with the Company logo: a green leaf inside a circle. No one from Oaktree would ever wear something like that, but the lower-rung employees seem to think it's the height of sophistication. We see three purple ones and a tie-dye version before we even get inside.

The Woodland River Centre has a glass pyramid-shaped frontage ten storeys high, which is branded with the Company logo. The cloudless sky reflects off the glass, the sun so bright it hurts to look. We get swallowed up by the streams of people shuffling through the automatic doors. As soon as we're inside we get straight on the longest escalator, which sweeps us up to just outside the Look. The double doors swish open either side of the massive curly 'L' in the centre of the storefront. We walk past the rows of touchscreens, displaying dancing models in the Look's latest clothes, to the large atrium at the back.

A woman at a curved desk glances at us for a second. 'Can I help you?' she says without smiling. She's been a bit too heavy-handed with her iris drops this morning and they're almost piercingly acid green. It's oddly disconcerting.

Shell steps forward. 'Yes, we've got an appointment for ten fifteen?'

The assistant flicks open a screen above the clear glass of her desktop. 'Name?'

'Er, it's booked under our school, so Oaktree, I suppose.'

She straightens up, suddenly seeming to notice us. 'Of course, ladies, we have your pods all set up for you. If you'd like to come this way.'

She takes us through an archway, past an empty waiting room and into a long corridor with pods on both sides. As we enter a cleanbot is on the way out, holding a box of fabric scraps. They must have only just finished cleaning the pods out after the people before.

The cleanbot spots us and immediately rushes backward. The assistant, ahead of us, frantically shoos it away with her hands, looking furious.

'It's all very easy,' she says to us. 'When you're inside, align yourself with the footholds and hand rests, and the pod will take you through a series of options. It measures your dimensions to the nearest 0.01 mm and offers a choice of a thousand fabrics, styles, colours and prints to create your perfect garment.' She sounds like she's reading that last bit from a teleprompter.

The assistant takes us along a line of pods and stops halfway, pressing buttons and unlocking the doors. 'Miss Thomas, you're in pod twelve, Miss Bryson, you're in pod fifteen, and Miss Hendrick, you're in pod eighteen.'

She presses a series of buttons and the door of pod eighteen slides open.

'Thanks,' I say, and step into the pod, placing my feet in the footholds straight away. Lasers surround me, marking out my exact measurements. Every time I move they have to readjust, so I try to stay as still as possible. In front of me, filling my whole vision, there's a screen with the Look's logo on it. In a second, when the pod has registered my presence, it'll offer me a range of options based on what I've chosen before.

The screen abruptly goes blank. With a skull-shakingly loud beep it flashes up an error message, which at such close proximity feels like it's inside my head.

ERROR, it flashes at me between beeps. ERROR. ERROR.

I scream, gripping my head. The doors slide open and I almost fall out.

'I'm so terribly sorry!' says the assistant, frantically jabbing at the door controls. 'Our pods hardly ever malfunction! It's really very rare!'

She helps me out and then presses buttons randomly on the control panel, trying to stop the alarm blaring. The cleanbot lurks behind her, as if it's interested. I have to put my hand up to my face so I can't see it looking at me.

'What happened?' I say. 'I just got in and then it . . . started doing that.'

'I'm really very sorry,' she says. 'I don't know what's wrong with it. I might try turning it off and turning it on again.'

'Can I just use another pod?'

'I'm afraid they're all booked up at the moment,' she

says. An incident number flashes up in luminous green on the control panel. 'Oh. It seems that when it tried to read your IndexChip, it failed.'

'Oh!' I say, worried. 'Is there something wrong with my chip?' What if I can't get back into school? What is going on?

'Oh no, not at all,' she says. 'If anything, it seems it was too advanced for our technology. Have you recently had a new one fitted?'

'Er, yes, about six months ago,' I say. 'But it's been working normally until now.'

The assistant turns pink. 'Ah well, our pods are not necessarily equipped to deal with the absolute newest technologies,' she says. 'I could refer you to an appointment at our store in London? The pods there were installed at the start of the year.'

I know Shell will kill me for saying no, but I've never actually been to London on my own before. I'd need Cranshaw's permission, and I'm pretty sure she wouldn't consider a dress fitting to be important enough. We generally don't leave the school at all, apart from going to the shopping centre and the occasional school trip. We have to visit our parents over the summer holidays and the Winter Festival, but apart from that we live at school.

'That's OK,' I say. 'I think I'll just pick something off the rack.'

'Oh, of course,' the assistant says with surprise. 'You'll find our non-bespoke dresses to the left of the atrium.'

As I walk out the cleanbot zooms after me down the long corridor. I step aside to let it pass, crushing myself against the wall so it doesn't touch me, but it just stops and watches me with its blank eyes. I can feel the panic rising up in my chest; I glare at it as hard as possible, until my eyeballs start to hurt, then I realise it probably can't pick up my facial expressions. I look around to check no humans are nearby.

I lean right up to the cleanbot's face. 'Go away,' I hiss at it through gritted teeth, like an insane person, then whip away before it can do anything to me.

I pick out practically the first dress I see with ruffles on the sleeves. It's a pale-grey satin with a flared skirt. I press the screen where the model's wiggling around, and it slides back, revealing the dress. There's not much point trying it on as my wardrobe will produce one in my size anyway, so I just look it over quickly.

The assistant types the dress number into her tablet to process my order. 'There we go,' she says. 'Your wardrobe will produce dress number 6473YG674 on 12 June.'

Because it's not bespoke, I'll have to feed it back into the wardrobe after the ball so it can produce clothes for the next day. It is a bit annoying that I won't get to keep my ball dress, but it's not like I'd ever wear it again anyway.

'How would you like to pay?' the assistant says, her eyes fixed on mine.

'Oh . . .' I say. This is awkward. 'Er . . . I'm an Oaktree pupil? So . . .'

'Oh, oh, of course,' says the assistant, typing into her tablet. 'There we go. No payment required, naturally.'

Now she thinks I'm completely spoilt. All of the Woodland River employees hate us because they think we're so pampered by the Company. But they have to be nice to us because our parents might be their bosses.

Shell and Riley emerge from the fitting area. 'Hey, you got finished quickly.'

'Oh, no. The pod malfunctioned, so I just picked something from the shop floor.'

'Oh, Millie!' says Shell, aghast. 'You could have ordered that from inside the dormitory any day of the week.'

'I know, I know, it's all right though,' I say. 'Did you get what you wanted?'

Shell's eyes light up. 'Yes. It's *perfect*,' she breathes. 'Completely toxic. I went for a pinky-purple instead of pink at the last minute, because I thought it brought out my eyes more.' She flutters her eyelashes at me.

'No,' says Riley. 'Someone's already ordered mine.' She pouts.

'Well, technically, there's nothing stopping you ordering the same dress as someone else,' I say.

'I know there's nothing *stopping me*, but I don't want to have the same dress as someone else,' she says. 'I had to go for my back-up option, which isn't as nice.'

'Oh, well, show me on your tablet later. I'm sure it'll look great.'

'Should we go and get some food in a minute?' says Shell.

We always take the opportunity to eat (delicious, but unhealthy) junk food when at Woodland River because we can only have (nutritious, but ultimately not that exciting) healthy food at school. We won't have another monthly health check until next September now, so we might as well eat as much junk food as we can. The only problem is that sometimes you eat more than your calorie intake for one sitting and your IndexChip won't let you have any dinner when you get back to school.

Finn and Lu join us from the basement, where they've been playing virtual-reality games – an alien exploded all over Finn and he keeps randomly shuddering and saying, 'I feel like it's still on me!' – and we travel up the escalator to the food court, which is at the very top of the centre, underneath a massive skylight. As we zoom upward, I spot Welbeck, eyes fixed on his tablet, standing on the down escalator. One of the teachers is often on duty at Woodland River on a Saturday, to keep an eye on the younger pupils.

'Let's go to Sammy's. I want to talk to the foodbot,' says Finn.

The main fast-food restaurant has a huge outlet right at the front of the food court, and though the customers literally zoom through the checkpoints, choosing their food, beeping their chips to pay and grabbing their bag of food from a Sammy's foodbot as they leave, the queue still has about forty people in it.

'Finn, it'll take way too long.'

'But we had a really nice conversation last time.'

Sammy's new thing is that the bots are programmed to speak to you, with three special phrases. Usually bots don't talk to humans at all, but clearly Sammy's is trying to mould them into being customer-friendly. Finn swears a Sammybot told him he had nice eyes the last time we were here, but Shell, who was with him, said she was pretty sure that it was malfunctioning.

'It was not!' says Finn, aghast.

'It kept flashing up an error message,' Shell points out, 'and it told the woman before you she had "lice thighs", so I think it's safe to say something was wrong.'

'Whatever.'

After we pass the chaos at Sammy's, the inside of the food court seems calm in comparison.

Shell wants to get some freeze-dried soy-extract mousse, and it turns out they're offering supersized sundaes with extra sugar shavings on top, so we all get one and grab a table at the edge of the food court, where you can see right down to the ground outside. Hundreds of people are still arriving, exiting the underground stations and moving towards the entrance like a huge herd of tiny sheep.

'It's actually quite hypnotic if you watch it for a while,' says Finn, staring outside.

'The endless cycle of consumerism,' says Riley smugly.

'Ooh, I might use that in my debate exam,' says Shell through a mouthful of cinnamon-flavoured mousse.

49

'That's what you think it'll be about then? Consumerism?'

'Maybe. It just sounds easy to slot in somewhere,' says Shell, shrugging.

'See, if we could disable our chips, we could do this every day,' says Finn.

'Are we still talking about this?' I say. 'We don't even know if that's what Daisy did.'

'Where is Nick anyway?' says Riley. 'I thought he'd come with you.'

'Oh no, he stayed at school. He said he had to get up early to go and talk to Cranshaw about stuff,' says Finn. 'He was gone when I woke up.'

'What stuff?' I say. A one-on-one meeting with Cranshaw is quite a big deal. Unless you're Jake, who has been her favourite for what feels like eternity.

'He might go home for a bit,' says Finn. 'I don't know if he'll sit his exams. It's all a bit up in the air.'

Shell leans back on her chair and looks out at the people milling around down below. 'For all we know Daisy could be here right now, in disguise.'

'Probably not,' Riley says. 'Either she will have been picked up by the Company representatives by now or . . .'

The 'or' just hangs in the air for a second.

Shell recovers quickest. 'Well, obviously that's the most likely solution . . . But imagine if she got away? She could be down there right now.'

'She wouldn't go to the mall nearest the school, would she?' I say. 'They'd find her right away, and if her Index-Chip is still broken she wouldn't be able to buy anything or enter any shops.'

'Some other shopping centre then. It's just nice to think about,' says Shell.

'Yeah, it is,' I say. Daisy disguised but free, somewhere out there, is a nicer image than that of her kidnapped or alone somewhere in the wilderness.

'Millie.' Jess appears behind me, surprising me.

'Oh! Hi,' I say. I don't think she's ever actually talked to me outside school before. In fact, most of Jess's interactions seemed to take place through sneering looks.

'I thought about not coming over here,' she says, her mouth a hard straight line, 'but what you said before the fire alarm yesterday really bothered me.'

'Oh,' I say. I don't actually remember what I said. 'You mean, in Welbeck's class?'

'Yes,' she says. I can only just hear her over the noise of the food court. 'You obviously have a problem with units. How can you think it's wrong for them to be given freedom?'

I'm knocked back for a second. 'Wait, what?' I say, my stomach curdling. 'I never said that—'

'You didn't have to. It was obvious,' she says, her tone incredulous. 'I just don't understand how you can think like that. You've grown up around units. They've served you all your life without ever hurting you or even inconveniencing you. Why do you want to oppress them?'

She glares at me. Her spiky blonde hair is backlit by the sunshine from the window behind her, almost like an angel's halo. She's definitely got the sanctimonious tone to match.

I open my mouth, and then close it. And then open it again. 'I don't think . . .'

Shell suddenly leans across the table. 'What? What did she just say?'

Jess gives her a contemptuous look. 'I'm just asking Millie her opinion on units, as yesterday it seemed like she was pretty against them to be honest.'

'I just think we should be *careful*!' I say.

Does no one else see what I see? Units aren't just appliances that do what we want them to. They have their own minds, their own motivations . . . And they're super strong, huge and pretty much indestructible. How does anyone not see that giving them freedom puts us at their mercy?

'They're not dangerous!' says Jess. 'It's completely *stupid* of you to think that.'

'Oh my God, Jess, shut up,' says Shell, throwing her spoon down. 'Millie can have any opinion she likes, even if it is wrong.'

Jess sneers at me. 'See. Even your friends think you're prejudiced against units.'

'I'm not!'

'I think you are, Millie,' she says, the sneer falling from

her face, to be replaced by a falsely sympathetic grimace. '*You* don't know what it's like to live in a world where you're persecuted for who you are.'

'Neither do you, Jess,' says Riley. 'You've been part of the Company your whole life. You've always had everything you want.'

'At least *I* know how to treat those with a lower social status than me. I don't go round thinking *I'm* superior to units because I happen to be human!'

'What *are* you saying?' Shell is incredulous.

'I don't think I'm superior to them. I never said that,' I say. 'I just think we need to be careful about how much freedom we give them all at once.'

I can understand maybe giving a few units freedom, and closely monitoring them to make sure they don't hurt anyone. But all of them at once – they could destroy the human race if they wanted. It's not because I think humans are superior. It's because I think we're *vulnerable*.

Shell, Riley and Finn glance at me oddly. Jess looks triumphant.

'See! You still think they're dangerous. You've clearly got issues with units, based on nothing.' She looks at me steadily, shaking her head slowly. 'You lot walk around the school like you're the best thing since cubed mudge. But really you're all completely ignorant.'

'I heard that!' says Shell.

'Jess, look,' I say, 'I'm sorry if I offended you—'

'I'm not looking for an apology, Millie,' she says. 'I don't want to do this, but if I have to I will.'

'Do what?'

'Yeah, do what?' Shell's leaning over the table, trying to catch every word.

Jess straightens up and folds her arms. 'I'm going to have to go and see Cranshaw and tell her what you think about units.'

My mouth actually drops open, like a cartoon character. 'You wouldn't.'

Cranshaw loves units. Not just Florrie. All of them.

'Jess, you can't do that,' says Finn. 'You know what Cranshaw is like!'

'Well, I don't really have a choice.'

'Jess, please, please don't,' I say, my stomach squeezing. If Cranshaw decided she didn't like me, for whatever reason, then even if I aced every exam I could still be moved to another school. Cranshaw has the final say on who starts at the school next year.

'I don't *want* to.' Jess pretends to look rueful. 'But I might have to.'

Shell looks sick. 'You might have to? You might *have to*?'

Riley has stayed eerily calm. 'Can you go away now, please, Jess? No one wants to listen to you.'

'Shell, I wouldn't expect you to understand,' says Jess, not moving.

'I wouldn't expect *you* to understand what it's like to

have friends!' Shell says, her face reddening. 'Apart from the units, of course!'

'At least *I'm* not an ignorant Humans First supporter!'

It happens in slow motion. Shell, flushed with outrage, stands up and chucks the melted liquid at the bottom of her sundae cup at Jess. It flies in a pastel-pink arc across the table. Jess steps calmly to the left and the liquid misses her by centimetres and splatters messily on the floor. A clean-bot immediately zooms forward and starts mopping up.

Jess looks at me, eyebrows raised. 'Always got other people cleaning up your messes for you, haven't you, Millie?'

Welbeck is suddenly next to our table, purple with anger, as Jess melts away into the background. 'You five, move now.'

We slowly stand and follow Welbeck through the food court. My heart thumps with guilt. This is all my fault. Welbeck marches us through the mall, our heads down. We travel on the shuttle in silence and trudge over the grounds towards the school. I just want to go to the dormitory and hide my red face under my bedcovers but Welbeck directs us towards his office at the back of the Main Building.

I'm not expecting to see Cranshaw sitting at his desk, Florrie behind her. I flinch back behind Shell. My first thought is that Jess has somehow got a message to the head teacher and she's here to tell me I'm expelled.

'I'm so sorry to interrupt your day out, children,' she

says. She always refers to us like that, even though all five of us are now thirteen. 'I have to tell you something before I announce it to the school. Another pupil has gone missing. A friend of yours.'

My heart freezes. Shell grips my elbow.

'I'm afraid it's Nick Hayes.'

Three

On Monday we're revising in the common room after dinner, going through endless notes from every lesson we've
had this year on our tablets.

'Millie, come on, we've done all we can do for today,'
Shell says, as Finn scrolls through the film choices on the
big screen in front of us.

'I just want to finish this bit,' I say.

I'm still trying to read her history notes from last
November, when I had to spend time away from school.
It's almost impossible – Shell writes by hand and all her
notes are in a stream-of-consciousness style, which is
almost like reading a foreign language.

'Wait, I don't understand this bit,' I say. 'You've put
something about Josef Goebbels sending a mass email to
promote the Nazi party in the 1930s?'

'What's not to understand about that?' Shell says.

'Millie, come on,' says Finn, slumped on the sofa. 'Are we watching this film or not?'

'Two seconds . . .' I say, scrolling down the page.

'You do know it's pointless revising,' he says. 'Either we know it or we don't. Why bother even having exams?'

'Oh, cheer up, Finn,' Shell says, glancing at me worriedly. 'It's not that bad.'

We're actively not discussing Nick's disappearance. Yesterday we talked about nothing else. We'd tried revising, but nobody had got any work done; we'd all just sat around in the library, our tablets sitting unused in front of us, going over it again and again.

Finn couldn't understand. 'But how could he have run away?' he kept saying. 'It's not *like* him.'

'It's the only explanation, Finn!' Riley kept saying. 'Cranshaw said Oaktree is the safest place we could possibly be.'

When Cranshaw had told us about Nick, she hadn't come right out and said he'd run away – but when Finn asked if he could have been kidnapped, she'd said, 'Absolutely not. No one from outside can enter the school grounds without us knowing.' So that left really only one option for us to endlessly discuss.

Occasionally one of us – usually Riley – would make a big show of making notes or highlighting passages in a document, which would prompt the rest of us into working too, until someone – usually Lu or Finn – would suddenly stop and say, 'But we're never going to see him again.' This would start off another endless circle of whys and nevers and hows.

Today we all seem to have entered into a mutual, unspoken agreement of pretending everything is normal. In a way, it's worse than the directionless, never-ending pondering. Nick's absence prickles under the surface of everything we talk about. I can tell Finn feels it too; he's dropped into a bad mood we can't seem to shake him out of. Maybe I'm wrong and it is just the prospect of exams – or maybe it's because he's wondering where Nick is, if he's been found yet or if he's still out there somewhere in the wilderness. Like I am.

'I'm just going to turn the film on now, and if you're not done . . .' says Finn.

'I'm nearly done!' I say.

'Too late,' says Finn, as an ad for the Company's new extra-powerful cleanbot battery flickers on screen.

'Shouldn't we wait for Lu?' Shell says. 'She said she'd only be fifteen minutes . . .'

Lu had been summoned to Harrison's classroom for a remedial revision session after he'd been left speechless by her last Mandarin essay.

'She can catch up,' says Finn. His hair is twisted into an ice-cream-swirl style at the front of his head, but the top is drooping over his forehead, as if it's miserable too.

'What are we watching?' Shell asks.

'It's the new Ling Chang movie – it's number one on

the network because a unit plays a human in it,' says Finn. 'Although apparently a lot of people think it must be a human dressed up, as it's so realistic.'

'It's definitely a unit,' says Riley, entering the room with a box of ginger-nut mudge. I haven't seen her since she refused to leave the library at dinner time. 'You can tell by the eyes.'

'I've seen the trailer. He's really good,' says Finn.

'Maybe it's just a very blank actor?' I say, not hopefully.

'Millie, I thought you'd be well up for this,' says Finn. 'You love Ling Chang.'

'I know. I am.'

I do love Ling Chang. I even had a poster of her in my dormitory last year. But I just feel the whole acting-opposite-a-unit idea is a bit gimmicky for her. She's better than this.

'Millie hates everything now,' Shell says, settling next to me on the sofa.

'I don't *hate everything*,' I say, turning my tablet off. 'I just don't think a unit in a film is *that* interesting. People will just watch it to see if the unit looks like a human.'

'No, it's true,' says Riley, turning to me. 'You don't like X-cess any more either.'

'They're just a boy band!' I say. 'I outgrew them!'

'You haven't even read the new Alisha Atkins book, and it's been out ages,' says Shell.

Alisha Atkins is a series of action-adventure books written by a team from the Company's PR department. It's about a girl who goes back and forward in time to solve crimes. The latest one came out in January and was downloaded over a million times in the first three minutes. I used to be a massive fan – Shell and I once got up at 5 a.m. to be the first ones to download the new movie.

'Well . . .' I say. 'I haven't finished the set texts for English lit yet, and I feel guilty reading anything else until I do.'

'Maybe one of these days I'll just tell you who dies at the end, then you'll wish you'd read it,' says Shell, as the film starts.

When the unit first appears on screen, there is a moment when Shell leans over and stage whispers, 'Is that him?' and I'm not sure, then the moment ends and I can see the unit's eyes are unfocused and its face has that weird, slightly-too-perfect rigidity to it. But to its credit, it speaks the way a real person speaks and in certain scenes you can easily forget you're watching a unit.

Technology's moving on so quickly. I always forget that the school's newest units are still a few years older than the latest models already out in the world. There's no way you could ever mistake one for a human, even in the dark. But judging by the showbot we're watching, units are getting closer and closer to resembling humans every day. This one looks like it has skin. You can't even see the joins.

At one point there's a scene where the unit and Ling kiss passionately, and all four of us, even Finn, recoil and

61

shout 'Urgh!' at the screen, and then laugh because we did it in perfect unison.

'Oh God, could you imagine?' says Shell. 'It must be like kissing a lamp post.'

'Yeah, wouldn't it be cold?' says Riley.

Halfway through Lu suddenly bursts through the door, making us all jump.

'Oh, it's just you,' says Shell, moving up so she can sit down. 'How was Harrison?'

'It was fine,' she says vaguely. 'I just . . . saw something weird outside . . .' She trails off.

'Something weird?' I prompt.

'When I was walking back over the grounds from the Main Building just now,' says Lu. 'I saw the medical-centre staff . . . carrying something . . .'

Her eyebrows knot together again.

'What's this?' says Shell, leaning over. 'Who was carrying what? Have they started setting up for the ball already?'

'No, it wasn't furniture or anything,' Lu says slowly. 'I think it was a pupil.'

'A pupil?' Finn, also listening, snorts with disbelief. 'Who?'

'I don't know,' says Lu, her face still screwed up in concern. 'He . . . *they* were covered with a sheet.' Her eyes meet mine.

'Huh?' I say, just as Finn says, 'You what?'

Lu winces. 'I think they'd been hurt.'

'Wait, you mean they were carrying a *body*? Wrapped in a sheet?' says Shell.

'Yeah,' says Lu.

Finn shrugs. 'Probably just a kid from one of the younger years messing about in the grounds or something.'

'Yeah, idiots,' says Riley.

'Yeah,' I say quickly. The little twist of worry I felt when I saw Lu's face unknots. 'That's the only explanation. It's probably not a big deal at all.' I rub Lu's arm to comfort her but she shrugs me off.

'That wasn't the only thing,' she says. 'It—' She pauses, seemingly considering what she's saying, before she continues. 'The . . . er . . . the nurses yelled at me. They told me to go away.'

'They probably just didn't want you to see,' says Finn. 'Do you remember when we used to climb the oak tree when we were in the first year? I'm surprised none of *us* ended up in the medical centre.'

Shell laughs, turning to Finn. 'You were the one who always said we should jump off the top!'

'I was not! That was N—'

I remember who it was the second that Finn stops abruptly. Nick.

'Oh, look,' I say, gesturing at the screen for a distraction. 'Now he's swimming in the sea. Isn't that quite dangerous for a unit?'

'Must be CGI,' says Finn.

The others settle down to watch the film again, but I

63

notice Lu can't seem to concentrate. She's still staring into space, slowly twisting a strand of her hair round her finger.

'Lu,' I say quietly. 'Are you OK? Seriously?'

'What? Oh yeah, don't worry,' she says. She smiles at me but the worried crease in her forehead doesn't go away.

'I can tell there's something else,' I say. 'What is it?'

Lu looks right at me. 'I just . . .' She leans in closer, her face centimetres from mine. Her voice is barely louder than a whisper. 'It was a weird . . . shape.'

'What was?' I say.

'The body,' says Lu. 'I can't explain it . . . it looked like a person but . . .' She trails off.

'Well, maybe it was something else and you got confused,' I say.

'No, no,' she says. 'It looked . . . wrong. The whole thing was strange . . .'

I lean back away from Lu. I can't really grasp what she's trying to tell me. 'I'm sure, if it was a pupil, they can sort whoever it is out at the medical centre,' I say.

Lu sighs and puts her head in her hands. I know she's realised I'm not getting it.

Shell elbows me. 'Shhh, I want to hear this bit,' she says, leaning towards the screen.

Ling Chang's about to run away to Argentina and the unit is trying to persuade her to stay. I find myself a bit hypnotised by his lips every time he speaks. How did they

get them to move like that? They must have had to pro-
gramme him to mimic human speech. I shudder.

'Millie,' says Riley from Shell's other side.

'Shhhh!' says Shell, but Riley ignores her.

'I wanted to ask you, can you help me with maths
revision soon?' she says in her normal voice, as Shell
moves forward so she's practically sitting on the floor. 'I
just want to go over a few things.'

'Er . . .' I say, scrabbling around in my brain for an
excuse. 'Are you . . . are you sure?'

I'd tried to revise maths with Shell just a few weeks
ago, but I hadn't been able to recall a single formula. Shell
had gone from being gently encouraging to openly
shocked – she had gaped at me when I couldn't remember
how to calculate the tangent of a triangle.

'You really *are* in trouble,' she'd said, eyes wide. 'I
didn't realise you were still *this* bad.' It was the first time
she hadn't brushed off my worries about exams with a
breezy 'Oh, you'll be fine, stop worrying.' She'd understood then, for a moment.

I have no desire to go through the same thing with
Riley. Once was humiliating enough.

'Yes,' Riley says, surprised I'm not agreeing immediately. 'I need your help.'

'Er . . . well, maybe later in the week?' I say. 'I'm concentrating on history, and world culture, and English, and,
er, a few other things right now.'

'Shhhh!' says Shell again.

Riley glares at me with her dyed-aqua eyes, clearly thinking I'm trying to hog all the maths talent for myself. 'But don't you—'

Riley jumps like she's been hit with a cattle prod. Next to her Finn jolts, then Shell, sitting on the floor, and then Lu, next to me. There's a pause while they all look around blankly.

'Er . . . OK,' I say, a bit shaken. 'What was all that about?'

Shell's eyes come back into focus. '*What? What is going on?*' she says, looking at the others, horrified.

'I don't know,' says Lu, her voice squeaky with fear.

'Wait, what?' I say. I'm starting to wonder if everyone has gone simultaneously insane except for me when Finn rubs his ears.

'I'm half deaf now,' he says. 'She set that alert way too loud.'

Oh. Cranshaw must have sent out a school-wide message alert to everyone's RetinaChips. It beeps in your head so loudly it makes your brain vibrate. But why haven't I got one?

'This makes no sense, at all,' says Riley. 'It's nearly eight thirty, for crying out loud!' She jumps up, chucking her half-full box of mudge in the bin and heading towards the door.

'Wait, I didn't get the message,' I say, trying to log on to my chip as the others start picking their stuff up. 'What did it say?'

'Why didn't you get it?' Lu starts to say, but Shell cuts in.

'Cranshaw wants us all to undergo a mandatory brain-streaming session,' she says, shaking her head as if she doesn't believe her own words. 'Right now. In the Main Building.'

'What? Now? In the school? Why?' I grab my tablet and my water bottle and hurry round the table to join her.

Shell watches me, her eyes widening. 'You can't come!' she says. 'Your doctor said you can't brainstream!'

'It's *mandatory*, Shell; she has to come,' Riley says.

'Well, I—' I'd not thought of that.

'And what if her chip electrocutes her whole brain? What then?' Shell says to Riley.

'Shell—' I start to stay, but Riley turns to me.

'Millie, you have to at least tell them why you're sitting it out,' she says. 'Otherwise it'll look suspicious.'

'Suspicious?' I say, unsure what she's implying.

Brainstreaming was originally developed as a way for witnesses to give accurate evidence in court. They can also use it for victims of violent crimes, to help identify the attacker, but not for murders – it's illegal to download the brainstreams of the dead. It's also used on the accused to check their story, but there are a lot of regulations sur-rounding it. It's never been used on Oaktree pupils though, ever. Not even one pupil, let alone the entire school at once. We're just not the sort of kids that commit crimes.

About ten years ago brainstreaming was developed

for commercial use. Now everyone can use it. Everything seen through your eyes is saved automatically on to your RetinaChip; you can either watch your memories back in your own head or stream them on to your tablet, pick out the best bits and then post them on YouStream so everyone can watch. You just stick a sensor pad to your temple, plug the other end into your tablet and away you go. It doesn't hurt. Everyone I know downloads streams on a daily basis, and I only don't do it based on medical advice. The teachers hate it, and we're strictly banned from using it instead of making notes in class or in exams. But I know at least a few people (*cough* Jake *cough*) who use it as a homework shortcut.

I lose the others as we trudge across the courtyard, caught up in the slipstream of pupils exiting their dormitories on the right side of the courtyard. A whole houseful of sixth-years, a sea of aqua T-shirts, separates me from Shell and Riley. I can just see Shell's blonde head and Riley's chestnut one bobbing through the crowd up ahead, moving slowly towards the Main Building's side entrance, the one the pupils use. I can't see the others though. I log on to my RetinaChip and find my alert message from Cranshaw, tucked away in my spam folder.

'Why are you *there*?' I say, under my breath. A sixth-year girl with curly hair, her shoulder squished against mine, looks at me oddly.

There's another unopened message under it from the

medical centre. A check-up appointment with my doctor, Dr Tavish, has been moved from next week to tomorrow at seven in the morning, to avoid clashing with any of my exams. My fingers dig into the hard plastic of my tablet and my water bottle crunches together in my hand. I could have missed my appointment. Why can't my chip just work properly, like everyone else's? Why can't it do what I want it to do? The lack of control I have over it frustrates me like nothing else. I know the others tease me about wanting everything to be neat, but is it really so much to ask that my own inbox be in order? I quickly confirm the appointment and try to calm myself down.

It's *so* difficult. And I'm so sick of feeling frustrated. It's not just my chip, but my whole head. I feel like I've been trying to restart my brain over and over again for the last six months, but instead of bursting into life it crashes every time. All it can splutter out are those scraps of memory from the day of the accident. *The crowd closing in, the brush of metal against my arm, the screen above me.* And I don't even know what they mean. I'm so sick of feeling powerless over my own brain.

By the time I get inside the building a queue of pupils snakes down a staircase and halfway down a corridor. According to the alert message the brainstreaming is taking place in a classroom on the second floor. I throw my crushed water bottle away and walk along the queue, trying to spot my friends. Everyone is huddled in small groups talking quietly. Some pupils are using their tablets for a bit of on-the-spot brainstreaming right now, obviously checking for anything incriminating in their minds. But there's no way to delete anything from your brain. Whatever's on there, whoever's doing the brainstreaming is about to see it.

I keep hearing snatches of conversation. Nick and Daisy's names slip out of the hubbub of noise to reach me. I suppose it's obvious really; no pupils have gone missing before. The school wants to check no other pupils are going to attempt the same thing. There's no other reason why our parents would allow a brainstreaming session like this. It would have to be for our own safety.

But my mind keeps pushing the image of Lu's worried face at me. An injured body, covered up, is spotted being carried through the school grounds . . . and suddenly everyone in the school has to have their brainstreams checked? If it wasn't just an idiot eight-year-old messing about, and someone injured had been found on the school grounds, did that mean the brainstreaming was . . . for evidence? For witnesses? Or were they looking for the attacker? Do they think it was one of us?

'Millie, here.' Shell calls to me from the queue. She's huddled with Finn, Riley and Lu at the foot of the staircase.

'Oh, hi!' I say, jerked out of my reverie. 'Sorry, I got stuck in the crowd . . .'

'It looks like it's going to be a long wait,' says Riley.

70

'Yeah, I can see,' I say. 'Have they said why this is happening?'

'Isn't it obvious?' says Finn, his voice flat. 'They want to check no one else is planning to do a Nick and Daisy.'

'Or they want to find out if anyone else knows how to disable their IndexChips,' says Shell.

'You don't think it could be anything else?' I say, glancing at Lu, who's reading her tablet.

'Maybe they think someone knows where Nick and Daisy are,' says Riley. She's bouncing impatiently on the balls of her feet, craning her neck to try to see the front of the queue. I fight the urge to put my hands on her shoulders to make her stop.

'Well, that's if they haven't already been found,' says Shell quickly. 'I'm sure they're both safe by now.' She looks at me pointedly, flicking her eyes at Finn, as if I've strayed into dangerous territory.

'No, I mean . . . what if it's not to do with them at all? What about what Lu saw?' I say.

'Millie, that was nothing,' Lu says quickly. 'I don't even know what I saw.'

Riley snorts. 'They wouldn't need to brainstream the whole school about that, would they? Someone falling out of a tree or whatever?'

'No,' I say, checking no one around us is listening. I draw in closer to the others. 'You don't think an unconscious body being carried through the school grounds has something to do with the first-ever mandatory

71

brainstreaming session at Oaktree? You don't think it could be . . . *a criminal investigation*?'

Lu's eyes meet mine for a second. But Finn snorts.

'What? Why?' he says. 'Isn't that a bit of a big assumption, Millie?'

'No,' I say, hurt.

'Oh, Millie,' says Shell, straightening up away from me. 'You always assume the worst. Oaktree is the safest place we can be, silly.'

She smiles and rolls her eyes at Finn, seemingly unbothered by all this. But I can tell she's relieved that he's dismissed my suggestion so quickly. She doesn't want to believe anything bad could be happening. I don't know why we're pretending everything is OK, just because Cranshaw said it was. It's not.

'Come on,' I say. 'It's weird, isn't it, that these two things happened on the same day?'

'No one at Oaktree is going to attack anyone,' says Riley. Her jaw is rigid with impatience, so her words are coming out clipped. She's still bouncing. 'It's ridiculous.'

'OK, then, fine,' I say, shrugging one shoulder. 'Whatever.'

'Millie, come on, don't be grumpy,' says Shell, locking her arm round my neck. 'You know what you're like. If an acorn fell off the oak tree, you'd think the sky was falling in.'

She's been saying that to me since we started at Oaktree. In fact, she said it to me just last week when I told her

72

how nervous I was about the exams. But I refuse to be charmed. I fold my arms, leaning away from her.

'We shouldn't be talking about criminal investigations,' says Riley, looking at me reprovingly. 'Someone'll overhear and everyone will freak out. And then the rumours will start . . .'

'Like that one about there being an unexploded World War Two bomb under Cranshaw's office,' says Lu.

'That's true,' says Finn. 'I swear, that is true.'

'I can tell you what happened,' says someone behind me.

I turn round and Jake's standing there. 'Well,' I say, anger flaring up in my chest. 'We don't want to talk to *you*.' I turn round, folding my arms, my back to him.

'Millie!' says Finn, shocked. 'Jake, wait!' He dashes past me, after Jake's swiftly retreating back.

Shell grabs my shoulders. 'Millie, are you being serious?' she says, her eyes wide. 'What if he knows something about Nick?'

'He doesn't know anything, Shell!' I say. 'He's just saying that so I'll talk to him again.'

'What if Cranshaw's told him something?' Shell says. 'He's always in her office, he's obviously her favourite—'

My teeth are gritted. 'So? You really think if he heard something secret from Cranshaw, he'd tell us?'

Shell's eyes skitter over my face. 'Are you just never going to talk to him again? Your own brother?'

'I—' I automatically touch the stitches in my skull.

'You don't even know why,' she says. 'You're just

73

confused because of the accident. Cranshaw said he wasn't even with you, didn't she?'

'Yes,' I say, 'but . . . I don't know . . .'

Shell grabs my shoulders. 'Please, Millie, please please please,' she says. 'Can he just talk to us for a bit without you being all cross . . . for Nick's sake . . .'

'Fine!' I say. 'Fine. Ask him about Nick. But I'm not talking to him. And this doesn't mean I forgive him either.'

'Oh, Millie, thank you!' says Shell. 'I promise we won't be nice to him.'

Then, for the first time in six months, I find myself toe to toe with my brother. He's only an inch or two taller than me, but I feel like he's looking down at me from a great height.

'Millie,' he says.

His light brown eyes – the same as mine – flick around uneasily and he runs a hand through his scruffy hair. I snort and turn away from him.

'So what's going on?' says Finn. 'Did Cranshaw tell you something, or—'

'No, no,' says Jake. 'I just had my brainstreaming session and the nurse told me something weird—'

'The nurse?' says Finn. 'Doing the brainstreaming? It wasn't a Company representative?'

'No,' says Jake impatiently. 'It was just a nurse from the medical centre. He told me why . . .'

Suddenly Jake trails off and looks up and down the queue, as if he's worried someone's listening. I can tell the others are all hanging on his every word now. Inwardly I roll my eyes at his big show of secrecy – anything he says will show up in all their brainstreams anyway.

'Why what?' prompts Riley. 'Why we're being brainstreamed?'

'Yes,' says Jake, his voice lower. The others all lean in further. 'He said something about . . . a victim.'

Everyone jerks back. Even though I'm trying hard not to listen, I feel stunned. The vague feelings of trepidation I had before dissolve into real horror.

'The *victim*?' repeats Shell.

'The victim of what?' says Riley.

'Someone's been attacked?' Finn says. 'At Oaktree?'

'He didn't say who it was or what happened,' says Jake, his eyes flicking back and forth. 'He said all the medical staff are talking about it. He said . . . they need to check everyone's stream for evidence. Because the incident in question is . . . missing from the victim's brainstream.'

Shell gasps. 'What? How?'

'They have no idea how,' Jake says. 'I think that's why they've panicked and ordered the whole school to be scanned at once. I mean, they can already check our tablets . . . I suppose they thought this was the only way to find . . . evidence.'

'What . . . the . . .' says Riley. The blood has drained from her face.

'I thought removing brainstreams wasn't possible,' I say without thinking.

'Yeah, that's the scary thing,' he says, looking straight at me. I immediately look down at the floor, my teeth clenching automatically.

'I should go,' he says suddenly. 'Don't say anything to the other kids. You know what people are like . . .' He looks round at our shocked faces, as if he's regretting telling us.

'I thought you knew something about Nick,' says Finn weakly.

Jake pauses. 'I'm really sorry, we haven't – no one knows anything yet,' he says, his hands spread, like he's Cranshaw's official spokesman.

We stand in silence after Jake leaves. Brainstreaming is something we do so regularly now we don't appreciate it. After every day out, fun at the mall or even a joke someone's told, everyone wants to be first to plug in their sensor and download the memory to their tablets. Apart from that, it's been an infallible part of the justice system for years.

But someone reaching into the mind of another person and deleting their thoughts brings back the gravity of the situation. If the technology has been developed to remove parts of a person's memory, and someone at Oaktree is using it in this way, what's going to happen to us? How much of the victim's thoughts have been stolen? Will something like that affect their personality? Will they be a different person without their memories?

The body Lu saw. I can't believe it's a coincidence – things like this never happen at Oaktree, let alone twice on the same day.

'Who's *doing* this?' says Shell, looking around at the other pupils in the queue like it could be one of them.

'Who would know how?' I say.

It feels like no time until I'm at the front of the queue. Shell comes out of the classroom where the brainstreaming is taking place, still looking as flabbergasted as I feel. As she passes me she grabs my wrist.

'What are you going to say?' she says. 'About your chip?'

I'd forgotten, in all the commotion, that I'm not allowed to stream anything. Dr Tavish said *under no circumstances* was I to do anything with it until he said so. 'I'll, er,' I say. 'But, wait, if they don't see my brainstream, will they think *I'm* the one who ... the one who—'

'I don't know!' Shell says, close to hysterical. 'Don't you have a note or something on your tablet?'

I just shake my head.

'Next!' comes from inside the room.

'They'll know, right?' says Shell. 'They'll have your data on file, about the accident and everything. And about your appointments with your doctor and stuff.'

'Yeah!' I say. 'They'll know! They must know!'

Shell shoves me inside the room. 'They have to.'

They've set it up with the desks moved to one side and a long dentist's chair in the middle, next to a large screen.

'Hi, Millie Hendrick?' says the nurse. He's wearing the nurse's uniform of a plain white T-shirt and trousers, the Company logo stamped on the T-shirt's breast pocket.

77

As glad as I am that it's not a terrifying Company representative doing the brainstreaming, I can't figure out why it's not.

'Yeah, that's me,' I say.

'Right, this won't take a second. Sorry you've had to wait so long.'

'Er, I haven't been able to stream anything for a while,' I say quickly, before he opens the program on the screen. 'I suffered a brain injury about six months ago and the doctor told me not to access my brainstream until he said it was OK.'

The nurse looks at me for a long second. 'This is a doctor at the Oaktree medical centre?'

'No, no,' I say. 'He's from another hospital. He's not part of the Company . . . it's kind of a long story . . .' My voice is coming out weirdly squeaky. 'I have appointments with him. I have one tomorrow. I can show you . . .' I hold out my tablet for him to look at.

'I still need to check your brainstream,' he says.

'But-but—' I say. 'It's just – he said not to . . .'

'Is it a new RetinaChip?' he says, peering into my eye. 'Is that why?'

'Er, it is, yeah,' I say. 'Retina and Index. My old one was damaged.'

'Sometimes when a new chip is fitted, it needs a bit of time to settle in,' he says. 'A few weeks, at least.'

'Yes, exactly,' I say.

'But that's a brand-new chip, on someone who's never

had one before,' he says. 'I mean, you've had one already, haven't you? Since you started school?'

'Yes,' I say slowly. 'But . . .'

'I still need to check your brainstream,' he repeats.

My hands clench. 'I don't know what will happen.'

'Nothing should happen,' he says, turning back to the screen. 'It shouldn't be a problem anyway, but this machine—' he pats the screen next to him— 'is state of the art. It's not like streaming on to your tablet.'

'I'd still prefer not to,' I say. Even without brainstreaming my brain still isn't working properly. I can't let it get worse.

He sighs. 'It's mandatory, I'm afraid,' he says.

'But . . .'

'It's just not a good enough reason,' he says gently. 'There are no medical grounds not to stream you, and your doctor isn't Company-trained, and we have to stream everyone. It is man—'

'Mandatory. I know, I know,' I say. I don't have a choice but I just can't shake off the feeling that Dr Tavish knows something the Oaktree medical staff don't. 'Fine.'

I drop into the chair. My eyes are screwed shut and my hands are in fists, up by my face. The nurse attaches a sensor to my forehead, murmuring, 'It'll all be over in a second.'

There's a beat of silence, and I wait for my head to burst open. For my chip to explode. For my brains to splatter all over the room.

79

'It's all fine,' the nurse says. 'It's very clear. Extremely clear, in fact. Want to have a look?'

'No,' I say out of the corner of my mouth, my eyes still shut tight. I'm still braced for the impact. It could still happen . . . any second . . . Then the sensor is pulled off my head. I open my eyes and the nurse is smiling at me.

'All done,' he says. 'You can go.'

Four

I stumble out of bed in the half-darkness the next morning. At least today I can avoid staring at the ceiling for hours, what with the excuse of getting up early for my doctor's appointment, but it doesn't stop me feeling gut-churningly tired. I groggily get dressed in today's colour (burgundy), smooth my hair into a ponytail to keep it neat, apply my eyelash fibres and take about ten minutes to carefully apply tiny dark red gems along the tips of my nails. When I'm finished, I hold out my hand close to the window, squinting to see if the gems line up properly.

'Millie!'

I jump, not expecting anyone else to be awake so early. Shell's sitting bolt upright in bed, her hair sticking up at the back like a bundle of hay.

'Millie,' she says again, surprisingly alert. 'You're going to the medical centre.'

'Shell, you scared me,' I say, my hand over my heart.

'You need to find out what's going on in there,' she says seriously.

'What? With the . . .' I stop before I say *the attack*.

'If someone's been attacked, they'll be in the medical centre,' says Shell. 'You need to listen and see if the medical staff are talking about it.'

'Shell,' I say, sitting down at the foot of the bed. 'That's stupid. The . . . the victim might not even be in the medical centre any more.'

'Where else would they be?' Shell says.

'Well . . . the medical centre staff aren't going to be talking about it in front of me, are they? I don't see how—'

'I'm not asking you to hack into Cranshaw's chip and access the medical records or anything,' says Shell, slumping back on her pillows. 'Just keep an ear out. If you hear anything, we'll know it's true.'

'Oh, all right then,' I say. I know she won't let me go until I agree. 'I'll try to listen in.'

'Go, girl,' says Shell, flipping over and putting her pillow over her head. I grimace inwardly, as my RetinaChip beeps with a new message. I open my inbox, hoping it's from the medical centre to tell me Dr Tavish can't make it, but instead it's another totally blank post: no sender, no content and no title. Who's sending them? Are my messages getting wiped before they reach me? Or is there a glitch on the system?

I reach the medical centre, bleeping my chip at the entrance, and walk up to the desk. The receptionist, whose powder-blue hair is always styled in a solid-looking bee-hive, glances up and smiles at me.

'Millie! How are you?' she says.

'Oh, er, I'm fine, thanks,' I say. She's nice to me but I always feel bad that I can't remember her name. 'How's everything been here? Busy?'

'Oh, no. Everyone stays out of trouble around exam time,' she twinkles at me.

'So, er . . . nobody here for a long stay or anything?' I say, nearly rolling my eyes at my own lack of subtlety.

'Nope,' the receptionist says, looking through her tab-let. 'Now, we've had a message from your doctor . . .'

'Dr Tavish,' I prompt.

'Yes, Dr Tavish. He's running a little late, so you might have to wait for a bit.'

'Oh,' I say. I hate waiting.

I sit down on one of the seventy empty chairs and check the network for the first time today. I scroll past *Millie Hendrick is waiting in the medical centre*, but not many people seem to be up yet. Although I see Riley is already in the library.

I drum my fingers on the chair, watching the gems sparkle in the early-morning light streaming through the window, resisting the urge to start picking at them already.

The medical centre is almost always empty, apart from three days every term when the whole school has their health evaluated, one at a time. Then it's mayhem, the waiting room full around the clock and a constant stream of pupils coming and going. Exam week can be busy too, as the really hardcore pupils burn themselves out revising all hours of the day and night and get checked in for exhaustion. Now though it seems particularly quiet. Is it just because it's so early in the morning? It feels less and less likely that someone is being treated for horrible injuries in here.

The minutes tick by. My brain itches in my head with impatience. I feel like I've been sitting here for hours, but it hasn't even been five minutes yet. I start making a mental list of all the things I still have to revise, but it's so long by the end I've forgotten what I put at the top of the list.

A nurse with a bleach-blond quiff enters the room holding a tray with a bowl of mudge on it. 'Nope,' he says, clattering the tray down on the desk. 'He didn't even want—'

The receptionist coughs loudly across him, nodding in my direction. The nurse glances round, spots me and immediately starts to gather up the tray again. I look back at him, frozen like a rabbit, and he turns round and walks away quickly.

The receptionist eyes me warily for a few seconds. Inwardly I'm slack-jawed with my eyes popping out of my head, but on the outside I manage to cobble together a bored, barely listening expression, which seems to pacify her. She looks down at her tablet, squinting fixedly at the screen.

So there *is* someone in here. Someone who couldn't eat their breakfast . . . Could it be the victim of the mysterious attack? My mind whirls. Is it too much to assume? Why else would they try to hide it? If a patient was just in here to have their appendix out or something . . .

I log on to my RetinaChip, debating whether to message Shell about what I've just seen. I can't decide if she'll be hysterical at such priceless gossip or disappointed that I've come back with a set of assumptions and suspicious facial expressions. I know how quickly she can go from 'If you hear *anything*, anything at all, tell me,' to 'You saw *a tray*? That's it?'

A cleanbot whirrs into the room, picking up a discarded cup from under a chair. I jump and accidentally log off my RetinaChip. I check the receptionist to see if she's about to yell at me for being prejudiced towards units, but she's concentrating on her tablet. The bot moves closer to me, to wipe down the table in the middle of the room. I turn, folding my arms and crossing my legs away from it, but keep a close eye on its movements. As it bends down, I notice a subtle red blinking at the base of its neck below the Company icon. Its battery is low; it must be at the end of a night shift.

I look at the receptionist still hunched over her tablet. The tiny bud of an idea is blossoming in my brain. Quickly, making sure not to step too close to the cleanbot, I move over to the vending machine and select a drink. I don't look at the flavour, but it comes out impressively green and viscous. Perfect. I turn round and, when the receptionist isn't looking, throw the whole cup on to the floor. It hits the table on the way down, splattering the whole area, plus my shoes, with liquid.

'Whoops!' I say, and casually sit back down. The receptionist barely looks up. The cleanbot, however, immediately jumps into life, zooming over to the mess, brandishing a cloth. As it begins to mop up the goo on the table, I stare at it, as if I can will it into submission. Sure enough, its movements slow and eventually it flops like a rag doll from the waist, completely silent.

'What on—' says the receptionist, putting her tablet down and moving round to inspect the cleanbot.

'These things are more trouble than they're worth sometimes,' she says to me, tutting as she opens the cleanbot's back control panel. I nod vaguely, as though I'm not really paying attention.

'Yep, used all its battery up,' she says, rolling her eyes. 'I'll have to get a booster pack. You'd think they would know their own limits.' She walks back behind the desk and disappears into a small back room, closing the door behind her.

I throw myself across the room and stretch up and over the desk. The receptionist's tablet lies on the top. I grab it and minimise her Tetris game, and underneath it is a line diagram: a layout of the medical centre. My eyes skitter over it. I've only got a few seconds. The only text on the diagram is inside one of the rooms, but it's so tiny I can barely make it out. I zoom in.

Room 57: Nick Hayes.

I blink at it. Nick Hayes? Nick Hayes. That's what it says. But it doesn't make any sense.

There are footsteps behind the door, and the handle turns. I throw the tablet back on the desk and zip back into my seat, trying not to look out of breath.

The receptionist leisurely installs a replacement battery pack in the cleanbot, which beeps into life and starts cleaning up my mess straight away. It's all happened so quickly. Did I really just see that? *Room 57: Nick Hayes.* The image of the text burns into my brain. Has he been here all along? The body Lu saw . . . was that Nick?

Thoughts are filling my head too quickly, jostling for space, but I'm too shocked to work it out. Nick could be in the same building as me right now. Stupidly I look around the waiting room, as if he's been sitting across from me all this time and I just haven't noticed. What about his brainstream? How bad is he really?

There's only one way I can find out. But I'm dismissing the idea almost before I've thought of it. *I can't.* What if someone catches me? There must be a reason Nick being here is a secret. I can't think what, but there's a part of me that doesn't even want to *try to* think what.

But . . . it's *Nick.* I've known him since I was born. What if this is my last chance to see him, *ever*? What if

I spend the rest of my life regretting that I didn't summon up some bravery from somewhere and go and see if Nick is in that room?

'Er, I might just pop to the loo,' I say casually, ignoring the thump of my heart, still pumping from my sprint across the waiting room.

'OK,' the receptionist says.

I go down the corridor, then, checking she's not watching, take a right. Room 57. The medical centre is all one floor so it can't be too hard to find. I turn down another corridor and almost smack into a nurse with white-blonde hair. My brain's scrabbling for an excuse when I realise she's already passed me with barely even a glance. Maybe she recognises me from other health checks and thinks I'm just on the way to an appointment.

Suddenly there it is. Room 57. I put my hand on the door, then have to take a deep breath, suddenly feeling anxious. I remember Lu talking about the body she saw, the way she winced when she said, 'It looked . . . wrong.'

I steel myself and go in. The first thing I think is, despite seeing the name on the list, that it's not Nick, after all. It doesn't look like him. Then I realise and my brain skitters around in shock.

The broken boy in the bed *is* Nick. His injuries are staggering, like nothing I'd prepared myself for. His head is heavily bandaged, with just a tuft of dark hair sticking out of the top, and he's wearing a neck brace. His face is covered in a million tiny cuts and grazes. One arm is bandaged up to the elbow, the other is so mottled with plum-coloured bruises you can't even see the flesh colour of his skin. His leg is in plaster, hoicked upright. For a second I can't see the other one and I panic that they've had to remove it for some reason, but then I see his foot poking out of the end of the blankets, also in plaster. He's not conscious, but he doesn't seem to be asleep exactly; he's lying rigid and stiff, and he's got an oxygen mask over his face. His face isn't relaxed in sleep – it almost seems screwed up, contorted with effort. Or pain.

My heart's drumming against my ribcage like a marching band and I feel almost on the verge of tears. I've never seen anyone in such a state – even his ears are bruised. I have to fight down nausea.

I only wanted to see him, but his eyes suddenly flutter open. For a second he looks totally confused and bewildered, and I wonder if he really could have had part of his memories removed. But then he recognises me.

'Millie,' he says, slowly removing his oxygen mask.

'Oh, Nick,' I say, keeping the tears back through pure willpower. 'You remember me!'

He laughs huskily. His voice is so weak. 'It's been an odd few days,' he says, his eyes fluttering closed.

I think he's fallen back to sleep, but he speaks again. 'I'm sorry,' he says.

'Sorry? Why are you sorry?'

'I missed you earlier,' he says, his voice only just louder than a whisper.

'What?'

'Earlier, earlier . . . I didn't see you,' he says.

'Oh, it's OK. It doesn't matter now,' I say, having absolutely no clue what he's talking about. 'What . . . happened?'

His eyelids flutter. 'I don't know,' he wheezes. 'It just . . . cuts off.'

'What does?' I say.

'The . . . the memory . . .' he says. 'I don't remember . . . it's gone . . .'

His brainstream. A weird pressure settles on my lungs, the horror trickling into my stomach. At least I know why *my* memory's patchy, and it's not because someone's reached in and taken it.

'Are you . . .' I gesture to his injuries. 'Is it . . . bad? Really bad?'

His eyes open and his face contorts with pain again. 'It hurts,' he says.

'Oh, Nick,' I say, biting the inside of my lip to keep from crying. 'I'm so sorry.'

'It's OK,' he whispers. 'Not your fault.'

His eyes close again and this time he is asleep. I stumble out of the room, back towards the front desk, the image of Nick's purple-and-black skin imprinted on my brain. Who – or what – could have done this to him? I feel dazed, like I've been smacked in the head with a frying pan.

'Where have you been? Dr Tavish is waiting for you . . .' the receptionist starts to say when I walk back into the

90

waiting room, but trails off when she sees my face. 'Are you ill?' she says, looking horrified. I can only assume all the colour has drained out of my face. 'Shall I tell Dr Tavish you need to go home?'

'No, no, I'm OK,' I say quickly. I can only imagine what Dr Tavish would read into that. When I saw him after the Winter Festival last year I had a cold, and now he asks me every time if I've had another cold recently. 'Can I go straight through?'

'Millie,' Dr Tavish says when I enter the appointment room. He always looks so happy to see me; I suppose he just loves fiddling around with people's heads. 'How are you?'

Dr Tavish is the only person outside the Company I've ever spoken to. Instead of a uniform like the medical-centre staff, he wears a long white coat with no logo. He works for a hospital in London, but it's not a Company hospital. I suppose it must belong to another company. My Company lets me see him because he treated me for my injury originally and he's the best head-injury specialist in Britain. Like Welbeck he wears glasses, though I've never been a hundred per cent sure they're not for show. They're very thick. I sometimes wonder if the company he was born into didn't provide eye surgery.

'Er . . . I'm fine, thanks,' I say, hopping on to the long chair in the centre of the room. I still feel stunned – my mind keeps turning back to Nick's bruises. Everything Dr Tavish is saying sounds like it's coming from far away.

'No recurring headaches? Eyesight problems? Anything like that?' he says, prepping his equipment.

'No, no,' I say.

'Any more of those horrible colds?'

'No,' I say, 'although . . . my RetinaChip has been a bit dodgy lately; I don't know if that means anything?'

'You have problems accessing it? Difficulties seeing it?'

'No, no, I just . . . don't get messages right away sometimes,' I finish lamely.

'That's probably more to do with the technology, Millie,' he says. 'It'll settle down. It's only a matter of time.'

'OK, yeah,' I say.

'Now,' he says, getting out the little gadget he uses to check my eyes from his bag. 'You're still having short-term memory issues?'

'Yes,' I say, blinking as he shines the light in my eyes.

'Not very helpful for studying, is it?' he smiles.

'No,' I say, 'definitely not.'

He looks in both my eyes, checks my ears and examines the texture of my scalp with a magnifying machine.

'It's healed up well, there won't be much residual scarring at all.'

'Even the stitched-up areas?'

'Yes, they're fine,' he says. 'The stitches have disappeared very nicely.'

Dr Tavish tends to talk about the surface of my head proudly, as if it's a work of art he's created. In a way, I suppose it is. He puts the magnifying machine away in his doctor's bag and takes out the laser he uses to check the surface of my brain for damage.

'So the memory problems haven't improved?' he says, slowly scanning the laser over the back of my head.

I let out a long sigh, one I feel I've been holding since I stepped in Room 57, and slump down in the chair. 'No,' I say. 'I can't remember anything. Even short term.'

'I know it's hard, but I promise it will get better,' Dr Tavish says. 'With these sorts of injuries, the first few months are always the most difficult—'

'But it's been six months now, and it just seems to be getting worse!'

'You must be patient, Millie,' he says. 'Putting extra pressure on yourself will not help you get better any quicker.'

'I know, I know. I just wish I had a little more time before the end of the year.'

'The Company is fully aware of your problems, and they know it's only a temporary condition. I'm sure they'll take that into consideration with your exam results.'

I'm sure they won't, especially as Cranshaw told me that while the school would do everything to help me, they didn't want to give me an unfair advantage over the other pupils. But I nod along anyway.

He moves my hair to one side so he can check the other side of my head. I wonder what will happen to Nick now. Will Cranshaw tell him the same thing?

'Did you ever make up with your brother in the end?' he asks.

Immediately I can feel my body tense up, as it does every time Dr Tavish mentions Jake. 'Er, yes. I mean, no, actually.'

Dr Tavish laughs. 'Well, did you or didn't you?'

'Well, I *saw* him,' I say, my back teeth clenching together. 'But I didn't— I haven't— He's just really annoying.'

Dr Tavish laughs again, like it's all a big joke. 'Siblings,' he twinkles, but I look away.

'Oh,' I say, suddenly remembering. 'They brainstreamed us yesterday. It was mandatory, so I had to do it, but it was all fine.'

The brain scanner stops moving over my head. 'You *what*?'

'I . . . they looked at my brainstream,' I say. 'I tried to say no. I told them what you said, but I had to!'

'Millie,' Dr Tavish says.

'But it was fine, nothing happened,' I say. 'It didn't even hurt!'

'Millie,' Dr Tavish says again. 'Do you realise how delicate the balance of your brain is at the moment? How easily the healing process can be disturbed?'

'Erm,' I say.

'Can you . . .' He sighs. He doesn't sound angry, just disappointed. 'Can you promise me you won't use your brainstream or let anyone else use your brainstream again? Please? For your own good?'

'I promise,' I say in a very small voice. 'It was only five seconds—'

'*One* second could be too much,' Dr Tavish says. 'There's no way of knowing how much those five seconds could have set your recovery back. If someone tells you it's *mandatory*—' he spins the word out— 'you just tell them to talk to me first.'

'All right, I will,' I say.

He resumes his scanning for a few more minutes as we sit in silence.

'OK, well, I think that's all done for today, Millie,' he says, putting his scanner away. 'I don't think you'll need another appointment till after the summer now.'

'OK, cool, thanks,' I say, hopping down from the chair.

'See you then,' he says.

I leave the room and I'm halfway down the corridor when I realise how close I am to Nick's room. Would it be tempting fate to try to see him again? I dither at the corner, and then decide not to. I turn into the corridor to the exit door at the back.

'Excuse me!' someone at the far end of the corridor shouts. I jolt with shock. It's the blonde nurse I passed in the corridor before, but this time she's definitely noticed me.

'You can't be here. Please leave,' she says, rushing towards me with her arms out, like she's trying to herd a cow out of a field.

I genuinely don't want to annoy her further, especially as she already looks pretty angry, but to leave I have to walk past her, exactly where she doesn't want me to go.

'Er, actually I was just leaving.'

95

I carry on walking forward, and bizarrely she keeps on striding towards me, flapping her arms.

'No, no, no, you can't be here!' she says, her voice rising.

'What is—' I've stopped, but she lunges towards me, trying to escort me back up the corridor. 'OK, look, I don't know where you expect me to go; the exit is down that way,' I say.

'Go to the bathroom and lock yourself in for five minutes. I don't care,' she shrieks, her face red as she tries to twist my shoulders in the opposite direction. Her eyes keep flicking away from my face to the exit door behind her. I attempt to slip out of her grasp but it doesn't really work, and she shoves me firmly in the back.

'*Go!*' she says, properly panicking now.

'What—' I turn round, and in the same instant two nurses and a teacher enter through the door, holding a stretcher between them. On the stretcher is an unconscious girl with dark brown hair, whose skin is covered from head to toe in red and purple bruises. Her leg is angled strangely and there's a flash of white around the knee.

It shocks me like a punch in the stomach, pushing all the air out of my body. I can only stand there and gape, as the three people holding the stretcher stand and gape at me.

The nurse takes her opportunity. She pulls me out of the corridor and into the bathroom.

'Right,' she says, her face centimetres from mine. 'You

didn't see that. She . . . she fell from a tree. The girl . . . she was climbing a tree and she fell. That's all that happened, she was just climbing a tree.'

I nod obediently in shock.

'You don't tell anyone,' says the nurse. 'It's very important . . . The Company can't find out.'

On the last sentence, her voice goes from a demanding bark to a broken whisper. She looks at me, terrified. I don't know what on earth could be going on.

'OK . . . OK . . .' I say, my head reeling from Nick's injuries and the girl's injuries, so many bruises swirling in my mind . . .

'All right, go quickly,' she says, shooing me out of the room. I hurry down the now empty corridor, through the exit door and out of the medical centre, stunned.

Five

Everyone else has fallen asleep, but every time I think I've finally pushed all of Nick's injuries – the bandaged arm, the purple-and-blue mottled skin, the neck brace – out of my mind, another one pinballs its way in, the horror flaring up all over again. I only saw the girl for a fleeting second, but just thinking about the angle her leg was twisted at instinctively makes my stomach roll. What is happening? Does Cranshaw know, and is she trying to keep it a secret? But why?

And why the mandatory brainstreaming yesterday? Do they really think another pupil could be responsible for this?

I haven't told anyone about what I saw. Not even about Nick. I couldn't think of a way to say it without sounding totally ridiculous, and when Shell said, 'How was the medical centre? Any sign of—' I opened my mouth, and then I just shook my head. She shrugged and said, 'Knew it was a long shot.'

She was almost more interested in what Dr Tavish had told me about brainstreaming. 'I told you,' she kept saying. 'I told you not to let them brainstream you. Didn't I tell you?'

I can hear Lu gently snoring in the bed next to mine, and I pull the covers over my head, trying to think of something happier. I will not think about bruises. I squeeze my eyes shut, focusing on a long-ago memory of climbing the trees in the school grounds, Jake moving up the branches higher than everyone else, balancing right at the top and calling down to the rest of us, 'I think I could jump from here!' and my head starts to swim, the image turning hazy – I can feel myself drifting off, my limbs turning weightless . . .

The crowd closing in, the brush of metal against my arm, the screen above me—

I jerk awake, one leg half out of bed, my heart battering against my lungs. I was barely even asleep and now I'm completely awake again, adrenaline thundering down my veins like I've just lapped Shell in a cross-country run. If only I could remember what happened that day in London when I hurt my head. These little fragments, scraps of memory floating to the top and washing up again and again on the shores of my brain – I just want to know what they *mean*. When I was recovering, Cranshaw told me

I had been separated from the group on a class trip, wandered into the road and got hit by a car. The crowd I was in, that could be people in the street in London . . . but why do I keep remembering the screen? What was on it? Was a unit beside me? Why?

And why can't I see a unit without my chest clamping down with fear? Why can't I look at Jake without wanting to punch him in his stupid face? He wasn't even near the car, Cranshaw says.

I touch my head, where the stitches are, and then I remember the brainstreaming the other day. I did it – well, the nurse did it – and my head didn't fall apart. I know what Dr Tavish said. I know I promised I wouldn't. But if it's healed enough that I can look at my brainstreams . . .

My breathing is laboured and my hand is quivering as I lift my IndexChip and bring up the brainstreaming screen. I'm willing my skull to stay in one piece as I scroll back through my brainstreams of the last weeks and months.

The RetinaChip automatically saves your brainstreams as you live them. If you want to post them on to the network you can chop them up and leave out all the embarrassing and/or boring bits – although I do know a few of the boys think it's really funny to post a whole load of toilet clips all together. For the last few months all my brainstreams are marked with a blue dot, which means they've never been downloaded or posted.

One date is marked INCOMPLETE: 16 November. It cuts off halfway through. Dr Tavish had said something about the effect of the trauma on memories leading up to the accident – as if my brain had helpfully deleted anything that might help me figure out what had happened. Just looking at that date makes my lungs clench. I can't – I cannot – start with that one, so I scroll past it quickly to last September. Up here I haven't lost so many whole days – just stretches of time here and there, dotted about, like teeth missing from a mouth.

The first brainstream with a bit missing is early on in the month, when we'd just got back to school after the summer. I can still remember bits and pieces from back then. It doesn't seem as scary as delving right into the murky depths of my brain. More like paddling in the shallows.

I take a very deep breath, my stomach jittery, then, before I can picture my skull cracking apart, I press play and the brainstream begins. Usually I watch other people's brainstreams on my tablet, but replaying my own on my RetinaChip is just like living through it again, remembering every detail. I'm sitting in my history classroom from last term, as Llewellyn starts the class. I can remember this – at least, I know what's going on. These lessons were the first Jake and I had had together for about six years, and at first Llewellyn couldn't seem to get over the fact we were twins – she kept saying really cringy things like 'double trouble' and 'I got two for the price of one this term!' despite us both having changed so much since we started at Oaktree that we barely looked related any more, let alone like twins.

Jake was there for the first lesson, but didn't turn up for the next three. This just doesn't happen at Oaktree. The first time, when I realised Jake wasn't sitting next to me as the lesson started, I expected Llewellyn to be horrified. I expected there would be a search for his IndexChip tracker, units scouring the grounds, our parents sobbing in Cranshaw's office (although to be honest the likelihood of that happening would depend on how busy their schedules were). But instead, she glanced casually at the seat next to me and said, 'Oh yes, no Jake today,' and then just carried on.

It was only after the lesson, when I messaged him, worried he was either critically ill or fatally injured, that I found out he'd been in Cranshaw's office the whole time. *She invited me for a cup of tea,* he messaged. *Got the teachers to let me out of lessons for the afternoon. It's not a big deal.*

Does this happen often? I messaged back.

Sometimes, he replied.

But it happened the lesson after, and the lesson after that. I couldn't quite put my finger on why I felt so resentful of it. 'What do you talk about?' I said, one day as I helped him 'catch up' (i.e. download my brainstream of the lesson on to his tablet).

He shrugged. 'I don't know. Just stuff. She tells me things about the Company.'

'Things about the Company?' I said. I didn't even know if that was allowed.

I'd always known Jake was Cranshaw's favourite – everyone did. Any special job, any example she wanted to present to the rest of us to look up to, the congeniality prize every year. And I knew he'd met up with her and Florrie privately. In our first year at Oaktree he spoke of nothing else but seeing Florrie up close and became the go-to expert for anyone with a question about units, or indeed whether Cranshaw's office was built over an unexploded World War Two bomb.

But Cranshaw merrily signing Jake out of lessons so they could have a chat seemed like a step too far. 'Doesn't she worry you'll fall behind?' I said.

Jake looked at me like I was insane. 'Nah,' he said.

'I don't get . . .' I started to say. I didn't know how to put this without him getting defensive. 'Why does she like you so much?'

Jake shrugged. 'She just likes interesting people, she says. People who like units.'

'That's it?' I said. 'That's the whole reason?'

Jake looked at me. 'You don't know what it's like for units like Florrie,' he said. 'On a level intelligence-wise with humans, but everyone just treats her like an appliance. Only people like me and Cranshaw really get it. We're the only ones who really understand units.'

I couldn't think of a good response to that. 'Pfft,' I said.

The next lesson, Lu and I were two minutes late for history – *two minutes* – and Llewellyn stood us up in front of the class and lectured us on the importance of time-keeping and 'no excuses' and 'What would happen if every Company executive didn't bother to turn up on time to meetings?' I started to say, 'But, Miss, it's not like we skipped a whole lesson—' but that just prompted another wave of 'disrupting the lesson' and 'lack of respect' and on and on and on. Jake was slumped in the front row, barely listening. I tried to catch his eye, so I could somehow telepathically let him know this was *not fair* and all his fault somehow, but he was playing something on his tablet.

The brainstream starts in the next lesson. *I'm sitting at my desk, inspecting my fingernails, aware of the door out of the corner of my eye. If Jake turns up, fine. If he doesn't, I – well, I don't know yet. A sarcastic comment is the best I've come up with so far. 'I suppose a lack of respect isn't such a big deal when Cranshaw says it's OK?' I'm still working on it.*

Llewellyn arrives and shuts the door. If Jake turns up now he's officially late. I comb the end of my hair with my fingers, my insides curdling with tension. I wish I didn't care so much about what Jake does. The problem is, when you're twins, you're always compared.

Then a message from Jake bleeps through on my RetinaChip. Hey, Mills, not going to make it to history today. Emergency. Can you tell Llewellyn? Thanks.

I sit with my mouth open for a minute. He wants me to cover for him now? I could just not say anything. I could just see what happens when Llewellyn doesn't have a note from Cranshaw excusing Jake.

But of course I can't. I put my hand up. 'Miss, Jake isn't going to be in today. He's got some sort of emergency.'

'Oh,' she says, and presses something on her tablet. And

that's it. No disappointment, no anger, no lecture. She even has a half-smile on her face.

'Miss,' I say again. 'Don't you think . . .'

'Don't I think what, Millie?' she says.

'Well . . .' I say. Am I really going to demand my own brother gets in trouble? 'Jake's missing a lot of lessons, I was wondering . . .'

'Lucky he's got you to help him catch up then, isn't it?' she says in an issue-closed sort of way, then swipes the lesson plan on to the main board from her tablet. 'Now, Winston Churchill . . .'

I slump in my seat, my stomach curdling with anger. I hate it when the teachers do this. It's like they consider Jake and I to be two halves of one person and he gets the personality, the humour and the naughty streak and I'm stuck with the conscience, the work ethic and the obedience. Everyone always expects me to clear up his messes after him. My face prickles at the injustice. What kind of emergency could this be anyway? Cranshaw has an emergency cup of tea she needs to drink with him?

It's a Tuesday, so it's beautifully sunny, and there's just a hint of a snap in the air. I'm looking out of the window as Llewellyn drones on, following a tiny bird's progress round and round the courtyard, when one side of the Main Building's double doors opens a crack, then a bit further. Cranshaw walks out, followed closely by Florrie. I immediately sit up straight. Is Jake not with her after all?

Cranshaw's gait is hunched and she keeps glancing around, as if she's up to something she shouldn't be. She runs down the steps quickly and motions Florrie to hurry up. Cranshaw usually holds herself up high, her walking pace slow and deliberate. But today she's bent over, scuttling around, as if she's afraid of being spotted.

She has something in her hand. At first I think it's some sort of bright-red box. Then I realise it's a paper book. Outside. In contact with the air. For a second my insides actually quiver with the . . . wrongness of it all. I know if I was to take a paper book out of the Old Section of the library, let alone outside, I would probably be expelled – all the books belong to Cranshaw. Well, they belong to the school, under Cranshaw's responsibility. If she wants to take all the books on a jaunt around the grounds I suppose that's her own business.

I recognise the cover of the book. It takes me a moment to place it as I've only ever seen it on my tablet before. It's the first Alisha Atkins book, the one where she travels back in time to World War Two and roundhouse-kicks Hitler in the face. It was immortalised in paper due to how successful it was. This just makes the whole thing even stranger. Why would Cranshaw be reading Alisha Atkins? Everyone my age has read it. We were practically brought up on it. But Cranshaw is old.

She crosses the courtyard quickly, disappearing momentarily from my view when she walks under the oak tree, and then stands still, Florrie next to her, at the very end of the courtyard, towards the Left Building. I have to twist all the way round in my seat just to keep her within my sight. I check to see if Llewellyn's looking, but she's so busy talking about the Battle of Britain she doesn't even glance my way.

When I turn back, Cranshaw has moved, just slightly, so I can only see the top of her candyfloss hair. But Florrie has turned round. I can see her face, and I'm momentarily taken aback by how animated it seems. Florrie's nodding while someone, just out of view, is speaking to her. She might even be making eye contact with them. I lean over the windowsill, straining to see who it is. My nose is nearly pressed up against the glass.

Then they all move, and I see Jake. He's smiling and chatting with Florrie, then turning to Cranshaw and offering her his arm like something out of a black-and-white movie. Cranshaw takes it, and they stroll leisurely on to the lawns, as if it's the most natural thing to be out for a walk round the grounds. There's no urgency to their movements whatsoever. Jake has the Alisha Atkins book in his hand.

I snap out of the brainstream in surprise, instinctively flicking my IndexChip and closing the screen. What? None of that makes any sense. Putting aside the weirdness of seeing a unit have a conversation with a human – which I wouldn't believe myself if I hadn't just seen it with my own eyes – what has this got to do with my head injury? Why did my brain suppress this memory in particular? I can't work it out.

I lie back into my pillow, my brain buzzing, and switch back into the brainstream.

As soon as lessons are over I rush over to Jake's dormitory. If I message him he'll just ignore it. At Chestnut house someone else lets me in and I run up the three flights of stairs and batter on his door.

Jake opens up and when he sees it's me his face drops. But in the next second he's already recovered. 'Millie! Hey! How was, er, history? Was Llewellyn OK?'

'Fine,' I say, half out of breath. 'I was just wondering if I could borrow your copy of the first Alisha Atkins book?'

'Wh-what?' says Jake. Clearly he expected something angrier. 'Don't you already have it on your tablet?'

'No, I mean the paper version,' I say.

Jake looks at me, his gaze slowly moving from my right eye to my left and back again. 'Millie—'

'I saw you,' I say. 'I saw you and Cranshaw earlier. And Florrie. Emergency all sorted out, was it?'

'Millie, you really don't know—'

'I just don't understand the book,' I say. 'What was the book about, Jake? Have you got it? Can I see it? Are you and Cranshaw starting a book group now—'

Jake suddenly jerks forward, grabbing me by the shoulder and putting his face right up to mine. 'That's a secret,' he says in a low voice. 'Don't talk about it. To anyone.'

'Jake—' I say, but he slams the door in my face.

Six

'Millie,' says Shell. *'Millie!'*

I jerk out of a daydream, pulling my fingernails away from my mouth. 'Wha-what?' I say.

Shell looks at me beseechingly. 'I need your he-eeelp,' she says.

It's Thursday evening, and we're in the library. We're supposed to be revising. But Riley stomped over to the other side of the room in a sulk about an hour ago after shouting at Finn for singing the Sammy's jingle, Finn got bored and left shortly after, and Shell has been secretly reading the third Alisha Atkins book on her tablet ever since, thinking I can't tell. And I'm staring into space, thinking.

Watching my brainstream the other night has just left me feeling more confused than ever. I had the same dream

I always have – *the crowd closing in, the brush of metal against my arm* – except I looked up and it was Florrie standing next to me, holding a red paper book. But then it changed to the showbot from the Ling Chang movie we watched the other day. When I'm not thinking about that, my brain immediately reverts back to Nick and the girl in the medical centre. It almost seems like a horrible nightmare now. I could almost believe it didn't even happen.

'Can't Riley help you?' I say. 'I'm reading about . . .' I have to look at my tablet to remember.

'I don't really fancy getting my head bitten off again, thanks,' says Shell.

We look over to where Riley's sitting hunched over a table, her hands over her ears as she reads. There's a litre bottle of the energy drink Rush in front of her, nearly empty. She's had her status set to *Riley Thomas is revising in the library* for the last three days.

'OK, OK,' I say, rubbing my eyes. I feel half asleep. 'What is it?'

'*If* the debate exam is on brainstreaming,' says Shell, leaning in to me, 'how amazing would it be if we could quote from some really old book about the introduction of brainstreaming into the justice system and how—'

'Book?' I say.

'A paper book,' she says. 'So much more authentic—'

I'm already shaking my head. 'Oh no, Shell. No.'

'What?' She looks up at me, eyes wide with pretend innocence. 'You don't even know what I'm going to say.'

'Yes I do. You're going to trawl through all the paper books in the Old Section by hand and you're going to force me to help.'

Shell's eyes flicker from side to side. 'Well—'

'*No,*' I say a little too loudly. The people at the table next to us turn round. 'It'll take all night! It's already eight o'clock, and I want to go to bed some time before midnight!'

'Millie, come on,' she says. 'You're the only one who knows the system in there!'

'That's not true, you all *know* it,' I say. 'You just think you don't. Anyway, Riley knows it, ask her.'

'First of all, *no,*' says Shell. 'And second, she doesn't know it. She just pretends to because it makes her feel superior. We got stuck in there ages last time because she couldn't work out where they'd filed a Brunel biography.'

'Can't you just . . . Is there nothing on brainstreaming on the library database?' I say.

'No,' says Shell. 'Well, not the history of it.'

'All right, all right!' I say, getting up. 'Let's get this over with.'

The problem with the Old Section of the library is that, unlike with a document you can access with your tablet, there's no way to search for a word or topic mentioned in a paper book. Apparently, the pages can't be scanned because Cranshaw is incredibly paranoid about somehow damaging them, so they're all just logged in with their titles and a basic description. If you want to find something specific in an old book, you actually have to go and look through them. Physically.

It's not even that simple (and, believe me, with nearly five thousand books, that's not very simple). Cranshaw is so hysterical about the old books falling apart and so insistent that we remember they're all museum pieces and parts of history blah blah blah, she only allows one group of pupils to be admitted to the Old Section per day, *and* you have to wear cotton gloves to handle the books, *and* there's this really weird rule about breathing. She's worried that oxygen will break down the ink compounds faster, so the room's kept completely drained of air most of the time. If you want to use it the librarybots have to turn on the air dispensers and you have to wait while the oxygen is pumped in. Also, you can't talk too loudly or gasp or sigh or yawn or sneeze or the librarybots kick you out (the yawning rule is a particularly hard one to avoid). And you can't take any books out, and you have to check in your tablets when you go in. So the only way of keeping track of any information you learn is to download it later from your brainstream. The whole thing is a massive pain. (Obviously none of these rules apply to Cranshaw herself. Because she's so *careful*.)

Having said that, quoting from an old book is an absolute guaranteed way of getting an amazing mark. Teachers literally light up when you say, 'As it says in the *paper edition* of (whoever's book) on (something boring) . . .' It's like the information itself doesn't actually matter, just the amount of effort you put in to finding it.

'Ooh, you know who hasn't been running for a while? Megan Wickham,' says Shell as we cross the library floor, one eye on her RetinaChip. 'That's good, isn't it?'

I stop dead, my heart jolting. Megan Wickham has dark brown hair. Megan Wickham must have been the girl in the medical centre.

'You all right?' Shell says, looking at me. 'You look a bit freaked.'

'Ah . . .' I nearly blurt it all out.

Shell raises her eyebrows expectantly. 'What?'

'N-nothing,' I say eventually.

I can't tell her – I should be trying to stop thinking about any of it, not dragging more people in. Everyone else is doing their best not to mention Nick any more – Finn didn't even flinch the other day when we saw he'd been deleted from the network. A company works on team-work, as they always tell us – and teamwork doesn't work if one person keeps blathering on about something every-one else wants to forget.

Shell side-eyes me. 'We're still going to the Old Sec-tion, loser,' she says.

'Yay,' I say weakly, following behind.

Megan Wickham. I didn't know her well, but my mum once left a family holiday early to go and yell at Megan's dad. They both sit on the Company's board and he'd disa-greed with her on something. After we got back to school, Riley had pointed Megan out to me in the canteen and she had raised her eyebrows at me, as if to say, 'Parents, eh?'

113

'They probably won't even let us in,' I say as we approach the desk. 'Everyone's revising at the moment; why wouldn't they all be in there?'

'We'd like to enter the Old Section please,' Shell says to the librarybot on the desk.

We hand over our tablets – I'm careful not to make contact with its hand – and the librarybot presses a button on the desk. Shell gives me a withering look. 'See, easy,' she says.

From outside we can hear the air dispensers in the Old Section whirring. The meter next to the door, displaying the oxygen level, rises up and up until it hits somewhere near seventy per cent and dings. The librarybot unlocks the door and lets us through.

The Old Section is laid out completely differently from the rest of the library. I think the Old Section is actually bigger than the main library, but it feels almost cramped because it's so full of bookshelves. In the daytime, the light pours through the tall window into the main library. It's full of space – bright and airy with big windows and rows and rows of desks for people to work at, a few check-in machines along the wall in case you can't log on to the network with your chip, and that's pretty much it.

The Old Section, on the other hand, is *full* of books. The bookshelves stretch into eternity and all the way up to the ceiling. Even standing in the main aisle and looking straight down, you can only just about see the far wall. The windows are as big but the sunlight comes through fractured, squeezing through gaps between the book-shelves. Even at night-time it's gloomy, as the electric lights are motion-sensitive and only come on when you walk near them.

That familiar smell of the plastic, machine-pumped air combined with the mould-and-damp smell from the books hits us as we enter. Everything's arranged by number, so I direct Shell to rows 185 and 186, which cover mid-twenty-first-century history.

'Oh God, I actually forgot how much *history* there was,' Shell says as we approach the shelves. 'We should skim-read titles until we find something good.'

'I don't know, Shell,' I say, pulling on a pair of gloves from a box at the end of the shelf. 'This all seems general. We'll need something specific for the debate exam.

'Maybe we should look by subject instead,' I say, thumbing through books about the colonisation of the moon.

Shell sighs loudly, and we both look around for the librarybot.

'I might see if there's anything in technology about brainstreaming,' she says. I knew she'd get bored of this quickly.

'Well, we shouldn't give up on finding something about its history,' I say, wondering how *I* ended up talking *her* into this. 'I'll look by subject for a bit.'

'OK then, library-system girl,' says Shell, turning back to the shelf. 'I'll message you if I find anything.'

I walk down the endless aisles to Row 102. It's all the other books they can't fit in anywhere else, arranged alphabetically by subject.

I find 'J', for justice, and flick through the titles. Finding nothing, I move up a few rows to 'R' for rights, just to see if I can find anything on legal rights.

A title suddenly catches my eye. *Units in the Home: 2065– present* by Chester A. Hughes. Units only came into general use in the early 2070s, but they were being developed by scientists for years and years before that. I think the really rich had household units by about 2065, and they were basically the predecessors of today's cleanbots.

I pull the book out from the shelf and flick through it. It's weird handling paper when I'm so used to my tablet. The pages are so . . . strange. I can't help rifling the pages back and forth with my fingers. This title must have been a huge bestseller when it came out to be preserved in paper. There are a lot of pictures of early units looking like hunks of metal. The original housebot, which I think was meant to be a cleanbot and a foodbot combined but ended up not really being able to do anything that well, looks more like a waste-disposal unit with a mop in its hand than anything else. I flick through the pages quickly, only looking at the pictures. I actually find some of the older units quite cute, better than the almost-human-but-not-quite look they have today. The housebots were really small as well, barely up to the average human's waist; I think today's units are too tall. Maybe it's because I'm short, but it unnerves me the way the cleanbots and food-bots in the canteen tower over me. They've got to be an average of at least six foot these days.

I flick further on in the book. There's loads of stuff about whether units can be considered equal to humans or not. The 2060s viewpoint does seem to be closer to mine than Jess's – there's a lot of talk about the import-ance of keeping robots segregated from one another. But then I knew it was an outdated opinion. Chester A. Hughes has devoted a lot of time to pointing out possible signs of robots being capable of a greater intelligence – the movement of their eyes, for example, or their ability to ape human mannerisms. I flick forward a few more pages and a title jumps out at me – the Unit Rights Act 2068.

This surprises me. I had no idea unit rights were even considered so long ago. I read on. It had been really popu-lar and many high-profile figures had spoken out in favour of it, but it didn't go through Parliament. The day before the decision, a politician called Perrin Rodgers stood in front of Big Ben and gave a stirring speech about the importance of protecting ourselves against units and not allowing them to get too close – and then without warning a bomb went off in the crowd. Several people were killed, including Rodgers. It was later found that a cleanbot, working on the street, had malfunctioned and caused the explosion.

I'm frozen with shock. All this time they've been

telling us over and over and over again that units can't hurt us, that they've never hurt anyone, and to think any other way is wrong. But it's not true – the evidence is there. I'm right – they're dangerous. I wonder if the cleanbot even malfunctioned. It's very convenient that it just happened to explode and kill the leader of the group opposing unit rights at that particular moment.

The act, of course, was thrown out of Parliament the next day and people began to question the safety of using units. The demand for unit rights went quiet but they were still used for factory work and industrial cleaning. They didn't feature so much in households any more; they'd gone out of fashion. I suppose now they're beginning to come back in. For years Cranshaw was the only person I'd ever heard of having a unit as an assistant, but last summer a lot of my parents' friends and neighbours seemed to have them.

Recently the support for freedom for units has increased. A timeline of units' development at the back of the book shows that a law for unit rights has been debated in Parliament several times in the last few years, but the anti-units group, Humans First, always came up with an irrefutable piece of evidence at the last minute that had to be looked into or something. Now I wonder if that's all just a cover up for horrible unit atrocities.

I close the book and put it back on the shelf. I almost can't believe what I've just read. The thing that really makes my blood boil is the fact that I'm right, units *are* dangerous, but people like Jess are always going to make out that I'm the one with the problem. And maybe one day they'll put themselves in danger without even realising it and end up dead or maimed or injured at the hands of a bloodthirsty unit . . .

A thought flickers at the back of my brain, but before it can burst into being I'm distracted by a movement at the end of the shelf. I can't tell if it's the librarybot checking we're not breathing too much or someone . . . or *something* else. I nearly call out, 'Who's there?' but that'll definitely get me kicked out of the Old Section, if it is the librarybot. I slowly approach the end of the row, trying to keep as quiet as possible – but nothing's there.

There's a huge clank from one of the air dispensers in the ceiling, making me jump. I can't shake off the feeling there's a librarybot looking over my shoulder; it unnerves me. This is the problem – they're always around you. In the library, cleaning your room when you're at lessons, in the grounds, in the canteen, in the school corridors, all over the Woodland River Centre – and how does anyone know what they're thinking? At Oaktree, in particular, they've got us completely surrounded. If they decided—

And suddenly the little spark of a suspicion from a moment ago blazes into flame like the world's biggest bonfire. The attacks. The disappearances. It's not another pupil. It's the units.

My absolute conviction and my complete terror hit me at the same moment, so hard that my legs buckle. It all makes sense. The attacker has to have incredible strength, to hurt Nick and Megan so badly. The attacker has to be able to destroy an IndexChip's tracker. And the attacker has to be able to remove brainstreams from a person's mind. Units can do all these things. They can definitely read IndexChips. You can download brainstreams on to them. And the monstrous strength is a given – they're made of the highest-grade titanium. How easy would it be for a unit – or even a whole group of them – to corner a pupil and attack them?

I want to cry and I want to be sick. *The units are rising up. The units are rising up.* I have to tell someone. I retch suddenly, my stomach squeezing in on itself like a fist.

All this time I've been right. I think about Jess gloating at me about the Unit Rights Act – the new one – and clutch my face. My worst fears are going to come true and *no one will believe me.* It can't be a coincidence that these attacks are happening when the units are about to become free – what if it's a way of blackmailing the Company to vote in favour of the act? Nick and Daisy both have parents who sit on the board – so does Megan. *I* have a parent on the board. And Jake too obviously . . . who else?

There's a beeping coming from somewhere. I can't concentrate through the noise; I can't focus on the important things. I need to think about what to do next, but the beeping's getting progressively louder, filling my head and pushing out any reasoning. I put my hands over my ears but that doesn't help.

'What? What is it?' I hiss into the empty row. There's nothing but beeping in response. It sounds as frantic and panicky as I do. I tentatively stick my head round the bookshelf, wondering if this is some strange way for the librarybot to lure me into a trap, but then I locate the noise. It's coming from the door. I creep up to it, my eyes flicking from side to side like a frightened rabbit.

The meter beside the door shows how much oxygen is left in the room. It's usually at around seventy to eighty per cent. As I approach the door I can immediately see why it's beeping – it's at fourteen per cent. And dropping.

I stare at it, my eyes popping out of my head. It must be broken. It *must* be. Then I realise the air dispensers are humming; they're draining the air out of the room.

I grab the door handle and wrench it so hard I nearly pull my arm off – but it's locked. I rattle the handle desperately, but it doesn't budge. The door automatically locks whenever anyone leaves so no outside air can get in. But *we're still in here*. I batter at the door with both hands, yelling out. Surely the librarybot outside will hear me? But nothing happens.

I call out Shell's name, but I've got no idea where she is. My breath is coming in short little gasps. I can't use up too much air, I keep thinking, but I can't stop. I need to keep calm, but the panic's rising in my chest. Does the librarybot think we've left somehow? Does it think the room's empty? Or . . . is this deliberate?

So easy to say the system simply malfunctioned, and a couple of unlucky pupils got trapped inside. Tragic, obviously, but no one's fault. I gasp, a big shuddering breath, and straight away clap my hands over my mouth, as if I can push the air back in. My heart thuds against my ribcage and I feel dizzy, which scares me even more. The meter, still beeping, drops down to ten per cent. I haven't got much time.

Riley's still in the main library. I message her, but I know she won't check it until she leaves. Anyone else won't get here in time. I weave my way down to the glass wall that divides the main library and the Old Section. It's getting hard to walk straight and I nearly wobble into a bookshelf. When I make it, I lean against the glass, trying to focus. There's pressure on my lungs, like I'm holding my breath underwater. I can see Riley across the nearly empty library, still hunched grumpily over her tablet with her fists over her ears.

'Riley!' I yell, banging my hands on the glass. 'Riley!'

But she doesn't hear, and neither does anyone else. My fists go *bunk-bunk-bunk* against the glass, and I know it's too thick to let any sound through. 'Riley,' I say again, but there's no power behind my voice. She remains motionless.

I'm so conscious of every breath I take. They're wheezing in and out; my head swims with each one. I have to think of something else I can do. There must be a way out I haven't thought of.

But it's so difficult. I feel vaguely as though I'm

floating. The panic and the terror are slowly ebbing away from me, and I know that's not a good thing. I stumble back to the door, weakly trying the handle again, but it's no use. The meter is now at six per cent. It's still beeping, but it sounds distant. I breathe in again and my vision breaks up into dots. Will I pass out before the meter reaches zero? Is Shell already unconscious somewhere? There has to be another door, another exit. But of course Cranshaw wouldn't want the books being damaged . . .

My eyes suddenly alight on a big red button just above the meter. The thought takes longer than usual to properly crystallise in my brain – *the fire alarm. The fire alarm will open the fire escape.* My mind jolts with understanding and suddenly everything seems to rush back into focus again. I slam my fist down on the button. The sudden *weyo-weyo-weyo* of the alarm, impossibly loud and clear in my ears, is the sweetest sound I've ever heard. I stagger down the bookshelves, on my last reserves of energy, drawn to the glowing green light of the fire escape like a moth.

The air hits me like a wall as I crash through the door. Momentum propels me forward – I practically bounce down three flights of fire escape stairs and slam straight into the person standing by the last step. We both fall to the ground. I don't realise it's Riley until she starts telling me off.

'Millie? What are you *doing*?' she says, jumping up and brushing herself off. 'Did you just come out of the Old Section? Cranshaw is going to kill you!'

I want to lie on the grass outside and sleep forever. The night air is blissfully cool on my skin. The few pupils ejected from the library are milling around in the darkness, but I can see the dormitories are emptying too, everyone with their hands over their ears. More and more people are making their way towards us, talking excitedly.

'Shell . . .' I try to say, but it just comes out as a wheeze.

'You didn't really think there was a fire, did you?' Riley says. 'I don't think Cranshaw's going to let you off contaminating the books just because you thought a fire drill was—'

'Riley,' I say, my voice strengthening a little. 'Shell's still in there . . .'

'What?' she says, bending closer to hear me over the sound of the alarm.

'I was trapped . . .' I say, taking another lungful of air. 'I was trapped in the Old Section with the oxygen running out . . .'

'What?' says Riley. 'That doesn't sound—'

'I set the alarm off!' I say, pulling myself up. 'There was no way out, but Shell's still in there! We need to get a teacher or something—'

'What's going on here?' Welbeck arrives at the scene, pushing past a group of pupils to get to where we're standing, and I nearly collapse with relief.

'Sir,' I say, 'we've got to find—'

'Sir, Shell's trapped!' Riley says suddenly. 'We've got to get her out of the fire!'

'What?' I say. 'No—'

'Wait, it's a real fire?' says a boy in a group of people behind us. 'I thought it was just a drill.'

'No, it's real!' Riley says. 'Millie saw it!'

'No,' I say. 'It's—'

'There is no fire,' says Welbeck. 'None of the other smoke detectors have gone off. Someone pulled the alarm in the Old Section.'

'Yes, Millie did!' says Riley, her voice rising with panic. 'We can't waste any time. Shell's in there!'

'Have you got an explanation for this, Millie?' says Welbeck, his jaw set.

'Sir, no, you don't understand,' I say, tumbling over my words. 'We . . . Shell . . . I got trapped in there, and the oxygen started running out, so I set off the fire alarm—'

'What?' he says. 'That's impossible, there's no way the librarybots would allow that to happen.'

'You don't understand,' I say. 'Shell . . . the meter . . . the – there's no oxygen!'

Welbeck sighs. 'If you can't give me a straight answer about what happened, Millie—'

'No, look, I just can't think with all this noise!' I say. The facts of the situation are slipping away from me. I have to try to hold on to the most important one. I keep imagining Shell, unconscious on the floor of the library, the shadow of a unit looming over her . . .

'Shell's trapped in the Old Section. There's no oxygen, and I'm worried that—'

Riley gasps. 'She's trapped by the fire?'

'There is no fire!' I yell.

'Look,' says Welbeck, 'the librarybots will check if Shell's still in the Old Section—'

'*Not the bots!*' I yell at the top of my voice. At the same time, the alarm cuts off abruptly. Welbeck and Riley reel back.

I know what the alarm shutting off means. The librarybots have to check every inch of the building for a fire before they can turn it off, even in a drill. Which means they've found Shell. My whole body goes cold.

'Millie, it's too dangerous for a human to go in there,' Riley starts to say gently.

'They've got her,' I say. 'They've got her already—'

'Millie,' Welbeck says sternly. 'Answer me this clearly – and I don't want anyone else chipping in,' he says, glaring at Riley. 'Did you set off the alarm?'

I can feel my face crumpling on the brink of tears. 'Yes,' I say.

'Was that because you saw a fire in the Old Section?' he says, looking down at me.

'No,' I say, 'but the units—'

'Finally, an answer,' he says. 'I don't know what story you were trying to spin, but it won't help you when Dr Cranshaw hears about this.'

'Wh-what?' I say. 'But what about Shell—'

'Millie, you've let outside air into the Old Section by opening the fire escape, not to mention forcing the whole school out on to the grounds,' Welbeck says. I can tell he's trying not to completely lose his temper at me. 'What did you expect would happen? We'd all say well done on the hilarious prank?'

'Sir, it's not a prank!' I say. 'Shell's . . . Shell's . . .' I burst into tears, shoving the heels of my palms into my eyes. I can't think, I don't even dare to take it in. Shell. We've been together since we were born. I've seen her nearly every day of my life. The image of the four-year-old Shell running around the gardens at Heathersdown with me flickers through my brain. I can't stand it.

'The units have got her. She's the next one . . .' I try to say in between sobs, but I'm barely comprehensible. Welbeck walks off, shaking his head.

'You're not making any sense, Millie,' says Riley. Her dyed-grey eyes are wide, trying to understand. '*What* about the units? I don't understand. Where is Shell?'

'I don't know. I don't know!' I say. 'I don't know what they'll do to her . . .'

Riley's hand suddenly drops from my shoulder, and a second later she says, 'OK. She's behind you.'

I whip round and Shell's standing there with Lu, waving at me tentatively.

'Shell!' I say, overcome with relief. Then that passes and I'm furious. 'Where were you? I thought you were in the Old Section with me. I thought you were trapped!'

'Sorry!' she says, wincing. 'I sent you a message! I just . . . got a bit bored.'

I grab her in a hug, angry and relieved all at the same time.

'Wow, I should disappear more often,' she says.

'But I don't understand, where did you go?' I say, logging on to my RetinaChip. There's a new message from Shell sitting in my spam folder. Of course there is.

'I didn't go anywhere,' says Shell, looking appropriately shamefaced. 'I mean, I went to the dormitory for a bit. It just . . . gets so claustrophobic in that room.'

'Really. I hadn't noticed,' I say tonelessly.

'Anyway,' says Shell, 'the fire alarm went off so we all had to leave. I didn't know *you* had set it off though.'

'Cranshaw is going to kill you when she finds out,' Riley says again with relish.

'What were you thinking?' says Shell.

'I was trapped,' I say for the hundred-thousandth time. 'The air dispensers had stopped working—'

'Millie, that's impossible,' says Riley. 'The bots would have let you out if that had happened.'

I take a big deep breath. 'Well—'

'Wait a minute . . . wait a minute,' Riley suddenly interrupts. 'Are you sure the *meter* didn't break? And you convinced yourself you were running out of oxygen.' She rolls her eyes.

'No,' I say. 'That's not what happened—'

'That is so typical, Millie,' says Shell. She punches me on the arm, and I can tell both her and Riley are delighted they've seized on an innocent explanation for all this. 'If an acorn fell from the oak tree, you'd think—'

'Oh don't be mean, Shell,' Lu says, but she's laughing too. 'You'd be just as scared if it happened to you.'

'No – it was . . .'

I can't say what I want to: I think the units are rising up. Suddenly, with normality restored, it sounds ridiculous. I know what the others will say. *It's not possible. It doesn't make any sense. You shouldn't say things like that.*

'What, Millie?' says Lu.

I open my mouth, but then close it again. 'Oh . . . nothing,' I say. But, as we make our way back to Hawthorn house, I can't help looking over my shoulder, checking for a glint of metal in the darkness.

Seven

I have to look at my brainstreams again tonight, even though just the thought of it makes my heart thump in my throat. I pull the covers over my head, waiting until the others stop giggling and whispering to each other and practising Mandarin vocabulary (Riley). When I can hear two sets of deep breathing and Shell's snuffly snores I flick my brainstreaming screen up.

I'm just as scared this time, my hands shaking so much I can barely scroll down, but not because I'm worried my head might fall apart. The memory of that unit brushing past me in the crowd, already terrifying, seems coloured by what I now know they're capable of. What did I see? What did they do to me? The need to find out and the absolute terror of what it might be are tugging my brain apart. But I *have to*.

I can remember more from last autumn on my own now. After Alisha Atkins-gate, as Shell dubbed it, and the door-slamming, I didn't speak to Jake for a few weeks. If I passed him in the corridor, I and whoever I was with would just give him the evil eye as we walked past and he would either ignore us or say, 'Oh, really mature.'

The next brainstream marked with a blue dot starts with Riley and I sitting in the canteen eating blueberry-flavoured mudge. Jake comes up to our table.

'Millie, can I talk to you for five seconds?' he says.

'No,' I say, and he immediately turns away and walks off.

If it was Shell sitting with me, she'd have said, 'Your brother is so awful,' or 'Does he really think he can just talk to you again? Pfft!' or maybe shouted after him, 'Enjoyed any paper books lately? I hear that Alisha Atkins is good.' (I had immediately told everyone the whole story.) But I'm sitting with Riley, so instead I get a raised eyebrow and: 'Are you still bearing a grudge about that whole history class thing?'

'It's not just about that, Riley,' I say. 'He wouldn't even tell me why—'

'Millie, can you look at the big picture here?' Riley's world-weary tone surprises me. I look up at her, thinking she's about to launch into a speech about the importance of family in these alienated times. Her (lilac that day) eyes bore into mine. 'Cranshaw's favourite pupil in the whole school is your brother. Are you not going to exploit that connection, like, at all?'

'What?' I say. 'She doesn't even know I exist—'

'Yes, but Cranshaw tells him stuff she doesn't want anyone

131

else to know,' Riley says. 'What if he's trying to tell you Alisha Atkins is the set text for English literature next term and you're telling him where to go? Won't you think of the rest of us, Millie?'

I know by 'rest of us' she means her. 'I don't think Cranshaw tells Jake stuff about school though,' I say.

'But you don't know,' she replies. 'How do you know this isn't his way of making amends?'

The brainstream abruptly ends, and with a jolt I find myself staring intently into my own pillow. Well, that was hardly enlightening. I don't really think Jake was being fed information about schoolwork that no one else was getting. He always passes everything easily, yes, but he doesn't exactly work hard for it – he's just good at getting away with things like that. If he read one chapter of one book all year, that would be the chapter the exam was on. I scroll down to the next blue-dotted brainstream a few days later.

Shell and I are in the library when I see Jake again. As soon as he spots us, he starts moving round the tables towards us. By the time he arrives, Shell is practically spitting fire.

'What do you want?' she says. 'We're trying to get some work done here . . .' (We're actually secretly playing Killer Zombie Fun Fair III, *while keeping half an eye out for the librarybots.)*

'I just want to talk to Millie for two seconds,' Jake says.

'Well, she doesn't want to talk to you—' Shell starts to say, as I get up.

'Three seconds,' I say to him. 'That's it.' I'm sick of not knowing what's going on, and my curiosity has finally outpaced my annoyance with him.

'Millie,' says Shell, but Jake shakes his head.

'Not here . . .' he says. 'Not in front of . . .' He gestures at Shell.

'Well, thanks very much,' says Shell.

'What?' I say. 'Why can't you just tell me here?'

'It's too important,' Jake says in a low voice that Shell can't hear. 'I'll message you.'

He walks away. For the first time I start to wonder if Jake is in some kind of trouble. Though Shell brushes off the whole thing by saying, 'Your brother is such a drama queen,' I can't help worrying he knows something about the Company that Cranshaw has told him, which he thinks I should know. Are our parents being made redundant? Is the whole Company in danger of collapse?

The brainstream ends and I select the next one at ten past midnight. Jake messages me. I'm already in bed asleep. I never bother to turn off my RetinaChip notifications at night – everyone I know has to be in bed by ten – so when the message beeps through I jerk awake and end up half sitting up with one leg out of the bed before I realise what's going on.

Meet me by the oak tree in five, the message says.

I so nearly delete it and go back to sleep. Am I so interested in Jake's secret that I'm going to get out of bed in the middle of the night and start wandering around outside? But . . . the lengths he's going to . . . what on earth could this secret be?

Surely it can't be anything as simple as knowing the set text for next term? I have to find out.

I pad down to the oak tree, squinting through the darkness to try to see where Jake is. The outside temperature was lowered a few weeks ago and my breath puffs out in a cloud in front of me. There's no sign of him as I duck under the lowest branches and walk up to the trunk. I decide to stay thirty seconds and then leave if he hasn't turned up, and then something grabs my wrist from behind.

I scream and try to twist free, but my attacker starts laughing.

'Jake!' I say, as he moves out from behind the trunk. 'You-you—'

'I couldn't help it. It was just so easy!' he says.

'So all this was just a trick?' I say in a voice much higher and shriekier than I would like. 'You never actually wanted to talk to me?'

'No, I did, I did!' Jake says. He's stopped laughing.

'I was asleep, you know, before,' I say, suddenly thinking about how cosy my nice warm bed is inside. 'Why should I stay here and listen to you?'

'Millie, this is important,' he says. 'I can't tell anyone else. You're the only person who I can trust . . .'

This is a typical Jake trick – lavishing you with compliments to get you to do what he wants. 'Jake, just tell me or don't tell me,' I say.

'You have to promise not to tell anyone,' he says.

'Well—'

134

'You have to promise, Millie,' he says. 'This is big.'

'OK, whatever,' I say. I'll have to tell Shell obviously. And Lu, and Finn, and Nick, and Riley. But apart from that, I won't tell anyone.

Jake takes a deep breath, then moves his face right up to my ear. I try to elbow him away, but he blocks my arm and says, 'Cranshaw's the leader of AIR. She founded it.'

'Cranshaw's the what of what?' I say in a much louder voice than Jake has just used. I didn't know what he was going to say, but I definitely didn't think it would be that.

'Shhh – shut up,' says Jake, looking into the darkness beyond the tree. 'Artificial Intelligence Rights – AIR. It's a political group, a protest group. They want units to be given freedom. They're campaigning the government for it.'

'They what?' I say. 'Does the Company know?'

Jake gives me a look. 'What do you think? Do you think we'd be talking like this if they did?'

I just gape at him for a few minutes. Cranshaw is involved in something the Company doesn't agree with, and Jake knows about it?

'But—' I say. There are about a million conflicting thoughts trying to shove their way into the front of my brain. 'Why wouldn't the Company— What has Cranshaw done— Does this mean— Is this because Florrie—'

Jake puts me out of my misery. 'The Company wouldn't like it, because they can't link themselves to anything this drastic politically when they're advising the government,' he says slowly. 'And if they find out, Cranshaw will be gone.'

'But, Jake, if Cranshaw's doing something bad . . .' I say. 'You need to tell them! What if they find out—'

'It's not bad,' he says. 'It's good. You can't think denying units their freedom is a good thing, can you, Millie? AIR is working for them.'

I feel like my brain is a couple of steps behind. For a start, Jake's logic is making sense, which never happens. But it's against what the Company wants.

'Millie, don't look so alarmed,' Jake says. 'There's a law that's going to be passed soon, and then supporting unit rights won't be so controversial. Everyone will know it was the right thing to do. But until then, Cranshaw's involvement has to be a secret.'

'B-but if she's the leader . . . if she founded the whole thing . . .' I stammer. 'Doesn't she have to give speeches and stuff?'

'She's never shown her face in public,' he says. For some reason he looks slightly uncomfortable. 'Only the very high-up members know she's the leader.'

'How do you know then?' I say. 'If it's such an important secret?'

'We talk about this sort of stuff all the time,' Jake says. 'We've always talked about units and unit freedoms. In fact . . . I might sort of be about to become . . . a junior member. Cranshaw's helping me apply.'

'What?' I say, clutching my head. 'Jake, but what if the Company find out? What if Mum and Dad get made redundant and we all have to leave? What if—'

Jake shakes his head. 'You don't need to worry about that—'

'I think I do!' I say. 'We could all be left with nothing—'

'Cranshaw leads the whole thing and they've never discovered her, so I really don't have much reason to worry,' he says, his voice flat and hard. 'And anyway it's more complicated than that.' He folds his arms.

We glare at each other for a few seconds.

'Is that what the Alisha Atkins book meant?' I say, as it occurs to me. 'It was information from Cranshaw about . . . AIR?'

'Yeah,' says Jake. 'Everything digital leaves a trail. She has the minutes from AIR meetings written out by hand and put in a paper book for me to read.'

That seems a bit much for a potential junior member to have access to.

'Er, OK,' I say. 'So you know everything they're planning to do?'

'Yes, but I can't tell you anything about that,' he says. 'I had to get permission from Cranshaw just to tell you this much.'

This throws me. 'So why are you telling me?' I ask.

'You know about the book,' he says. 'I couldn't risk you telling someone who knew, or finding it and showing it to someone who could work out what it meant.'

I feel strangely hurt. 'So it's not because I'm the only one you can trust?'

Jake looks at me, his eyes wide. 'Do you think I'd be telling you this if I couldn't trust you?' he says. 'Do you know what would happen if a pupil we didn't trust found out about this and started talking?'

'We?' I say, but he talks over me.

'We'd have to totally discredit them. We'd have to make them look crazy, so no one would believe them.'

'You would— You—' I start to say, but I don't have any words.

'Promise me, Millie,' Jake says. 'You have to promise me you won't breathe a word about this. To anyone.'

Eight

I'm crushed in a crowd of people. If I look straight up, I can see a square of clear blue sky – but there's a video banner up there, curling and snapping in the wind. I can't see what's on it but I know it's bad, and I don't want to see the banner unfurl. I try to push through the people around me, but there's no give in the crowd whatsoever, and the more I push and shove the more they close in around me. I try to look in their faces, but they're as expressionless as units. The wind's dropping, the banner's going to open – and I have to move. Panic's filling up my chest like water in a bath. Flailing about, I stamp on a child's ankle, body-slam a woman in a sundress and suddenly I get a tiny slither of space and it's like breathing air after being held underwater and I'm free, I'm getting away, when I thwack face first into some-one's shoulder, which appears from nowhere, and I fall back on to the ground, cracking the back of my head as blood spurts out of my nose. I'm coughing, snorting and choking on my own blood, lying like an upturned tortoise on the ground, when I realise the person I bumped into is Jake.

'Jake!' I splutter, trying to jump up. 'The banner—'

But he's looking straight through me like I'm not even there, his eyes blank and glassy like a stuffed animal. I grab his T-shirt, close to hysterical.

'Please,' I say, gasping. 'Please—'

'Move,' he says, sweeping me away from him in one swift movement of his arm, and as I trip on someone's foot and catch my ear painfully on an elbow on my way towards the floor, I realise that's it, I'm looking straight up, and the banner has finally unfurled . . .

I wake up, my heart hammering against my ribcage, and I sit up so fast I nearly fall out of bed, tangled in my cover. It takes me a few seconds to realise it was a dream and I lie back, prickly with sweat. Then it hits me why I woke up so suddenly and I remember the three bottles of water I drank before bed last night. I need the bathroom *now*. I launch myself across the completely dark room in almost one movement, sliding a few metres on Lu's discarded jumper from the day before and stumbling through the bathroom door.

The loo is flashing up an error message. Oh no. I hop from foot to foot. Now I'm really desperate. There's another loo on the ground floor next to the common room but it must be about four in the morning now, and as it's Saturday the school won't start waking up until way past ten.

Though there's no actual rule about leaving the dormitories in the night, I've only done it once.

I slowly open the dormitory door, trying not to wake anyone. Outside in the corridor, it's even darker, and the automatic lights don't come on even when I move my arms. My breath catches in my chest and for a second I consider waiting until morning to use the loo, but I know it's not an option. I fumble quickly down the stairs, hoping none of the teachers are around, waiting to catch pupils trying to run away, when suddenly there's a noise through the deathly quiet. Just a tiny movement from somewhere further up the stairs, a clank or a shift of machinery, but my whole body freezes in fear like an animal being hunted and my stomach fills with ice. I suddenly can't get the image of Nick's injuries out of my head. Since the incident in the library two days ago, I haven't said anything to anyone about the units, but I can feel them watching me at every moment.

'Calm, calm, calm,' I repeat to myself, as the back of my neck shivers with goose pimples. Do not think about units right now. Just run down the stairs, dive into the bathroom, and then run back up. If I do it quickly enough it'll be like it never happened.

I brace myself, then lunge towards the stairs, my feet barely touching them as I race down. I reach the bottom then turn at breakneck speed and hurtle down the second set of stairs. My breath rasps in my throat but it doesn't matter; I'm nearly there. I barrel down the last set of stairs

141

but halfway to the ground my foot hits something and I tumble over, my head and elbows and knees crashing and bouncing off the steps, and I land with a bone-quivering thump on the floor. All the breath is knocked out of me and I just lie there for a second, hoping my head hasn't caved in. I've just made so much noise that if there is something lurking in the shadows, it will definitely know I am up and about by now.

I sit up and clutch my head. It seems to be in one piece. I still have a fear that it'll just crack like an eggshell one day. My knees and elbows are grazed but after everything that happened the other day in the library, it doesn't seem like such a big deal. I glance up the stairs to see what could have tripped me up. There's something dumped across two steps in the middle, but I can't quite make it out in the dim light. Saturday morning's first rays of sunshine are coming through the glass panes of the front door now, but even if I squint I can only see the outline of whatever it is. I wonder if someone from the younger years left a bag on the stairs or something.

I get closer. From this angle it looks like a sleepsuit, but it felt so much harder when I went tumbling over it. I touch it, and realise it's not a sleepsuit; it's a body wearing a sleepsuit.

Oh God. I pull back the hood, and an unconscious face lolls forward on to the step. I nearly fall back down the stairs. The face is so covered in bruises and tiny cuts I can't even tell if it's male or female. Deep blue circles ring the eyes, the nose is clearly broken, oozing blood down to the lips, which are so puffed up and bloody my breath chokes in my throat. I'm so shocked that for a second I just look, my mouth gaping, frozen like a statue, before I realise I should probably check if he or she is still alive. I pull the hood down further and press my fingers against his or her neck, which is just as blackened as the face.

There's a pulse. It's faint, but it's there. I'm so relieved it feels as though the terror has gone, but then it floods back in like a wave. What do I do? Is the unit that did this still nearby? I feel choked, paralysed with fear, and I clutch the body in front of me as if it can offer me protection. I suddenly recognise the short blond hair, though it's matted with congealing blood – it's one of the boys from the year below. His dormitory is just paces away from where he's been dumped.

The clanking is there again. I can hear it. It's closer now; it must be in the corridor above me. My pulse beats in my throat so hard my breathing feels constricted. But I can't move. Does it know I'm here? Or is it coming back to finish the boy off?

The silence is deafening. My ears are straining to hear movement but all I can hear is my own heartbeat. I look up the stairs, expecting at any moment to see a blood-splattered unit towering over me, but nothing appears. The seconds tick by. Every moment I think I should move, but I'm terrified if I make a movement something will pounce on me.

143

My legs brace in preparation to run, the adrenaline flooding through my body – and then without even thinking I launch myself away from the boy, down the stairs, across the hall and through the front door, slamming it closed behind me. I don't know if something is chasing me but I'm not going to hang around to find out. I race down the stone steps, hurtle down the path and round the building. I whack straight into someone standing just behind the corner, and stumble back. I'm about to cry out for help when I realise it's a groundbot, busily weeding the flower beds in the half-darkness.

'Argh!' I scream, holding my hands up to defend myself.

The groundbot just looks at me, making no attempt to move. Their vacant stare made me feel uncomfortable before, but now it chills me right to the bone marrow. I run away from it, gasping and choking, propelling my body forward on no energy until I get to the teachers' house.

There's a rule about ringing the bell once and waiting for an answer, but I just press the bell down and hold it. Llewellyn answers, wrapped up in a silky dressing gown with her hair all over the place.

'Millie! What *on earth* is going on?'

'Miss,' I gasp, barely able to form words. 'There's been another attack.'

She looks at me, flabbergasted. 'Attack? What?'

'There's a boy. On the stairs. In my house. Not moving.'

I sit on the doorstep, trying to catch my breath.

144

Llewellyn looks shocked, her mouth and eyes wide, but Welbeck appears behind her.

'I'll handle this,' he says.

Llewellyn just stands there, glaring at me and shaking her head slowly, as Welbeck grips me by the shoulder and walks me back across the grounds. I think we're going back to Hawthorn house but instead he takes a left turn and we end up in the medical centre.

'Wait, what? Not here—' I start to say, when a nurse comes out to meet us.

'A room for this one, please,' Welbeck says, and I know by the way the nurse nods that he's already messaged ahead somehow.

'But . . . I . . . but . . .' I gibber as Welbeck lifts his hand off my shoulder and the nurse's hand comes right down to replace it.

'It'll all be sorted out now, Millie,' Welbeck says. 'No need to worry.' But he doesn't smile.

They lock me – actually lock me – in a room inside the medical centre. For hours. They block my chip from the network so I can't message anyone. From time to time the nurse with white-blonde hair comes in and tries to force me to drink what she calls superfuel, which is basically just concentrated flavourless mudge, as far as I can tell. I try to ask her questions but she won't let anything slip.

'What happened to that boy? Is he OK? Is he alive?' I ask.

'What boy?' she says pleasantly.

'The one on the stairs; the one who was attacked!'

'*Attacked?* I don't know anything about that,' she says, raising her eyebrows. I resist the urge to grab her by the shoulders and shake her.

'Please just talk to me. Is he alive?' I say. 'I know you know. And you know I know!'

She shakes her head. 'You're very confused. Eat some more superfuel. You might want to take some deep breaths to help you calm down.'

I pick up my spoon to pacify her, but I'm far too jittery to eat. 'Can I at least message my friends so they know where I am?' I say. 'It's nearly seven.'

'Why would they need to know where you are?' She clucks her tongue at me. 'You'll see them soon enough.'

'Well, they might think I've gone missing.'

She looks at me. 'I'm sure they don't think you're *that* silly.'

I take a deep calming breath. But it doesn't work. My brain is *itching* to tell someone what I've seen. Why did I think saying nothing and keeping quiet was a good idea? This is *bad*. I'm filled with nervous energy. My hands haven't stopped shaking since I saw the boy this morning.

'Look, I just need to access the network for, like, two seconds,' I say, kicking my heels against the floor. 'I'm supposed to call my parents this morning; they'll wonder what's going on if my chip is blocked.'

'I'm sure your parents are much too busy to be

worried about things like that,' says the nurse dismissively. 'Now settle down. There's no way we can let you out of here until we can confirm you're no longer acting irrationally.'

'I'm not acting irrationally!' I say, but she's left the room.

I can't sit still; there's too much information pinballing around my head. I'm not even pretending not to bite my nails any more; with no gems to distract me I stick my fingers in my mouth and chew. Only cleanbots and pupils can access the dorms, and no pupil in Hawthorn is strong enough, or insane enough, to inflict those kinds of injuries. I flinch when I remember the boy's bleeding nose. And no pupil could download someone else's brainstream either.

Hasn't Cranshaw told the Company? No Company representatives patrolling the grounds, no hysterical parents swooping down to protect their children. She can't have told them. I should have got hauled into her office the day after I set the fire alarm off, but nothing happened. I wonder if there's any point in warning her about the units; she must know. Maybe, as the leader of AIR, she wants to protect them. We all know how fond she is of Florrie. But surely she values our lives above the existence of an appliance? There's no doubt that if the Company knew the units were turning against us they'd be in here in seconds, exhuming the school grounds of any trace of them. Cranshaw would be sacked and Florrie would be destroyed.

I can almost picture helicopters descending on to the

Main Building roof, packed full of Company representatives. They'd fan out across the grounds, tracking down every single unit. I'd imagine they'd deprogramme them first, leaving them empty metal shells, then hopefully bash their metal carcasses to bits just in case any lingering intelligence remains. I'm so weirdly cheered by this image that my whole mood lifts considerably. No more units, no more attacks, no more fear – the exams would feel like a breeze afterwards.

As I'm picturing a thousand units dismantled to their component parts and spread across the courtyard like bodies on a battlefield the door opens. I take a deep breath to ask the nurse again why I can't leave – but it's not her.

'Millie,' says Dr Tavish. 'How are we this morning?'

I gape at him, as he starts unpacking his equipment. 'Dr Tavish?' I say. 'I thought we didn't have another appointment until next year?'

'I got a call this morning,' he says, wiping a speck of dust off one of his tools. 'They said you'd been acting out of sorts, and asked me to check you over . . .'

'That—' I say. I can't believe this. 'I'm not acting—'

'You caused some kind of disturbance?' he says, moving round to the back of my head. 'Early this morning?'

I exhale roughly out of my nose. 'No. Well, yes, but – did they tell you *why*?'

Dr Tavish doesn't say anything, just runs his tool along my skull.

148

'Dr Tavish?' I say.

'No,' he says vaguely. 'Have you . . .' The tool digs into the base of my neck. 'Have you been downloading brain-streams again, Millie?'

'No,' I say automatically. Technically I haven't; I've just been rewatching old ones. 'Why? Is . . . is everything OK?'

'I . . . think so,' he says, rooting around in his bag and bringing out a magnifier, which he attaches to his glasses. He's never done that before.

'What—' I say, my heart rate picking up. 'What's wrong?'

'I'm just checking you over, Millie,' he says. 'Don't worry.'

How can I not worry? I should have never rewatched those brainstreams. Dr Tavish keeps bringing out more and more equipment from his bag with one hand, while the other presses tool after tool against my skull. He doesn't chat away like he normally does. Occasionally he says, 'Hmmm,' in a very un-reassuring sort of way.

'Dr Tavish,' I say, 'can you just tell me . . .' My eyes sink down to his tablet, lying on the table next to me. A new message has pinged up on the screen. *Your Membership Account* is across the top. Is this how the hospital organises their employees? I squint at the tiny logo at the very bottom. There are two words curved in a circle. *Humans . . . First.*

'Right,' Dr Tavish says abruptly. 'Everything seems fine physically. You may want to use the network a little less, Millie, but no long-term damage caused.' He starts to pack up all the tools, including his tablet. 'I'll tell the medical-centre staff you just need to get some rest, and—'

'You're part of Humans First?' I say, too shocked to be subtle.

'What?'

'The group that . . . the group that doesn't like units?' I say. 'The one that doesn't want units to have equal rights? You're part of them?'

For a second he holds my gaze, then his eyes drop and he packs his bag much more quickly. 'So . . . I'll see you at some point in September, I imagine,' he says much louder than before, and I realise what's going on.

'I won't tell anyone!' I say, my voice automatically dropping to a whisper, terrified at the thought of Cranshaw discovering a Humans First supporter on the school grounds. I grip his arm. 'I need help . . . there's something happening . . .'

'Millie . . .' he says, gently unclenching my fingers.

'No, you don't understand,' I say. 'The units . . . on the school grounds . . . they've been . . .'

'No, Millie,' Dr Tavish says, 'I can't help you.'

'You don't even know what I'm going to say!' I half shriek.

'No, *I* can't help you,' he says. 'I'm leaving now.' He looks at me as if I should be cottoning on to what he's saying. But I'm really not.

'If you just give me a second to explain . . .' I say. Will

even the unit-hating Humans First members accuse me of prejudice?

'Maybe you should talk to someone else,' Dr Tavish says, grabbing his bag. 'Like your brother.'

'Jake?' I say. 'What?'

'I'll see you very soon,' he says, and backs out of the room.

I should never have let him know I saw the Humans First logo. I should have just asked for his help. He's clearly way too stressed about being found out. The door opens again suddenly, and I look up. 'Doct—'

It's Welbeck. 'Dr Cranshaw wants to see you,' he interrupts. 'Now.'

Nine

'What?' I say. 'Why?'

Welbeck doesn't answer me, but just motions for me to come with him instead. I consider resisting for a split second, but I'm aware this could be my only chance of getting out of this room for a while. And I want to hear what Cranshaw has to say.

Welbeck escorts me to the room outside Cranshaw's office and tells me to wait. She's clearly not that desperate to see me – she makes me wait ages. This doesn't help my nerves. I start to wonder what she's doing in there. I keep logging on to my RetinaChip to message Shell so she knows where I am if I go missing and then logging off, because that's ridiculous. Log on. Log off. Log on. Maybe I should just quickly message my parents, so they know what's going on? Would they care?

I log off and suddenly realise Cranshaw is standing over me.

'Millie,' she says, smiling.

'Ah, er, hi,' I say, jolting. Stay calm. She's just another person.

'Shall we?' she says, leading me into her office.

I've never actually been in here before, and I hadn't realised how big it is. Shell and Lu were sent here after Lu hit Shell in the face with her lacrosse stick, but all Shell said was that Cranshaw kept telling her to stop dripping blood on the floor. Then a call from the Company's board came in – and suddenly Cranshaw changed completely, offering her cake, promising her the best medical care, and arranging for the removal of lacrosse from the school syllabus.

The office is the size of at least two classrooms. It must be big if it's built over an unexploded World War Two bomb, I think absently, before I remember that's not actually true. The five huge picture windows along the back wall face the sun, but with the blinds down there's hardly any light inside. The wood panelling of the walls and the dark green carpet give the room a gloomy, severe feel. She even has a green-glass desk lamp switched on. There are shelves everywhere, holding awards and stills of every class to graduate from Oaktree in the last fifty years, and above Cranshaw's desk hangs a massive framed print of the Company logo.

Cranshaw's puff of candyfloss hair doesn't tremor at all today, but the skin on her face seems to sag from the bones, as though her skull has shrunk. It's strange seeing her up close. She's usually in the distance on a podium, like when she gives her annual speech every June about this graduating year group being the most promising employees the Company's ever seen. From far away she looks the same as always: the white hair, the glasses on a chain round her neck. But this close I can see how transparent her skin is; the veins near her eyes stand out, vividly purple. Her face seems fragile, almost withered, under her cloud of hair.

Florrie trundles in from a side room, holding a tea tray. She fixes me with her round eyes and her vacant stare makes my bones shiver. I have to turn away from her. How could I not have seen this before?

'Now,' says Cranshaw, sitting down at her desk. 'Would you like a cup of tea?'

'Oh,' I say, taken by surprise. I've never actually had tea before. 'Er, yes please.' I sit down opposite her.

Cranshaw nods to Florrie, who moves right up to the desk. I lean away from her, looking up at the ceiling, fighting the scream in my throat. Cranshaw is not going to treat me kindly if I seem repulsed by her companionbot. Florrie sets down a floral cup and saucer in front of me, and then pours tea into the cup from the pot. She straightens back up, and I look down, watching the steam curl off the liquid. Suddenly Florrie's face is right next to mine again and I reel.

'She's just pouring your milk, dear,' says Cranshaw, looking unimpressed.

'Oh, sorry,' I say.

Florrie pours milk in from a tiny jug, her eyes fixed on my face. I can't meet her gaze but my skin prickles, knowing she's looking at me. I focus on a little ornament on Cranshaw's desk directly in front of me, pretending Florrie isn't there. Why is she staring? Does she suspect that I know something? My heart beats harder. Cranshaw barely notices. She's scrolling slowly through something on her tablet.

'Now then, Millie,' she says, without looking up. 'It seems I owe you an apology. You were in the Old Section the other night and the air dispensers failed.'

I'd so been expecting her to talk about the boy on the stairs, I had actually put getting trapped in the Old Section to the back of my mind. 'Yes,' I say.

'I'm really very sorry,' she says, sounding more bored than apologetic. 'The system shuts itself down at night, long after the library is closed. After you reported that the air had cut off, we checked it and it turned out the timings were set a few hours too early. A simple glitch.'

The units must have tampered with the system when we first entered the Old Section. I bite my lip for a second, to stop myself from saying, 'A "glitch" that nearly suffocated me!' I need to keep calm. If she's playing the ice-cold exterior, then so am I.

'Thank you,' I say. 'And I'm sorry if the books got damaged.'

Cranshaw flashes me a tight smile. I can tell she

doesn't want to let on how angry she is that I opened the exit door.

'But,' I say, bracing myself, 'I don't think it was just a glitch that caused the air dispensers to malfunction.'

Cranshaw looks at me for a second. 'It was a simple timing issue. I'm sorry you were inconvenienced but there's no one at fault, Millie.'

'I'm not so sure that's right, Dr Cranshaw,' I say, trying to keep my voice from wavering. 'I think it was done deliberately.'

'Why on earth do you think that?' says Cranshaw, her voice pleasantly dismissive.

If I start with 'the librarybot gave me a funny look' I'll be kicked out of here in ten seconds. The words stick in my throat. I can't tell my unit-loving, companionbot-having, AIR-founding head teacher that I think the units are to blame. She'll dismiss it straight away, no matter what proof I have to back it up.

'I-I just can't understand why the librarybot didn't hear me yelling from the other side of the door,' I say.

'They're very thick doors,' she says, like I'm three. 'They have to be, to keep all the air out.'

'It's not just what happened in the library,' I say. 'There are other things happening, like what about the boy I found on the stairs this morning? He'd clearly been attacked!'

'What boy?' she says, as opaque as the nurse from earlier.

156

'Dr Cranshaw! I know what I saw! There was a boy from the year below. I tripped over him on the stairs this morning. He was covered in bruises and cuts, his nose was broken, and he was unconscious! *Something* attacked him!'

'Oh, Millie, I think you've got a bit confused,' Cranshaw says.

Florrie leans forward, eyes locked on mine, to refill my teacup. I automatically flinch back.

Cranshaw, unaware, continues. 'You've let your imagination run away with you a bit here. Poor Joseph did get himself into a bit of a scrape, but he wasn't unconscious and he certainly didn't have a broken nose. Unfortunately he has a tendency to sleepwalk, which was why he was still wrapped up in his sleepsuit when you found him. He slipped on the stairs and took a tumble, got a little bit of a bump on his head, but he was in such a deep sleep he didn't even wake up.' She rolls her eyes. 'He's fine now, and already back with his friends.'

She looks at me, lips pursed in a smile. 'Really, Millie, is this what the commotion you caused this morning was all about? You thought Joseph had been *attacked*? Ms Llewellyn will be interested to hear. She didn't appreciate your wake-up call. She's really not a morning person.'

I'm knocked back. I have to regroup. 'But what about all the other disappearances? Daisy? Nick? Megan?'

Cranshaw clearly looks surprised I know so much. 'Megan? You mean Megan Wickham? I'm afraid she had to go home early this summer; there was a death in the family. I didn't think anyone knew about it though, only her very closest friends.' Her eyes narrow.

'I saw her, Dr Cranshaw. I'm not just spreading gossip!' I say. 'I was in the medical centre when they brought her in and she was all covered in bruises and cuts.'

Cranshaw's expression doesn't change. She continues to look steadily at me.

'And don't tell me Nick's run away either because I know he's in the medical centre too!' I say, my voice rising. 'Something is going after the pupils! Something's attacking us!'

'Millie, I don't know why you think you're in danger here,' says Cranshaw. 'Why are you imagining these terrible things have befallen your classmates?'

'I'm not,' I say. 'If I'm imagining it, then why are all these pupils turning up with these horrible injuries? I've seen them up close. I saw Nick in the medical centre and I—'

'Millie, Nick Hayes is not in the medical centre,' says Cranshaw firmly. 'I don't appreciate lies.'

'I saw him, Dr Cranshaw, he was covered in bruises—'

'You saw him?' she says, her eyes hawkish. 'You saw your friend Nick covered in bruises? You'd swear to this in a court of law?'

'Y-yes,' I say, trying to push down the memory of when I first stepped into the hospital room and I wasn't sure if it was him or not. 'It was definitely him. And besides, I saw his name on the patient list!'

'Patient list?' says Cranshaw. 'What patient list? There's no list.'

My brain skips. 'I saw the list! It was on the receptionist's tablet! Nick's name was on it!'

'Millie,' says Cranshaw, her voice barely concealing her anger now. Her hair quivers again, but this time not with worry. 'That can't be right. Patient information has to be kept confidential.'

'Well, I saw it!' I say, rolling back through the memory in my brain. I did see it. Didn't I? Could it have been something else? But Nick's name was on it. I was sure. I *am* sure.

'Wait!' I say. 'Lu! My friend Lu saw Nick too, as he was being taken to the medical centre!'

'She saw him?' says Cranshaw, raising an eyebrow. 'She saw it was him and she saw the same horrific injuries you described?'

'Well . . . kind of,' I say, losing steam. 'She saw the medical staff carrying a body.'

'So she didn't see if it was actually him?'

'Well . . . no . . . but who was it then? *Someone's* been injured!'

'Oh, the second-years have developed a new game of climbing trees and seeing who can jump from the highest point,' Cranshaw says. 'They've been clogging up the medical centre with scrapes for weeks. Apparently there's a rumour going round that some of the trees are fitted with airbags that cushion your fall if you jump high enough. It's not true of course.'

She eyes me as if I might be thinking of trying it.

'But everyone's been talking about the disappearances,' I say. 'It's not just me that thinks something weird's going on.' Even as I say it I know that's not true; we all stopped talking about it days ago. But we shouldn't have. I don't know why we all have just been pretending everything's fine.

'I don't blame them for talking about two students running away – that is very out of the ordinary,' Cranshaw says. Her eyebrows come together in concern. 'But there's no reason to indulge in extreme fantasies, Millie.'

It's like we're playing a game but she keeps changing the rules every time I make a move. I try to straighten out the facts in my head, but my brain won't stop skipping around haphazardly. I can't think through the timeline of events logically.

'If Daisy and Nick did run away, what happened to them?'

'It's in the Company's hands now,' Cranshaw says. 'They're dealing with it.'

I know Cranshaw has secrets. And she's lied to me about sixty times in the last ten minutes, despite that famed honesty policy of hers. But even though I know this, I'm starting to doubt my own memories. She's just so believable. Answering every question without pausing. I scrape the sides of my mind, trying to find something to throw her.

'Why did you make us have mandatory brainstreaming then?' I blurt out. 'And not explain it at all? That got everyone talking. We felt like criminals.'

'That was a new initiative from the Company; they simply wanted to know if anyone had any further information on Nick and Daisy's disappearances,' says Cranshaw. She sits back in her chair casually. 'They didn't trust the pupils to betray their friends, and they wanted to check no one else was planning the same trick. For their own safety,' she adds quickly.

'But I thought it was only legal to do that to criminals, people who had already been accused of a crime, without asking permission first,' I say.

'You were all defined as witnesses, and the Company has the right to subject you to any process it deems to be for your own good.'

'So it wasn't anything to do with Nick's brainstream being stolen then?' I lean back in my chair and fold my arms.

Cranshaw looks up at me quickly. 'What? Where did you hear something like that?' she says, tense with either disbelief or alarm, I can't tell. 'It's not even possible. It's ridiculous.'

'Jake told me,' I say, watching her reaction. Something flickers in her eyes – but it passes so quickly I'm not sure if I've seen it.

'*Jake* told you,' she repeats. 'Well, Jake likes his little stories, doesn't he? He does have a tendency to elaborate.'

'What?' I say. 'But you . . .' I can't say anything, but at

the same time I can't believe she'd accuse Jake of lying when she must – *must* – be lying herself.

Instead of meeting her eye, I glare at the ornament on the desk again. It's only then that I realise it's actually a little metal statue of a unit. Typical. I lean over to move it away from me, but Cranshaw flicks my hand away, hard. I flinch back, shocked.

She takes my outraged silence as an opportunity to lecture me. 'I think I've answered quite enough questions now, Millie. Why you think someone is targeting you and your fellow pupils, I have no idea. Oaktree is the safest place you could possibly be. I'm sure when you graduate in a few years, you'll realise what a protected existence you have had here.' She eyes me beadily.

I should have known it would be impossible to make Cranshaw listen. I didn't think she'd let me get away with saying anything about units, but she's not even admitting there's anything untoward going on. I move my teacup across the desk towards me, remembering I haven't taken a sip yet. As I do, Florrie, standing behind Cranshaw's desk, suddenly jerks to attention with a clank. Her eyes are focused on my face again, her neck craning forward.

Instinctively I push the tea back. I don't know what she's put in it but there's no way I'm drinking it now. This whole thing is insane. I know what's going on and nothing Cranshaw can say can persuade me I've misunderstood. Suddenly everything seems backward to how it was before, when I felt so safe. I can't stay here, trapped, waiting for the units to finally corner me. This is it. I'm done.

'Dr Cranshaw,' I say, trying to keep my voice firm, 'I think I need to leave school for a while.'

Cranshaw laughs. 'Millie, you can't be serious,' she says. 'You've got exams starting on Monday.'

'I'll be back by then,' I say. 'I just need permission to make a quick trip to see my parents.'

If I can just see them face to face I know I can convince them about what's going on. And I know, if I stay here, they'll get me.

'Oh, I see what this is,' Cranshaw says suddenly. She leans forward, looking at me. 'It's a ploy to get out of exams. Are you worried you haven't done enough revision? Well, I'm sorry; you've only got yourself to blame for that. Is this what this has all been about all along?' She twinkles at me as if I'm some mischievous scamp she's caught in the act.

'No!' I say.

'Now, Millie,' she says, 'I know you've had a few problems with schoolwork after that knock to the head you had last autumn—' she pauses, probably to check that was definitely me in her records— 'but the Company has given you more than enough time to recover. It would be unfair to the other pupils to make allowances for you.'

'That's not what this is about!' I say. 'I . . . ah . . . I need a few days away, after the trauma of being locked in the Old Section with no air—'

She's not even listening. 'I should have known,' she's saying. 'After that bizarre story, I was starting to think you'd gone funny in the head!'

She smiles, but her words hurt like she's kicked me in the stomach. I'm completely frustrated with her.

'You have to let me out, if I want to go,' I say. 'It's Company policy. We're free to leave whenever we want.'

'Not if I think you're just trying to wriggle out of exams,' she says. 'If you want to leave forever, you're very welcome to. But if you want to go and come back, you'll need my permission.'

I gape at her, furious. 'So I can't leave?' I say, my teeth clenched. 'I have to stay here, even if I don't want to?'

'No one *wants* to do exams, dear,' says Cranshaw, smirking. 'But I'm afraid I'm not going to let you waltz into your next school year without doing any work for it, just because you had a little bump to the head six months ago.'

I have to bite the inside of my mouth to keep from shouting. I would *love* to show Cranshaw how 'a little bump to the head' feels. She has absolutely no idea.

'Now, I'm sure you've got revision to be getting on with,' says Cranshaw, standing up. 'I'm sure you don't want me distracting you any longer.'

I stand up, my mind whirling. This could be my last chance to convince her. I've been thinking about this the wrong way; it's not me versus Cranshaw, no matter how much she's trying to hide. There's an actual real threat to my life, and it's standing in the same room as both of us.

I have to tell her about the units. It's the only way the whole thing makes any sense.

Then my eyes meet Florrie's, still staring at me with that unfathomable look, and I know I can't say anything with her right there.

'Dr Cranshaw, do you think I could talk to you about something . . . alone?'

Cranshaw looks confused. 'But we are alone,' she says.

'I mean . . . Florrie,' I say, my eyes on the floor. I can feel my face flushing red. 'Can I please talk to you without Florrie listening, just for a minute?'

Cranshaw's eyes immediately narrow, her frail skin pleating around the edges. 'What are you saying?' she hisses.

'I would just rather talk to you without Florrie here,' I say, looking at the carpet.

'Whatever you want to say to me, you can say in front of Florrie,' says Cranshaw, her mouth a hard line. 'She's completely trustworthy.'

'No, it's just . . .' I look up and Florrie's eyes are boring into mine. She knows. She knows *I know*. A prickling coldness rushes through me, like I've seen a ghost.

'I think it's about time you left now, Millie,' says Cranshaw. She knows exactly what I was trying to say.

'OK, yeah,' I say, my voice catching. I wrench my eyes away from Florrie's, nearly tripping over my own feet in my haste to get out of that room.

'Oh, Millie?' says Cranshaw, just as I reach the door.

'Yes?' I say, turning.

Cranshaw smiles slowly and deliberately. 'If you're still worried about events at the school, don't be afraid to send your parents a nice long message,' she says. 'I'm sure they'd love to hear all about it.'

Ten

I stomp along the corridor, out through the back of the Main Building and into the courtyard across from Hawthorn house. A few pupils are dotted about, lying on the grass, but I barely register them. Thoughts are jostling for space in my head. I can't contemplate the full horror of one before another elbows its way in. Cranshaw must be monitoring the outgoing messages from the pupils to the Company. Why else would she suggest telling my parents about all this? She doesn't want them knowing anything. I quickly check the last few messages I sent to my parents – they haven't been answered. I just thought they'd been ignoring me, but could Cranshaw be blocking messages? I have to tell someone.

But Florrie knows I've worked it out. Just the memory of the look in her eyes sends my pulse speeding and makes the hairs on the back of my neck stand up.

All the things I should have said to Cranshaw keep popping into my head. I should have told her how the units have been looking at me. Even the staunchest of AIR supporters would realise that was weird. And Nick spoke to me! He said my name. How could I have confused him with someone else?

I scroll through my messages again and see yet another blank message, with no sender registered. I quickly delete it but something clicks in my brain; I did this the day Daisy disappeared, and the day Nick disappeared, and the day I saw Megan in the medical centre . . . The timestamp was minutes before I found the boy. My heart thumps like it's trying to bash its way out of my ribcage. They're messages from the units; no human could send a message without a sender. They want me to know. I'm next.

Nausea hits my throat. All those little looks and acknowledgements I've had from units in the last few weeks, which I thought were so weird – did they all mean *that's the next one*?

I'm so lost in thought I'm nearly across the courtyard when I realise someone's waving to me from a hillock just beyond the Left Building.

'Millie! Millie!' It's Lu, dressed in pillar-box red.

'Millie,' she says, coming over. 'Are you . . . OK?'

'Huh?' I say. Then I realise I'm still dressed in my grey sleepsuit, hair in disarray. I kind of forgot to think about my appearance since about 5 a.m. this morning.

'Where did you go this morning?' Lu says. 'We thought

you'd got up early to revise. We decided to sit outside today instead. We're over there.' She points out a little ridge, shielded from the sun, where Finn and Shell are sitting with their tablets.

'OK, I should go and get dressed and stuff and then I'll join you,' I say.

'Were you sleepwalking?' she says, looking me up and down. 'Is that why you're still in your sleepsuit? You . . .' She squints at me, clearly comparing the usual neat-as-a-pin, clean-as-a-whistle Millie with this dishevelled oddball. 'You don't look like yourself.'

'I'll, er . . . tell you later,' I say.

Lu shrugs. 'OK, see you in a bit,' she says, turning to go.

'Lu, wait,' I say, and she turns back. 'Do you remember when you saw someone being carried to the medical centre?'

'Yes,' she says, eyeing me warily.

'I know we went over it at the time,' I say. 'But what did . . . did you see his face at all?'

She shakes her head. 'No, no.'

'A bit of his hair? The clothes he was wearing?'

'He?' she says. 'I couldn't tell if it was a boy or a girl, Millie.'

'Oh . . . I was just wondering. You didn't see *anything*?'

Lu thinks. 'I saw their . . . the shoes. They were poking out of the bottom of the sheet. Fawn trainers.'

'Right, right,' I say. That would be so helpful, if

everyone hadn't been wearing fawn that day. Inwardly I curse the Look.

'You haven't been getting weird messages by any chance?' I say desperately. 'Messages with no sender?'

'No . . . are you really OK, Millie?'

I turn towards the dormitory and almost come face to face with a groundbot, trimming the grass near where we're standing. It gives me such a shock I yelp.

'What? What?' says Lu. 'Did you step on something?'

'No, no,' I say. The groundbot looks at me briefly and carries on trimming. My mouth has gone completely dry.

'Millie, what is it?' says Lu. 'You look really weird.'

'I'm fine, I'm fine,' I say, trying to breathe normally. I've suddenly realised I can see at least five groundbots from where I'm standing, all supposedly engrossed in work.

'Could you let go of my hand then?' Lu asks. I'd grabbed her hand when I jumped without realising.

'Oh, sorry,' I say, letting her go. I'm desperate to ask her to come with me to the dormitory, but she's already giving me an odd look.

'OK, well, see you in a bit then,' I say, trying to sound casual.

As soon as Lu turns round, I run into Hawthorn house, not looking back to check if anything's following me. I run up the stairs – there's no hint of the body that lay there – and burst through the door of our dormitory. Riley, sitting at the desk with her tablet propped up, jumps about a foot in the air.

'What—' she says, clutching her chest. 'You nearly gave me a heart attack!'

'Oh,' I say. 'Sorry. I thought everyone was outside.'

Riley shakes her head grimly. 'You can't *revise* outside! They're not taking it seriously enough!'

She has dark circles under her eyes and her skin has an odd greenish pallor to it. She squints at me and takes a gulp from the Rush bottle on her desk. 'Are you still in your sleepsuit?'

'Yes,' I say, crossing to the window. It looks out on to a stretch of green that dips down into a hillock, then spreads out into a wide grassy field, peppered with clutches of trees and bushes for miles. Though the outer part of the grounds isn't as manicured as the courtyard is, I can still see the occasional groundbot, working in the hedgerows. They're easy to spot because the metal catches the sun. How many of them could there be, surrounding me, in the school right now?

If I go out into the grounds alone, a groundbot could easily get me. Though a foodbot would never get me alone, as the canteen is always packed, they could slip something into my food. Cleanbots can enter the dorms, so there'd be nothing stopping one of them getting me in the middle of the night.

My lungs feel crushed with fear. I have to do something. I have to get away and I have to tell the Company – but *how*? No one will believe me. Even when I tried to tell Dr Tavish, he didn't want to help. He just told me—

Then *ding*, my brain goes off like a light bulb, and I

whip round, back past Riley, who calls after me, 'Aren't you going to get *dressed*?' and I clatter down the stairs. There's only one person who will have noticed what I've noticed – the only person who'll be able to make any sense of what I've got to say. I run across the grounds as fast as I can, keeping my eyes down, until I reach Chestnut house. I batter at Jake's door.

One of his friends answers. He looks at me, slightly alarmed.

'Er . . . whoa,' he says.

I'm struggling for breath. 'Is Jake here?'

'No, canteen,' he says.

But I'm already gone. I race back down the stairs, round the Main Building and burst into the canteen. Saturday morning is peak time; every table is filled and there are at least ten people in both the mudge and real food queues. A foodbot nudges past with a bulging bin bag and I squeak involuntarily.

Jake is at the front of the queue at a mudge machine.

'Jake,' I say, rushing up to him. He looks up and sees me, then steps back in surprise.

'Millie?' he says, clutching his cubed mudge to himself. 'Are you OK?'

'No,' I say, ignoring the giggles from the queue behind me. Yes, I'm walking around the grounds in my sleepsuit. It's not that weird. 'I need to talk to you.'

'Really?' he says. 'Right now? Do you not want to . . . get dressed, maybe?'

'No, no,' I say. 'It's too important. It's about *units*.'

Jake immediately looks wary. His shoulders slump and his jaw sets – as if he knows how this conversation is going to go, before we've had it.

'What about units?' he says, his voice hard.

'Can we go— Is there anywhere else—' I start to say, but he cuts across me.

'No,' he says. His face has darkened, his jaw set. 'If you've got something to say, say it here.'

I look around. I feel as though everyone in the canteen is listening. It can't be just my imagination that the noise level has suddenly dropped in here, can it?

'I think something weird is going on with the units,' I say as quietly as possible. 'I just wondered if you'd noticed too.'

'Weird how?' Jake says. There's no question in his voice.

'Just . . . weird,' I say, knowing I sound lame. I can't explain. I can't say anything without making him angrier. This is like talking to Cranshaw all over again.

'Weird . . .' says Jake. Then he looks at me with such hatred I'm actually shocked. I'm the one who's meant to hate him, not the other way round. 'Change the record, Millie.'

'Wh—' I say. The pupils in the queue have stopped laughing now. They're just looking down at their feet, embarrassed.

'What did you want to tell me? Anything new this

time?' says Jake. 'That units are dangerous? That we shouldn't be around them? I've heard all that about a thousand times. What did you expect me to say exactly?'

'I . . .' I can feel tears bubbling up behind my eyes. 'People are going missing. You said about the brain-streams . . . there's *something* going on . . .'

'I've noticed *you* acting weird,' he says. 'You've been acting crazy. Brain-damaged, some might say.'

I stare at him, trying to summon up my most withering glare, but my chin is trembling. 'Thanks,' I say.

'Maybe you should get your head examined before you start going on about units again,' Jake says, but I'm done. I turn round and run out of the canteen, back to Hawthorn house, past Riley, and lock myself in the bathroom.

In the mirror I look like a stranger, hair still matted from sleep and my eyes deadened from tiredness. I'm suddenly exhausted; I want to close my eyes and have everything – Jake's anger, Florrie's stares, Cranshaw's vague threats, the blood oozing out of Joseph's nose, Megan's splintered shin bone, Nick's broken everything – wiped cleanly from my brain like a stain from the canteen floor. My legs are so heavy I can barely drag myself into the shower.

I stand underneath the water for ages, not wanting to get out and face reality again. Maybe I could just stay in here until it's time to leave. Maybe the water will wash me down the plughole to freedom. I try to distract myself by thinking about all the revision I haven't done and come up completely blank. Even the thought of failing all my exams and being expelled doesn't scare me like it used to. At least I'd be alive.

If only I could tell my dad. I just need to get out for a few hours. I've never travelled to London alone before but I know where the Company headquarters is. I could be back before Cranshaw even realised I was missing, if I knew how to disable my IndexChip. Obviously in normal circumstances if the Company found out a pupil had left the school grounds against Cranshaw's wishes they'd be expelled and blocked from the network immediately, but if I tell them what's going on . . . They can't kick me out of school for breaking the rules in these circumstances, can they? Surely my dad will be on my side. I just have to tell him what Cranshaw's been keeping from them, about the fire alarm, and Nick and Daisy and Megan disappearing, and then he'll have to listen to me . . .

My mind scrolls back to that Mandarin lesson last week, after Daisy disappeared, when Finn was talking about how to disable an IndexChip. I couldn't cut my finger off; I can't even think about it without wincing. But shorting the chip by sticking my finger in a glass of water . . . could that be an option? *Nine times out of ten you get electrocuted*, Finn had said. Is it worth it? What are my chances of survival if I stay at school, trapped?

Eventually I get out of the shower and pull on a bright-red dress, the day's colour. Riley smiles at me as I emerge from the bathroom.

'Feeling OK now, Millie?' she says, as I sit by the window. I assume she's being gentle with me, until she adds, 'Fancy doing some maths revision with me?'

I make a non-committal noise and look out of the window. From here I can see the line of trees that indicates the border of the school grounds. Beyond that, freedom. I wonder if Daisy was attacked by the units, or if she somehow figured out they were plotting something and tried to stop them. The image of her struggling through the wilderness beyond the school grounds pops into my head, but instead of feeling worried for her, I get a huge rush of envy. She's free. What was it Shell said? Maybe she's in a shopping mall somewhere, indistinguishable in such a huge crowd of people.

My eyes snap from the line of trees to the shuttle station, which is just visible below a small hillock. A plan is forming in my brain so fast it's practically whirring. I've been on the shuttle to London before, from the Woodland River Centre, and OK, I don't *remember* it, but I know that once you've beeped your chip at the entrance and you're on the train, there's no going back. It doesn't matter who's tracking you, unless they're a step behind you when you head towards the station, they've got no chance of catching you. Permission or no permission. And that shuttle goes fast. I throw the comb on my bed, grab my tablet and slip into my shoes.

I quickly log on to the network and go to the personal settings page. I change my action feed setting from 'all' to 'none', so my every movement won't appear on everyone's timeline. It won't prevent Cranshaw from tracking my IndexChip, but at least she won't be able to work out what I'm doing as I'm in the process of doing it. She'll know when I've gone into the station, but by then it'll be too late.

'Riley, I feel like getting out of the school grounds for a bit,' I say, as offhandedly as I can. 'Fancy a trip to Woodland River?'

Riley whips round, eyes popping. 'What?' she says, jaw clenched. 'You don't have time to help me with maths revision but you do have time to go swanning off on a shopping trip?'

'I don't *have* to help you,' I say. 'It's a *favour*!'

She looks at me, furious. I can tell most of her anger is coming from the fact that I haven't just blindly agreed to help her, like I usually do.

'The exams start on *Monday*, you know,' she says, drawing breath like she's about to launch into a never-ending rant. But before she can speak, something occurs to me.

'Wait,' I say, quickly leaving the room and cursing myself for forgetting. He's already back with his friends, Cranshaw had said. I run down two flights of stairs to the lower-year boys' dormitory and knock on the door.

A boy with curly brown hair answers, but the rest of the dormitory is empty. 'Yeah?' the boy says, clearly looking at something on his RetinaChip at the same time. I hate when people do that.

It takes me a second to catch my breath. 'Joseph,' I gasp. 'He here?'

'Nah,' the boy says. 'He's gone.'

'Gone?'

'Er, yeah,' the boy says, finally logging off and looking at me. 'He had an accident in the night, he was sleepwalking or something, and had to go home. That's what Welbeck told us anyway. Only happened this morning.'

I don't feel the triumph I was expecting. Instead, dread clunks painfully into my stomach.

'OK, thanks,' I say. I run down the stairs and through the front door.

Shell doesn't want to go to Woodland River either.

'We still have to revise chemistry,' she says, sitting out on the lawn with her sunglasses on. 'And we haven't even started on world culture. That's going to be pure hell.'

'Yeah,' says Finn. 'And after Monday, we're going to be so tired from the exams . . . We need to cram as much as possible now.'

'I just . . . I really need a dress for the ball,' I say. 'And I heard they got those new pods in at the Look. They might be able to handle my IndexChip.'

'I don't know, Millie,' says Shell.

'Come on, it is Saturday,' I say.

'I thought you were the one who was all worried about revision, Millie?' says Lu. 'You didn't even want to go last week.'

'I know I didn't, but I've changed my mind,' I say. 'I mean, the ball is so important. It'll be the last time we're all here together before summer . . .'

I feel a little wobble of sadness when I realise that *now* could be the last time we'll all be here together. *Ever*. If my dad doesn't believe me. If Cranshaw won't let me come back. I shove that thought swiftly out of my head.

'Well . . .' says Shell.

'Well . . .' says Finn.

'I can always just go on my own,' I say, knowing that'll persuade them. I *could* always go on my own, but if Cranshaw is tracking my chip I'm sure she'll be more suspicious of me going to Woodland River by myself.

'Well . . . OK,' says Shell, minimising a document on her tablet. 'I suppose a few rounds of blasting aliens into nothingness will refresh our brains for the afternoon.'

'Yay!' I say. I'm so happy I'm almost giddy. I link one arm through Shell's and the other through Lu's and practically skip as we walk down. I'm getting out. I'm getting away. As long as we can get to the shuttle station without the units attacking us I'm practically free.

There's a tiny copse of trees about a mile before the entrance to the shuttle station, and as we approach it, the sun catches a glint of metal through the trees. All my senses are suddenly on high alert.

'Did you see that?' I say to Lu.

'What?' she says.

'That,' I say, but whatever it is has gone. I try to tell

myself I'm imagining it, but my heart's beating so hard in my throat I can't even talk to the others. I keep seeing Florrie's blue eyes staring out at me from the hedgerows. I almost physically relax when we reach the shuttle station.

Despite it being the weekend the station is totally deserted and there are only two other people in the shuttle carriage when we board it. I suppose everyone has end-of-year exams coming up. Finn, Shell and Lu look around uneasily at how many empty seats there are, and I know they're feeling guilty about not staying to work. I feel a pang of guilt for persuading them to come along, but I remind myself that when the Company does come to evacuate the school grounds of units and kick Cranshaw out, my friends probably won't be able to do their exams on Monday anyway. I wonder if the Company will delay them. What will happen to Oaktree if Cranshaw is removed? Will it still carry on like normal, albeit with a different head teacher and no units, or will they close it?

I'm lost in thought when I realise Lu's been trying to talk to me.

'Sorry?' I say.

'What do you think you're going to choose for your dress?' she says. 'What colour? Or a print? What style, what length?'

'Oh, er . . .' I haven't thought about it at all obviously. 'I was thinking pink, maybe.'

Shell's face drops. 'You can't wear pink! I'm wearing pink; I showed you!'

'Oh, don't worry, it's a darker pink I'm thinking of,' I say, desperately trying to remember what Shell's dress looks like.

'It better be. People get us mixed up as it is. We already have the same colour hair.'

'Oh my God, no one will care,' says Finn.

When we arrive at Woodland River it looks reassuringly normal. There are hundreds of people swarming in from the four shuttle stations, just like always. There's a cleanbot sweeping up outside the doors and I automatically duck behind Lu, although there's no way it could do anything with so many people here.

'We'll go downstairs and see you in a bit then,' says Shell.

I feel a sudden rush of affection for her. I squeeze her hand. It's a tiny gesture but I hope she remembers it.

She looks at me. 'Chill out, Mills. It's just a dress. You weren't that bothered last week.'

'I know,' I say. 'I'm just excited.'

She rolls her eyes, trying not to smile, and twists her hand out of my grip, laughing at me.

'Loser,' she says, walking away with Finn and Lu.

It only takes a few steps before they disappear into the crowd. I swallow down the lump in my throat and remind myself that I'm trying to save their lives.

I stand still and look around, checking the faces of the people sitting at the huge café near the entrance, the people on the escalators, the people flooding forward, the people flooding in the opposite direction, and the people standing still, watching the other people, like me. I can't see any teachers. But that's no reason not to be careful.

A crowd of youngish-looking men pass me and I slip into step with them, wondering why I thought it was a good idea to put a bright-red dress on earlier. I stick out like a beacon against their stone-grey Company-logo T-shirts. We march as a group down the escalator, as they look at me with confusion. They don't say anything though. At the bottom of the escalator the group splits to avoid a gaggle of middle-aged women, all with styled hair and double chins. Instead of passing them, I pivot and fall into step between two of the largest women, one wearing a yellow Company-logo T-shirt, stretched tightly across her belly. This makes me much harder to spot, despite the colour of my dress. They board the up escalator, going back the way I just came. Unlike the men, they simply stand and wait for the escalator to reach its destination, while gossiping about someone called Stella from the third floor who hasn't told the Company about her 'condition' yet. They don't seem to notice me, despite me being practically wedged between them.

We reach the top of the escalator and, luckily, the group heads straight for the main doors. Out we go, back into the sunlight. The women fall into step with the stream of people headed towards the shuttle station directly to the right of the doors. I don't know where that one goes, but I know it's not London. Before I get so far along I can't move, I quickly check for teachers. I can see the head of almost everyone in the crowd, and none of them looks familiar. Now is the moment.

I turn and cut across the woman next to me, treading on her ankle by accident. 'Ow,' she mutters, but I'm already gone, sidling past the people streaming from the entrance to the nearest shuttle station. There's a wall of people's right shoulders in front of me, but I move quickly. I knock people over, I stick my elbows in people's backs, I trip over feet and knees and ankles, but finally the crowd starts to thin out and I'm no longer pulling against the flow to the right. Just behind me I can hear someone else causing a ruction – lots of 'tsk's and 'excuse *you*'s, and I duck my head right down. I need to keep moving straight ahead to the shuttle to London, but I have to stay in the midst of the crowd. The huge metal arch of the shuttle station's entrance looms up ahead.

There's a big group of people moving towards the station who must be senior Company executives. They are meticulously groomed, wearing beautifully cut clothes and expensive shoes. One woman is wearing a pair of boots that could even be leather. I duck behind the last few of them and hope I don't stick out too much. I'm so close. I can see inside the entrance to the station. If I can just get past the IndexChip scanner, it won't matter if the teachers are tracking me or not. I'll be halfway to London.

The crowd crushes together as we funnel towards the

entrance. I get wedged between the tailored shoulders of the two executives either side of me. They're taller than me, so it leaves me quite well hidden. Is it my imagination that there are hurried footsteps behind me? I'm not looking behind, whatever happens. I can see the IndexChip scanners now. I'm barely metres away.

Suddenly, to my right, there's a disturbance. Someone's pushing their way through the crowd, and shouts of 'Hey!' and 'Oi, where's the fire?' reach me. I duck my head lower, staring down at my feet so my face isn't visible at all. Just a few steps more and I'm practically on the train. There's a scuffle and a shout of 'Watch it!' behind me but whoever it is is too late: I'm there. I stretch my arm out towards the scanner. It beeps me through. But before I can take another step, a hand grabs my wrist.

'Millie,' says Welbeck, leaning against the scanner. He's been there the whole time. 'You need to come with me.'

Eleven

'I don't know what you were thinking!' Welbeck yells.

There's a huge clock on the wall of his office, so I know he's only been telling me off for about twenty minutes. But it feels like forever.

'Your exams start on Monday,' he says, pacing up and down. 'I don't think I need to remind you how important they are!'

I sit hunched in the chair, tuning in and out. There's a window directly behind him and I can't help wondering if there's a unit just outside. The light is catching in an odd way, as if it's bouncing off metal. Is someone – or *something* – listening? Are they following me?

I can't believe I've failed. Of course Cranshaw wasn't just going to depend on remotely tracking my IndexChip. She must have told Welbeck to keep an eye on me. It occurs to me that's two weekends in a row I've been escorted home in disgrace from the Woodland River Centre.

'This will not be acceptable when you're a Company employee,' says Welbeck. 'You can't go swanning off whenever you feel like it!'

I keep seeing that scanner at the shuttle station in my mind. I was so close. If I'd only spotted Welbeck a few seconds earlier . . .

'Company employees do not just waltz off on a shopping trip in London when the work gets difficult,' says Welbeck. 'They demonstrate loyalty, commitment, tenacity . . . teamwork . . .'

When Welbeck caught me, he asked what I was doing, trying to get on a shuttle to London. I was so surprised, and as usual I couldn't kick my brain into gear, so I just blurted out, 'I need to go to the Look in London to get a dress for the ball.' This seemed to infuriate him even more.

'At a sensitive time like this . . .' said Welbeck. 'When two of your fellow pupils have . . . made themselves absent . . .'

Three, I thought in my head. Four, actually. I'd forgotten about the boy – Joseph – this morning. And it could have been Shell and me on Thursday too, suffocated in the Old Section. What am I going to do? They're closing in on me every day. My breath catches in my chest and I breathe in quickly through my nose, so I don't burst into tears. Welbeck already thinks I'm hysterical.

'Now, about your punishment,' Welbeck says, sitting down at the desk. 'The Company has put certain measures in place after the incidents of the last few weeks.'

'Oh,' I say.

What he means is, Cranshaw doesn't want me escaping and telling everyone about her precious units attacking the pupils. I glare at him.

'You didn't think I'd let you off your punishment, did you, Millie?' says Welbeck. 'Just because there's only a few weeks left? Think again.'

I resist the temptation to roll my eyes and look fixedly at my stumpy fingernails instead.

'Now,' says Welbeck. 'To avoid distressed pupils putting themselves in danger by running away, the Company wants us to identify those who could be a flight risk and . . . *restrict* them.'

'But, sir,' I say. 'I was going to come back! I'm not a flight risk.'

Welbeck purses his lips. 'I'm afraid the Company won't see it that way.'

'Really?' I say, folding my arms. 'You don't think the *Company* will see it that way?'

Welbeck glares at me, clearly trying to decide what I'm implying.

'Millie,' he says, his voice crisp with anger. 'Is this another demonstration of your lack of Company loyalty? Twice in one day?'

'It's not the Company I'm feeling disloyal to,' I say.

'Please, continue,' he says. 'I'm sure the Company will be delighted to hear your opinions on their . . . priorities.'

I don't say anything. Welbeck's eyes bore into mine. By attempting to protect the Company from the units, I'm being accused of a lack of Company loyalty. Ridiculous.

He starts up again. 'Pupils deemed to be flight risks will be moved on to the restricted-exit chip system, to prevent them doing anything they may regret.'

'What does that mean?' I say.

'It means from now on, your chip will no longer be able to scan you out of your dormitory or exam rooms or classroom alone,' says Welbeck. 'It will still track you, but doors will not open for you. Every time you want to leave a room, someone will have to go with you.'

'What?' I say. Scanning our chips when we walk through doors is so automatic now I can't even imagine mine not working any more.

'You're still free to enter rooms alone, but to leave you will have to have someone with you,' Welbeck says. 'This makes your chip easier to track and prevents any rash decisions on your part, without affecting your day-to-day activities. Dr Cranshaw felt that was fair.'

'But what if I'm alone in a room and I need to leave?' I say.

'Then you'll stay in that room until someone else joins you.'

'But—' I say. I know there's a flaw in this logic

somewhere. 'But what if . . . someone wanting to run away just got their friends to beep them through? It's not exactly an effective deterrent.'

'You think your friends would help you put your own life in danger?' he says. 'Would *you* help a friend run away?'

I sit back in my chair, defeated. I wouldn't. I'd think they were crazy.

'Oh, and of course your chip will be blocked from using the shuttle station,' Welbeck adds. 'That's a given.'

'But I thought I was allowed to leave, if I wanted? I thought we were free to do what we want?' My voice wobbles out of control.

'Dr Cranshaw is simply trying to protect you from making any decisions that you may regret,' says Welbeck.

I want to go back to the dormitory but Welbeck says he has to escort me. Before we can even leave the room he has to beep me out. The door won't open for me otherwise. I feel mortified.

'Remember, we'll be keeping a close eye on you this week,' Welbeck says as we reach Hawthorn house.

I try to look placid but inside I'm furious. I stomp up to the dormitory. Riley's not there any more, but I don't want to tell her anyway. She'll just think it's my fault that I'm in trouble. I need to talk to someone like Shell or Finn, or someone who isn't so blindly focused on sucking up to Cranshaw like stupid Jake. I rush straight to the window, to check if there are any units outside watching me. There aren't, but I suddenly become very aware that I am alone, in the dormitory, and the cleanbots can access the dormitories any time they want. I'm a sitting duck stuck in here. Was this Cranshaw's plan all along? Or has Florrie manipulated it this way?

I can hear a shuffling in the corridor. Are they closing in on me right now? I dive under my bed, but then remember cleanbots have to sweep under there. They'll find me in seconds. They're also allowed access to the bathroom, to clean it. The only place they don't go is inside the wardrobes, but I'm nervous about stepping inside one – what if I get caught up in the machinery and made into a jacket? There's another shuffling outside, right outside the door, and without thinking I run inside the wardrobe and slide the door shut.

It's completely pitch-black inside. The only sound is my breathing. My ears strain to hear if anything's entered the room, and if it knows someone's in the wardrobe, but I can't hear. At first this worries me, but after a while the darkness and the silence become strangely soothing. It's like being cocooned in a warm, impenetrable blanket. Occasionally the wardrobe's innards make a creaking sound, making me jump, but nothing happens. Why can't all machines be like this? I feel so safe. My whole body relaxes into the wall. I hadn't even realised how stiff and tense I'd been.

Automatically I gnaw at my fingernails. It's dark so I

can't see how horrible they look chewed down. It's oddly freeing, but at the same time a strange mixture of anxiety, dull resignation and, weirdest of all, excited anticipation settles in my stomach. I can't work out why, until the memory of sitting inside the cupboard in the dormitory at Heathersdown comes back to me. I used to hide there on the first Saturday of every month, Parents' Day. Jake would ignore it totally and go and play off in the gardens somewhere, but I'd wait excitedly by the window, trying to spot my parents arriving, until I got too nervous. Then I'd go and hide in the cupboard, categorising the bed linen inside it, in case they didn't come. They never came, not once. That familiar hotchpotch of disappointment and embarrassment and ridiculous hope – they could just be running late, I'd tell myself again and again – swoops over me, and I have to shake my head to remind myself I'm not six years old any more.

I understand now why they never came. My mum was named among the Company's top forty under forty when we were two, and from then on she fought tooth and nail for a place on the board, working 'every hour of the day and night', according to her. Then after that she was on the board of course and had to work even harder. At the same time, my dad was rising through the ranks of the finance department, which he's now head of. Neither of them could afford to spend a day entertaining children. I get it *now*.

I don't know how much time passes, and I'm not sure

if I fall asleep, but suddenly there's a tapping on the door, which makes me jump about a foot in the air. Have they found me? Is this it?

The door slides open, and I brace myself for attack, but it's only Shell.

'Oh, thank God,' I say, exhaling. 'I thought you were—'

'What the hell is going on, Millie?' she says. 'We were waiting for you at Woodland River for hours!'

'Oh,' I say. I completely forgot I'd left them behind. I haven't checked my messages all day either. 'I'm really sorry, I—'

'Don't worry, we've only missed nearly a whole day of revision!' says Shell. 'Then when we got back here, we wasted another half an hour looking for you! Why were you hiding?' She glares at me, obviously just as hurt as she is angry.

'Shell, I can explain it all!' I say, climbing out of the wardrobe. 'There's . . . something's going on.'

Shell sits down on her bed with a thump. 'What?' she says.

Bizarrely I feel my face crumpling, like I might cry. Finally I'm going to tell someone. 'I think the units are rising up against us,' I say, moving towards her. 'I have proof. I know it's happening.'

Shell freezes for a long second, looking at me round-eyed. 'Millie,' she says slowly, as though she's choosing her words carefully. 'You can't say things like that. It's not funny.'

'What?' I say. My stomach drops, as heavy as a bag full of cement. 'It's true. I know it is. You have to believe me—'

Shell looks concerned. 'Millie—'

'No, Shell, you don't understand!' I say. 'There are things going on that you don't know about—'

'Millie—'

'I've seen things. They're attacking the pupils,' I say. 'They're *attacking the pupils*. They're trying to kill us.'

I'm trying to shock her into believing me, trying to alarm her, but she just shakes her head slowly. 'Millie,' she says, voice hushed. 'If you say things like that about units, that they're . . . people will think you're prejudiced.'

I knew this would happen if I told anyone. I knew it. I'm trying to stay calm but I can feel myself getting frantic. She has to believe me.

'Shell, listen to me. This morning I got up early and I found a *body* halfway down the stairs,' I say, trying to keep my voice from wobbling. 'I tripped over him. It was a boy from the year below. He was . . .' I pause, remembering his battered face. 'They'd beaten him. And no one else can enter the house apart from the cleanbots.'

'Thingy from downstairs?' says Shell. 'I thought he was sleepwalking and slipped on the stairs?'

'Yes,' I say, 'but Cranshaw said—'

'Cranshaw?' says Shell. 'When were you talking to Cranshaw?'

'This morning,' I say. 'She wanted to talk to me about . . . after I found the . . . Well, it was actually about what happened in the Old Section.' I stop as Shell starts to look more and more confused. 'The point is, she said he was already back with his friends and *he's not*. I checked downstairs and they said he's gone home. He's obviously in the medical centre. Cranshaw's lying!'

'Millie, there could be a hundred different explanations for that,' Shell says. 'I don't think it necessarily means he was attacked by *units*. That's a big assumption.'

She doesn't add that it's an assumption only someone prejudiced against units would make, but I can hear it in her voice.

'Shell! You need to *listen*,' I gabble. 'Nick's been attacked, Daisy's still missing, Megan Wickham was attacked—'

'What? *Nick?* Slow down, I can't understand you,' says Shell. 'What was that about Megan? Didn't she go home because her grandma died?'

'No, that's just what Cranshaw told everyone!'

'Millie, look, you need to calm down,' says Shell, coming over to me. 'You don't think there's any chance this could be a really severe case of exam stress?'

'No!' I say, squirming away from her. 'This is what Cranshaw tried to do! I know what I saw, Shell! I saw the boy this morning, and I saw Nick injured in the medical centre—'

'You *what*? What are you saying?' Shell says, but I carry on, talking over her.

'I saw Megan! And I'm next! I know it!'

I slump down across my bed, covering my face with my hands. Shell moves round to sit by me.

'It's the only thing that makes sense of everything,' I say as calmly as possible. 'The units are rising up against us.'

'Millie . . .' she says, her mouth twisted.

'No, I know what you're going to say!' I say. '*This is real!* Just listen to me, Shell, please. Why does everyone always have to pretend everything is OK when it's not?'

'We don't *pretend*,' says Shell. 'Everything *is* OK!'

'No it's not!' I say. 'People are going *missing*. Just because Cranshaw says something, doesn't mean it's true! I don't know why we trust her! We *always* obey – we do whatever she says – and fall back in line to show how good we are at *teamwork*. And then, when something bad happens, we pretend it's all fine—'

'Millie, just because we aren't talking about it doesn't mean we're not . . . sad,' Shell says. 'We're trying to move on. And it doesn't mean the units are trying to take over!'

She doesn't raise her voice, but I flinch away from her. She takes a deep breath and closes her eyes.

'Shell,' I say. Her eyes open again, and when she speaks, her voice is soft.

'When did you see Nick? You didn't say anything—'

'He was in a room in the medical centre,' I say. 'I didn't say because— I don't know. It was horrible. He was all . . .' I gesture to my arms and legs, thinking about his bruises, but Shell looks confused.

'Millie . . . are you sure—'

'I can show you!' I suddenly realise. 'I can show you my brainstream from the other day – Nick and the boy on the stairs—' I lift my finger to access my brainstreaming homepage but Shell slaps my hand down.

'What are you *doing*?' she says. 'You're not supposed to be looking at your brainstreams!'

'I did it the other day and it was fine,' I say. 'Just look at this—'

'Millie,' she says, her cheeks flushed red. She puts her hand over mine. 'Your doctor – the one who literally patched your skull back together – told you not to look at your brainstream. So it worked once? So what? You don't know what it could have done to—'

'Shell! It hasn't done anything!' I say a bit too squeakily. 'I've even—'

Shell cuts across me. 'Wait. You saw Nick . . . and Megan . . . when you went to the medical centre for your appointment?' she says slowly. 'Wasn't that the day after we were brainstreamed?'

'What do you mean?' I say.

Shell rubs my arm. 'Maybe you're not thinking straight,' she says. 'After your head injury—'

'It's not my head injury!' I say. 'Why does everyone think that? I'm not crazy!'

'No, listen,' says Shell. 'You haven't downloaded your brainstream all this time, and then suddenly you start getting confused about things again? Seeing things you don't know for sure are real?'

'But,' I say. 'But . . .'

'And when you saw the boy this morning,' says Shell. 'You fell down the stairs, you said? Could you have hurt your head?'

I put my hand to my skull again. 'Well, I did bump it,' I say. 'But this still doesn't mean—'

'Why do you think Megan was attacked too?' she says.

'I saw her being carried into the medical centre, after I saw Nick,' I say.

'The day after you had your brainstream down-loaded?' Shell says, raising her eyebrows.

'Well, yes, but . . .' I say. 'You think my brain is just . . . making stuff up?'

'You know your memory still isn't quite up to scratch,' Shell says gently. 'You still get confused about things. I know you're not sleeping well, and I've seen you sleep-walking. You know you're not fully recovered yet. Maybe that combined with your . . . feelings about units and worry about the exams has just . . . produced a perfect storm? Making you think you've seen things you haven't?'

For a split second, I see the whole situation through Shell's eyes. The delicate links I've weaved between the missing pupils and the units disappear as completely as if they were never there. The story in my head, the narrative of the last few weeks, tumbles apart into a thousand pieces. Suddenly everything I've said about units, attacks and Cranshaw seems nonsensical. Absurd. But then, just as suddenly, I see Florrie's eyes in my mind and the fear falls back into my stomach, as heavy as a brick.

'I . . . I don't know,' I say. My mind whirls. 'But I *spoke* to Nick . . .'

'Are you *sure* you didn't just get confused?' says Shell.

'But he said my *name*,' I say.

'Right, and no one else at school knows your name?' says Shell.

I clutch my head. 'Shell,' I say. 'I'm so confused . . .' My mind's gone blank. I can't quite seem to grasp what I was so sure about a few minutes ago. I still feel queasy with long-buried feelings, brought too quickly to the surface. The strands of the story can't reform themselves; I can't back up my fears with fact. If I'm scared of units for no reason . . . what does that make me?

'Why the units specifically?' says Shell, rubbing my elbow. 'Is it just the fact you don't really . . . like them?'

'No! No,' I say. 'I . . . I got these messages. I thought I was next . . . and it just makes sense. Who else could steal someone's brainstream?'

Shell rolls her eyes. 'Just because Jake said it, doesn't mean that it actually happened,' she says. 'He could have been wrong.'

'I know, but . . .' I say. 'There were other reasons. They . . . keep looking at me.'

'That's because you jump about a metre in the air every time you see one,' says Shell. 'Everyone human looks at you when you do that as well, you know.'

'Oh, Shell,' I say. I could cry but I'm too confused. 'But I was so sure . . .'

'Well, you did bang your head pretty hard,' she says. 'The school never really gave you the time to get over it. It's not your fault you got confused.'

'Really?' I say. I don't know what to think about anything any more. The need for action that's been urging me forward has faded away. I suddenly feel limp, weak, unbearably tired.

'Just a week, Mills, and the exams will be over,' Shell says. 'Then your head can have a rest for a bit. Just don't do anything rash until then. If something happens when the exams are over, then I'll believe you.'

I nod, snuggling my face into the duvet. Could my mind have really been playing tricks on me? Have I been completely overreacting to everything? All the fear in my stomach has been churned into confusion. If I just ignore it all, will it go away?

For the next week I stick to Shell like a limpet. Obviously I have no choice, as I need to be chaperoned at every point. But I'm glad I have the excuse. I don't know what could happen to me if I was alone. We eat every meal together; we go to exams together; we revise together. We sit outside on the lawn together, but only for five minutes, because we feel too guilty about doing anything that isn't revision.

After every exam I have to wait by the door until someone can beep me out with them. I can't leave the dormitory at night unless someone goes with me, even just to use the downstairs loo or go to the common room. I pretend to find it frustrating, like the others do, but in a way it's comforting. I feel safe constantly surrounded by other people. I'm never left alone with my own thoughts. When we walk down the corridors or sit in the library I'm very careful about where I train my eyes. I immediately look at the floor if I catch sight of a unit. If I spot one looking at me, I flick my eyes away and repeat the last line of the periodic table in my head over and over again. If I don't look at them, the fear can't overwhelm me.

The exams are just as horrific as the teachers said they would be. By Thursday morning I'm totally drained. My nails are bitten down to less than stumps. Each day becomes an endless cycle of eat-exam-eat-exam-revise-eat-revise-revise-revise-sleep. In the maths exam on Monday afternoon I can't remember Pythagoras's theorem. I get so worked up I nearly cry with frustration. On Tuesday the history exam is all about the Night of the Long Knives, which I never even thought to revise, and the day after all three essay questions in the English literature exam contain words I've never heard of. Shell has a similar nightmare in physical science, forgetting the formula for acceleration. And the formula for pressure. And the formula for density.

After each exam we lie across our beds in the dormitory, as exhausted as if we'd just been for a run. Then we have to pull ourselves up and go and get some food or revise or go to another exam. It's like a mental version of a hurdles race, except it never ends.

By Thursday afternoon, there are only two exams left: today's world culture and tomorrow's debate. And then it's over for another year. Instead of feeling excited though, I feel more nervous about time off than any of the exams. I don't want to have room to think. Just thinking about the exams being over lets a little of the horror creep back in. I push the thought firmly out of my head whenever that happens.

We have to wait in the corridor outside the exam room in silence before we can go in. I watch the Thursday rain dribble down the windows, trying to list all the provinces in China in my head. Riley joins me. 'Hi,' she croaks.

'Oh my God, you look terrible,' I say. I don't think she's slept since the exams started. The circles round her eyes are deep mauve and she can hardly keep her eyelids up.

'Why is everyone so eager to tell me that these days?' she snaps.

I shrug. 'Aren't you meant to be at the end of the queue? It's alphabetical.'

'I know.' She rolls her eyes at me. 'I got a last-minute tip from McNabb.'

'What? About this exam? That we're just about to go into?'

Riley shrugs. 'Yeah, why not?'

'Well, it's a bit late, isn't it?' I say. 'There's no time to revise; we've literally got about ten seconds before the exam starts . . .'

Riley closes her eyes, ignoring me. 'The Tokyo subway system,' she says, swaying slightly.

'No *way*! That's toxic,' I say, delighted. I went over it again just last night. I can even picture the map in my head.

'Thought you'd like to know,' Riley says, half opening her eyes and baring her teeth at me, in what she probably thinks is a smile. There must still be part of her that thinks of the two of us as revision partners.

'Thanks,' I say, as she retreats to the back of the queue. 'Good luck!'

Thank God. All my nervous energy leaves me. At least I know one exam is going to go well.

The exam consists of twenty multiple-choice questions and one essay question. I begin typing as soon as Harrison, monitoring the exam, says we can start. I keep my head down, my brain practically whirring with ideas and information. It's been so long since I actually felt good at something. It's almost enjoyable.

I finish my essay and read back over it, looking for mistakes. I correct the spelling of a few words and change some punctuation but overall I'm really pleased with it, and there are still twenty minutes to go. I glance over at Lu, who revised Tokyo with me last night. She's still typing but she looks pretty confident. Finn, on the other hand, a few desks over, looks more concerned. His eyebrows are knitted together in concentration and he keeps deleting the last thing he typed, retyping it, then deleting it again. He opted out of revising with us last night.

'The exam's going to be on Beijing, that's been the focus this whole time,' he told us. 'It's just a waste of time even looking at Tokyo.'

I feel a small stab of sympathy for him. Is that what I've looked like in other exams? I'm tempted to twist round in my chair and see how Shell's doing – but then the exam door creaks open and all my senses go on red alert.

Florrie moves into the room, closing the door quietly behind her. I drop my eyes straight away but my whole body has already reacted, my heart pumping adrenaline into my limbs. Fragments of the biological science exam come back to me – *the flight or fight response*. What is she doing? Units don't come into the exam room. They're not teachers. I keep my eyes trained on the desk, too terrified to lift them, but I can feel her coming closer. She's heading straight towards me; I know she is.

I'm hoping if I don't look or acknowledge her at all she might just leave. But no. She comes right up to my desk, practically bumping against it, and pauses for a long moment. I keep my eyes down, refusing to look at her. Maybe she'll go away. Suddenly her face closes in on mine, and I jerk with surprise, scraping my chair back across the parquet floor. Everyone's heads turn at the noise.

'Quiet please,' says Harrison absently, focused on his tablet.

I can't look at anyone else. I can't look at Florrie. I sit, my whole body seized up with fear, as she leans further towards me, so close I can hear the tiny whirring of her head moving. She stops, her face centimetres from mine, and doesn't move. Her eyes bore into mine. I can't look. Whatever I do, I can't look.

She moves again, very slightly, and I look straight up at her face. Of course I do. Her eyes hypnotise me, sucking me in. My heart thumps against my ribs. She looks at me, triumph and malice and no expression at all mingled together in those cold blue discs. She's so close I can see the join between the blue and the white metal. My head swims with fear and my ears buzz.

She brings her hand up close to her face, so it's just centimetres from my neck. I want to knock over my chair and run but I'm frozen, every muscle straining as far away as I can get from her. But she keeps closing in on me. Her hand reaches towards my neck. Is she going to throttle me, right here, with everyone ignoring her? My breath's coming in short gasps. There's a scream building in my throat, about to burst out . . .

But suddenly Florrie stands up and moves away from me. She whirrs on past all the desks to the door at the back of the room and leaves. It's only then that I can breathe normally. I take a big shuddering gasp, squeezing my eyes shut and putting my fist over my mouth to stop myself from crying. She's going to kill me. I know it. I'm not imagining it. They're after me. Maybe it's not all the units, maybe some of it is coincidence and assumption and fear, but there is no doubt in my mind that Florrie wants me dead. I've never been so sure of anything.

I look around the exam room again, my eyes wet. How has no one else noticed? Why am I the only one who can see what she's up to? Are they all just wilfully ignoring her in case Cranshaw thinks they're criticising her companionbot?

I'm going to have to run away. I can't wait another week. I can't sit around and wait for death to find me. I'm suddenly gripped with the urge to get up, right now, and make a run for the border. It's so strong I have to hold my chair with my hands. I have to leave tonight. *Somehow.*

Twelve

I look out across the grounds from my dormitory, taking it all in for the last time. In the darkness, through the torrent of Thursday rain, the lawns seem endless. I'll have to run at full pelt to be gone before anyone realises. If I really squint, in the far distance I can see the row of trees that make up the boundary line, and just beyond that, the brambles that signify the wilderness. I've never walked that far across the grounds before, but I can't escape on the shuttle because my chip is blocked. This is the only possibility of escape.

Crossing the border line will mean I'll be blocked from the Oaktree network, but if my chip can connect to a city network I can finally send my dad a message without Cranshaw blocking it. Maybe my chip won't work, maybe he won't believe me, maybe the Company will expel me, but if they do, at least I will be free. I have no idea what life outside the Company would be like, but at least, even Company-less, I would be alive.

I've never thought like this before. I've never even considered a life outside the Company. I'm terrified. But there's no other option.

The groundbots won't be out in the middle of the night, and the other units shouldn't be outside anyway. There's no reason to think a unit will see me, unless they already know what I'm planning – but they couldn't. I have to keep telling myself that. They. Cannot. Know.

Everyone else will still be trapped though. I look over at the three sleeping figures in the beds breathing peacefully. Riley mutters, 'Some people have curly brown hair through proper brushing,' and Lu rolls over. I wish I'd been able to tell Shell, to persuade her to come with me. She could easily become a target after I leave, as her parents both hold high-ranking positions. Not to mention Lu, and Riley, and Finn, and almost everyone else at the school. Even Jake could be at risk. But what can I do? This is a chance to save everyone. Admittedly . . . especially me.

The rain tap tap taps against the dormitory window. I can't leave until midnight, when Thursday becomes Friday; the rain will just have dried up, but the grounds will still be empty. But there's something I've got to do before I go. I have to watch the brainstream of *that day* in November now, otherwise I might never get the chance. I don't know what's going to happen out there.

I've flicked on to the brainstream screen about sixty times and immediately flicked back off. I can't. I can't. I can't. Just thinking about it makes my throat close up.

I can now remember almost everything leading up to *that day* now. Every November, the fifth-years go on a history trip to London, to see Big Ben and Tower Bridge and visit the Downing Street Museum. It's all anyone was talking about. This would be the first time we'd go further than the Woodland River Centre as a class. Of course lots of pupils had already visited the Company headquarters to see their parents, but this was different. This was outside, in the real world. It was a very big deal.

In the weeks before the trip Jake and I had begun talking more. We hadn't discussed Cranshaw or AIR again, but when no one else was around we talked non-stop about units. Particularly Florrie.

'And so you think she understands what you're saying?' I said, for the thousandth time.

'Yes,' said Jake. 'She talks back! We have conversations. It's not just a recorded message or whatever.'

'And her face?' I said, pinching my own cheeks. 'Surely it doesn't . . .'

'Well, she doesn't have expressions exactly,' Jake said. 'But there's something *there*.'

He told me about Humans First too. AIR wanted units to have rights, but Humans First were the main group stopping them. 'They're all crazy,' he said dismissively. 'They hate units.'

'But why?' I said.

Jake shrugged. 'They don't want them to be equal to humans,' he said. 'They really don't trust them. They tried to stop them working at the World Cup last year.'

'Really?' I said. 'Isn't that kind of the point of units? To work for us?'

Jake frowned at me for a second. 'Anyway, there's so much support growing now . . .'

Back then, it had never really occurred to me that units had a consciousness, like we did. It was as baffling as finding out my wardrobe felt taken for granted, or the flushing mechanism on the loo felt embarrassed about its job. It was like having my eyes opened, and though I still took everything Jake said with a pinch of salt, I was beginning to see clearly. For the first time I started noticing the work the units did for us. I stopped doing what everyone else did when a cleanbot entered the dormitory, which was to completely ignore it except to lift my feet up off the floor so it could clean under them. I would never leave my clothes on the floor or my bed unmade anyway, but now I definitely didn't. I even started to tidy away my own plate in the canteen, so the foodbot wouldn't have to do it. I wasn't afraid of the units then. Just curious.

I take a deep breath through my nose, thinking about *the crowd pushing in, the brush of metal against my arm, the screen above me* – my skull throbs, but I have to do it. I have to *know*. I hover over the 16 November stream, squeeze my eyes shut and flick my IndexChip.

After eating breakfast early, we cross the misty grounds to the shuttle station. The history teachers make each class travel separately, with staggered leaving times – they don't want us to have too much fun – but Shell, in the group behind ours, keeps messaging me to keep me updated on her progress.

We're leaving the school now. SO EXCITED!

Finn just got told off for trying to hide coriander-flavoured mudge up his sleeve for a snack on the shuttle. Idiot!

Jess is wearing green walking boots. What a loser!

'Partner up, and then if you lose your partner, we'll know if someone's gone astray,' Llewellyn says to us casually, as if she doesn't want us to think about it too much. I can imagine the repercussions for a teacher if a child under their care goes missing in central London. The strain in her eyes says it all.

Jake elbows me. 'Where's Lu?' he says.

'Oh, she couldn't come,' I say, logging off my RetinaChip to talk to him. 'Her parents wouldn't give her permission; they thought it was too dangerous.'

Poor Lu. She'll be stuck in the library all day with no classes to go to, and then we'll all force her to watch our brainstreams when we get back.

'Guess I'm stuck being your partner then,' says Jake.

'Ugh,' I say.

'Double ugh,' says Jake.

The trip to London takes just under an hour, but we make several stops as we draw closer to the city. I flick my Index-Chip to speed the brainstream up, slowing every time the shuttle reaches a stop. *At each station more and more people get on, looking different from visitors to the school or the majority of shoppers at Woodland River. These people seem smarter, sharper somehow. Then something amazing happens. At the last stop before London, a unit gets on the shuttle and sits down.*

I don't know if it can feel the eyes of about twenty Oaktree pupils on it, but Llewellyn immediately starts clicking her fingers and making outraged facial expressions at us.

'Don't be rude!' she hiss-whispers, and everyone abruptly finds the shuttle's ads for clearer brainstreaming sensors extremely interesting. A fit of inward giggles suddenly comes over me, and as I shake and hold my hand over my face, I elbow Jake in the ribs. He elbows me back, rolling his eyes. 'Get used to it,' he says.

We get out at the last stop, Charing Cross, and climb the stairs to the ground floor. The first things I see are the skyscrapers, nearly blocking out the blue sky above.

'Wait here!' Llewellyn calls over our heads. 'Has everyone got their partner? No one missing?' She checks her tablet, no doubt tracking our IndexChips to make sure we all made it off the shuttle.

I can't take it all in at once. It's too much. I can only see it as a fragmented series of snapshots. People dressed identically in suits crowd the streets, all of them walking hurriedly in the opposite direction to us. Cars are lined up on the roads, barely moving. A black cab zips past, which makes me go 'ooh!' without meaning to. The buildings loom above us. A shuttle train, its tracks fixed to the side of a glass skyscraper, zooms over our heads. A huge half-built structure hangs over us, like two curved halves of a triangle, pointing up towards the sky. I feel repulsed by the dirt on the ground, the litter we're all kicking through like autumn leaves, but at the same time it's London dirt. It's thrilling.

Everywhere I look there's movement. Every conceivable space is filled with people. It's still early in the morning but there are lights everywhere. There are adverts too, flashing at me, moving and popping up everywhere. I spot one for Sammy's, but I don't recognise the others. They must be for other companies' products.

People are pushing past us, sidling through our group, shouldering us out of the way. I can't believe I'd ever thought of the Woodland River Centre as busy. Llewellyn tries to talk to us but it's like having a lesson in the middle of a tornado. Eventually she gives up and gestures for us to make our way through the crowd.

I go to follow her but Jake grabs my arm. 'Wait a second,' he says.

'What?' I say. I can hardly hear him. 'We've got to go!'

'Just two seconds, I promise,' he says.

I can see Llewellyn's blonde hair, bobbing away from us in the crowd. Then it's gone. I can't see her or anyone from our class any more. The people keep moving forward, never stopping.

'Jake, we're going to get lost,' I say. 'I don't know the way to Downing Street from here.'

'We'll meet up with them later,' he says. 'They'll never know we were gone. There's just something I need to do first.' He keeps looking over his shoulder at something I can't see.

'What?' I know he has something planned – something that's not allowed. I can see it in his eyes. 'I don't want to get in trouble!'

212

'You won't,' he says. 'It'll be fine.' And then he turns and falls into step with the crowd, going in the opposite direction to the way Llewellyn has gone, tugging me along after him.

'Please, Jake, I want to go back,' I keep calling. I've never been to a city before and now I'm lost in one, without a teacher or a parent. A message beeps through from Shell – Wow. Two units just got on our shuttle! So toxic! – but I can't use my IndexChip to access it because Jake won't let go of my hand. We cross two roads – one car flashes past just millimetres away from me – and then Jake stops. The crowd moves round us like water round an island.

'Look up,' he says.

A huge seemingly endless banner hangs above our heads. It moves in the wind, like it's breathing in and out. As it puffs up and out, I see the words: AIR Rally.

'What?' I say. 'Did you know this was happening today?'

'Yeah,' says Jake. 'Duh.'

'But . . .' Anxiety slowly creeps up my spine. 'What if we get caught? They'll know—'

'They won't know,' says Jake.

'But—'

'I've got it sorted,' he says. 'Don't worry about it.'

I understand – Cranshaw will cover for us.

I shake my head. 'I don't want to,' I say.

'Millie, come on, we'll just stay for the first speech,' he says. 'Then we'll go back.'

He starts to move forward, but I stay still.

He looks back at me, exasperated. 'Either way, I'm staying

for the first speech,' he says, his tone harsh. 'You can find your way to Downing Street on your own if you really want to.'

I can't go back on my own and I can't leave Jake. 'Just the first speech,' I say.

'Yeah, sure,' says Jake.

I cling close to Jake as we weave through the crowd. Nelson's Column looms above us as we enter Trafalgar Square. Cranshaw must have made sure the trip happened today so Jake could attend the rally. I don't know if this makes me feel better or worse about being here.

As we get to the fountain, the endless moving stream of people starts to clump together in increasingly larger groups, chatting and singing and waving flags. People keep turning round to look at us, pointing us out to their friends. I suppose the average political rally doesn't have many thirteen-year-olds in attendance.

'Maybe we should stay here,' I say, hoping to make a quick exit, but Jake shakes his head. 'Let's get closer to the front,' he says.

There's a massive stage at the far end of the square, with an empty podium set up, flanked by two giant screens. Above it is another banner. This one is really flapping about in the wind. It's playing some sort of video short, but I can't see it – there are too many heads in the way. I'm ready to stop but Jake keeps moving and sidling past people. We duck through a large group of people with AIR T-shirts on and past a man in thick glasses and a tatty white coat—

Dr Tavish? I jolt out of the brainstream. What was he doing there?

—until we're almost at the very front of the stage, just a few lines of people ahead of us.

'Amazing, isn't it?' Jake says, his voice straining over the loud music and people talking.

I want to shake my head but there's something in his eyes that I haven't seen before. He's looking over my shoulder at the audience, with what I can only describe as pride. He looks like he's surveying his empire.

'When do the speeches start?' I say.

'Er, soon.' He's distracted, turning to look at the side of the stage. There's a man there gesturing to him.

'Hey, I'll be back in a second, OK?' Jake says without looking at me. He dashes off, pushing past people and ducking out of my sight.

'Er, thanks!' I say to no one. Now I really am alone.

For a second, I consider leaving and trying to find my way to Downing Street before Llewellyn checks our IndexChip trackers again, but I'm too worried about getting lost. At least Jake knows where I am. If he ever comes back.

Something metal brushes against my arm. I look round and a unit is standing next to me. I can't believe how close it is; I can hear the machinery moving around inside it. It doesn't look at me. I try not to react to its presence, though I can feel another giggling fit coming on. The unit looks directly at the banner above the stage, which is still curled up in the wind. As quickly as it appeared next to me, it's gone, pushing towards the front. I realise I've been holding my breath.

The speakers on the stage crackle and at the same moment the giant banner suddenly fills out, as if it's been waiting to perform. And I can finally see the video it's playing over and over again.

It's Jake. Jake is in AIR's campaign ad. Jake and a unit I don't recognise. Over and over again, Jake puts his arm round the unit, they both do a thumbs-up to the camera, and the AIR logo blooms on to the screen.

I stand with my mouth open, transfixed, until a woman barges past me to get to the front. She's wearing a grey T-shirt with the AIR logo and Jake's face on it. I jump away from her, knocking into someone else, who says, 'Hey!' loudly in my ear. Someone a few metres away is holding a flag with Jake's face on it. There's another flag further back in the crowd, and another, and another. They're everywhere. Everywhere I look, Jake's face beams out at me.

I can't take it in. Jake is a part of AIR – a major part. He has secret meetings with its leader. He has notes from AIR meetings secretly passed to him. He has his face emblazoned all over AIR's campaigns. How did he let this happen? Doesn't he realise this could be dangerous? What if our parents see? What if the Company find out?

The speakers crackle again and a stocky man walks out to the podium.

He throws his arms wide. 'Welcome, everyone—'

A bang like nothing I've ever heard before deafens me and the ground shakes like it's trying to throw me off. People are screaming. The last thing I see is the two giant screens falling towards me . . .

Thirteen

I jump up, practically half out of bed, fired up by adrenaline. I have to clap my hands over my mouth to keep from shouting out.

The crowd closing in, the brush of metal against my arm, the screen above me – it all happened. I saw it happen, but I still don't know what it meant. I obviously didn't get hit by a car – I can't believe I ever thought that was true – but what did happen? An explosion? I need to watch more – I need to find out more – but as my IndexChip flicks to the brainstreaming screen I see the time. It's a minute to midnight.

I can't watch more. I have to go, now. I'm jittery with anticipation, my hands shaking, my insides all twisted round each other, and I can't sit in this room and find out what happened afterwards. I can't leave through the door obviously, as my chip will immediately alert Welbeck, but there aren't any chip trackers on the windows. It's just the three-storey drop that worries me.

I put my bag on my back and prepare to climb up on the sill, when Lu sits up suddenly in bed.

'Millie?' she says, her eyes half closed. She's wearing her lucky striped sleepsuit.

'Shhh, go back to sleep,' I say.

'What are you doing?' she says, her voice loud in the near silent room.

'Er . . . I'm sleepwalking,' I say. It makes no sense but it's the first thing I think of.

'Oh,' Lu says, and puts her head back on the pillow, asleep.

I wait a few seconds, holding my breath, hoping no one else wakes up, and then the rain stops.

Now. I hop up on to the sill and slide the window ajar. I can't open it too far or the alarms will go off. I squeeze through the gap, backpack over one shoulder. On the other side I balance on the sill and slide the window shut behind me. Done.

That was the easy bit. Now I have to work out how to get down. I glance back through the window into the dormitory, already missing my friends. I may never see them again.

But now is not the time to think about that. Now is the time for focusing on not falling off a window ledge three storeys off the ground. I sidle along the ledge, trying to grip the window frame with my hands. If I can jump from here to the roof over the door, I can drop from there into the bushes without too much of an impact. But if I miss the canopy, I'll slam into the concrete path and probably break both my legs. And if the units don't get to me overnight, I'll be trapped in the medical centre. I take a deep breath and try to block out Finn's words, which are echoing in my head from nearly two weeks ago, about Daisy ending up splattered all over the path.

I lower myself down on the ledge until I'm sitting on it, and then dangle my feet over to the canopy roof to see if I can reach it. Nowhere near. I'm going to have to get closer. I inch off the ledge, holding on to it with my hands, until my whole body hangs from the window. The ground seems dizzyingly far below me. But my feet still won't quite reach the top of the canopy, even if I swing my legs out. My hands, scraping against the concrete, are starting to sweat. I'm going to have to try to jump.

I swallow a lump in my throat, look over at the canopy – and then before I can think my way out of it, swing my body off the ledge. For a second I'm suspended in mid air and my inner organs all seem to leap into my throat at once – and then I hit the top of the canopy so hard all my bones seem to quiver. I'm scrabbling to hold on but the tiles are slipping out of my grasp and suddenly I'm rolling off the roof, hitting my knees and elbows and chin on the edge, and falling straight into the bushes below.

My brain doesn't think anything except ow ow ow for a

few moments. I grab my head, checking it's all still in one piece, but it seems to be the only part of me that hasn't taken a beating in the fall. My knees, my elbows and the palms of my hands are scraped and bleeding, the whole of my right side throbs where I hit the canopy, and when I stand up, one of my ankles wobbles and can't seem to hold my weight without pain. This is not good. If I'm stuck in the wilderness for a while, an inability to walk is not going to help.

But I'm out, I've made it, and so far, in the two minutes I've been getting myself up, Welbeck hasn't descended on me demanding to know what I'm doing and the whole of Hawthorn house hasn't been woken up by me crashing all over the front of the building. That's the hard bit over. The easy bit, making it from here to the border without being spotted, may be slightly harder now because of my ankle, but the alternatives could be so much worse.

I check all the windows of the house for a light or a face watching, but there's no sign of life inside. There's a hedge just to the right of the house, which, if I duck behind it, should keep me hidden from here to a small copse of trees, about 500 metres away. I half run, half hobble to the hedge, dive behind it, and look back at Hawthorn house, possibly for the last time.

My heart flutters and I remind myself that the last time I was this close to escape, Welbeck caught me at the last minute. As I look out towards that distant line of trees, which used to scream danger, I can't help but feel hopeful. I'm almost there. I'm so close.

I reach the copse and weave through it in the dark, glancing back at the school to check there's not a group of teachers on my heels. I trip over a log and nearly fall into a tree, and as I steady myself, I hear something. A tiny shift, a metallic clinking.

My skin prickles into goose pimples and my breath catches in my chest. I couldn't have heard it right, I tell myself. It must have been an animal shifting in the woods. A unit wouldn't be out in the grounds for no reason. My heart's thumping against my chest and I want to hide, but I straighten up, look all around me as far as I can see in the distance, and of course there's nothing there. I'm imagining things.

I move further forward, checking behind me more often now. I don't hear anything until I'm almost out of the shadow of the trees when – there it is again. It's unmistakable – a shifting, clinking sound I hear a thousand times a day. It's the sound units make when they move. I dive like an animal into a ditch, looking for a glint of silver. But the next stretch of land ahead of me is a wide grassy meadow, offering no cover and nowhere to hide. My heart beats in my throat.

I can't see anything anywhere. It's too dark looking back into the trees. Could something be in there? Should I run for it or keep hidden and wait for it to move off? I hear another clinking, closer this time, and without pausing I launch myself out of the ditch, wrenching my ankle, and hurtle across the meadow. The grass is so high and thick

221

I'm wading through it like water. My breath rasps inside my chest and throat and I wish more than anything that I was in the dormitory, curled up in my bed and dreaming all this up.

Only when I'm halfway across do I chance a look back at the copse, expecting to see something coming after me. But the meadow's as empty as it was before. I can't see anything watching from the shadow of the trees either.

There's another small patch of trees metres away. If I can reach that without anything spotting me, I'll be close to the border. I can even see the tops of the trees that line the division from here. I need to get out of the meadow and get hidden.

The meadow's uneven surface is not helping my ankle. With every step I take pain shoots up to my knee, making me wince, but I won't stop or rest until I reach the trees. I'm hardly any distance away now. Suddenly there's another clank – so close by there must be a unit in the field. I turn and lurch forward at the same time, wobble on my ankle and fall face first into the grass. The impact knocks the air out of my lungs and I choke.

It takes me a second to get my breath back, but as soon as I do I'm on my feet, preparing to defend myself against the attacker – but again, the meadow is empty. I don't stop to check if it's ducked into the long grass but instead turn and run towards the trees again. If I can get to the trees, I can hide.

Just ten steps away . . . I'm expecting a metal grip on

my shoulder at any second. Just two steps away . . . And I'm there. I made it. I look back, trying to spot the unit. It felt like it was close. Is that a ripple in the grass a few metres ahead? It'll have to move at some point. Another ripple. I focus my eyes on the spot, but a movement beside me makes me turn, and there's a groundbot barely a metre away from me. Its eyes lock with mine. I scream from the back of my throat and launch myself away.

My legs are jelly, but the adrenaline and the fear are pumping through me now, hurtling me forward. I steal a glance back, and start when I see that two groundbots are on my tail, both just metres away from me. One of them reaches out for me, its face blank, and its metal fingers scrape my head, but I duck out of its way. And suddenly I'm out of the copse; I can see the border. It's only a hundred metres away. The units won't be able to cross it. I feel a renewed burst of energy. I speed up, barely noticing the pain in my ankle. As I veer past a bush, I see a third unit, coming from my left. Through the darkness I can only see it glinting in the moonlight, but it's enough to know how fast it's heading towards me. How many are out here now? I just need to get to the border. Once I'm past it, they can't get me.

I can see the border trees, and see each individual leaf on them. I can hear the thump of the units' footsteps behind me. I can hear the tiny creaks their joints make as they run. They could grab me at any second . . . Any moment now . . .

But they don't.

I crash into the trunk of the border tree in front of me, practically kissing it with relief. My legs crumple beneath me and my lungs burn. I look back and the units have stopped, all three of them together. They're staring at me, but there's nothing they can do now. I grin at them stupidly, wobbly with relief, then start walking away.

I slam into something cold, hard and solid. Dazed, I step back to look, but nothing's there. I reach out a hand and feel a flat surface, and then suddenly I can see it. It's a wall made out of glass, just level with the trees. I look for the top, and have to crane my neck all the way back. It's at least as tall as the tree. It extends along the border for as far as I can see in either direction.

It takes a second for realisation to hit, and when it does, it thumps into my stomach like a ten-ton weight, so heavily I can almost taste it in my mouth. There's no way out. This wall must have been here the whole time we were being told we could leave whenever we wanted to. There's never been a choice. I'm trapped. We're all trapped.

I turn round. The units haven't moved an inch. The three of them glint at me through the darkness, their expressions as blank as always. They must have known the wall was here all along.

My heartbeat, still racing to catch up from the run, speeds up even further, filling my ears and my throat. I crush myself against the wall, desperately trying to think my way out. Slowly the units move forward together, advancing on me. They know I'm trapped. Wildly I pick up a fallen branch from the ground and wave it around like a weapon, but it's barely as thick as my finger.

'Don't!' I say, my voice coming out as a squeak, as they close in on all three sides. Desperately I throw the stick at the middle unit but it bounces uselessly off its chest, not even making it pause. My legs fail me again and I fall back against the wall, holding my hands up to ward off the inevitable attack . . .

The units stop less than a metre away. The middle one locks eyes with me. There's no expression there but I know it's going to kill me.

Then something happens that I don't expect. It speaks. 'TAV201198.'

It sounds like a bad recording of a human's voice. I gape at it. Then, its eyes still boring into mine, it speaks again.

'Millie Hendrick.'

Suddenly hearing my name changes everything. In a split second the fear breaks like a tidal wave and crashes into anger. In that moment the idea of cowering like a frightened animal at the mercy of a trio of walking *appliances* makes me furious. The anger and indignation and adrenaline fill every inch of my veins like burning-hot poison. In one movement, before the units can react, I spring from the ground like a cat. I slip through the gap between two of them, and run faster than a deer across the school grounds. I don't stop. Not to look behind me, even though

I know they must be a heartbeat away. I see Hawthorn house in the distance.

Without stopping, running on pure momentum now, I clatter through the door, hurtle up the stairs, bash into the dormitory door and leap on to my bed, wrenching the cover over my head. I take a deep, shuddering breath, gripping my backpack to me. It's only then that I let the terror, the knowledge that I'm caged like an animal, rushing in to fill the space the burnt-up anger and adrenaline left behind, overwhelm me. As soon as the tears start to slow and my lungs stop convulsing, I flick my brainstream screen up and press on.

Fourteen

I wake up and my mind is blank, like sand after the sea has washed over it. I don't know where I am. I don't know my own name. But I'm too groggy to be alarmed. I'm vaguely aware that I seem to be floating. Lights flash above me and the surface I'm lying on trembles. There are noises around me but they're far away and muffled. I float through a pair of double doors just as my eyes begin to droop again . . .

Later, when I open my eyes again, I'm in a hospital room and a man I don't know is leaning over me.

'Millie,' he says, like I'm his oldest friend. 'Our little survivor. You're awake.'

'Wh-what—' My voice is hoarse. Some part of my mind registers his white coat. 'Who—'

'I'm Dr Tavish,' he says, turning his attention to the

beeping machine next to me. 'You're in City London Hospital. You've been here since six this morning.'

'What? Why?' My brain feels cloudy and I can't quite follow what he is saying.

Dr Tavish looks at me through his thick glasses, his eyes grave. 'There was an explosion in Trafalgar Square,' he says. 'The paramedics found you, buried in debris, two days later. They couldn't believe it when they found a pulse.'

Tentatively I touch my head, which is wrapped thickly in bandages. Oddly it doesn't hurt at all, but my earlobes throb.

'My brother . . .' I say, struggling to remember. I knew Jake and I had been together, but where had he gone? 'Is he here too?'

'I don't know,' says Dr Tavish. 'I can check the patient list . . .'

'When you find him . . .' I'm starting to drift under again. 'When you find him . . . can you tell him I'm here?'

'Of course,' says Dr Tavish, as my eyes close.

I wake up and don't know where I am. A nurse tells me I've been 'claimed' by Dr Cranshaw, who'd tracked me down and alerted the Company and my parents that I was still alive. She also tells me my brother is already back at school. He was uninjured in the blast. Blast? I think. What blast? My thoughts drift along vaguely, like clouds. I can't seem to pin anything down for more than a few seconds.

Dr Tavish sits down and explains everything to me, although even as he begins he says, 'I don't know how much of this you'll be able to recall later.' An explosive had gone off at the front of the crowd, barely metres away from me. Many of the people who had come to the rally that day were killed, although Dr Tavish said

228

they were still picking people out of the debris. I had been found two days after the explosion. The paramedics took me to him, the country's leading head specialist. Luckily he works at a hospital only a few streets from Trafalgar Square. My skull is cracked 'like an eggshell', to quote Dr Tavish. He shows me scans of my brain on his monitor.

'See, it seems there were four large bits of metal that hit here, here and here,' he says, indicating different parts of my skull. 'This resulted in cracks along here . . .' He traces a line across the back of my head. 'And here . . .' He points to an area from my left ear to the middle of my head.

'Luckily we got to you quickly,' says Dr Tavish. 'We patched up your skull and that seemed to go well. There were several small splinters of metal that caught the left side of your head, damaging your RetinaChip. Though we managed to remove most of the pieces lodged in your skull, there may be some residual scarring of the skin on your face. And your RetinaChip was so badly damaged, we had to replace it, and your IndexChip had to be upgraded to go with it.'

He looks at the scans on the monitor, then back at me. 'Really,' he says. 'You are incredibly lucky to be alive.'

Over the next few brainstreams, there are only little shards and fragments of available memory. I link them all together in one long string.

I'm in a hospital bed, and I don't know where or why. My head is wrapped in bandages. There's also a huge plaster over half of my left eye and most of the left side of my face, making it difficult to move it. My hand is also bandaged, my index finger encased in plaster. I meet my doctor and he tells me why I'm here. He says, 'You are lucky to be alive. Very, very lucky.'

People keep saying that to me. I don't understand why. There are news stories everywhere about an incident in London, at a political rally, but I don't feel like it has anything to do with me. My RetinaChip is still all bandaged up, so I can't check it for news anyway.

Someone presents me with a tablet. An old lady's face is on it, a big puff of wiry hair filling the screen. It takes me a second, but I get there. Cranshaw.

'I hope you're recovering from your car accident, my dear,' she says.

Is that what happened? I don't know. 'Y-yes,' I say.

'This shows why you shouldn't walk away from the group on school trips,' she says. 'Cities are dangerous places.'

I nod along. 'Er, can I ask . . .' I say, my voice rasping. 'Where—'

There's a metallic jingle from her side of the screen, a low whirr, and automatically I flinch away from the tablet, the back of my neck goose-pimpling.

'What?' Cranshaw says, leaning closer to the screen. 'Florrie, put the tea here.'

It's just Florrie, I tell myself. But my heart is drumming against my ribcage.

'What did you say?' Cranshaw asks.

I take a deep breath, trying to calm down. 'I thought . . . I thought Jake was with me, when I – when this happened,' I say. 'What happened to him? Is he OK?'

Cranshaw looks at me steadily through the screen for a long moment. 'I'm afraid you're mistaken,' she says. 'Jake was not with you. He was briefly separated from the group, but quickly rejoined them before Ms Llewellyn realised anyone was missing.'

'Oh,' I say. 'But—'

'Jake was nowhere near you,' she repeats firmly. 'He was not with you at the time of your accident. You have remembered that wrongly.'

I go back to school. I still have a bandage wrapped round my head and padding on the side of my face, but apart from that I look almost normal. 'It's just what's happening on the inside that might be a problem,' Dr Tavish keeps saying.

'What about my new RetinaChip?' I say. 'It won't affect my brain, will it?' Dr Tavish has told me it was OK to start using it, but I'm scared to log on in case my whole head falls apart.

'There might be a few teething problems, but nothing major. The only thing that will need more time is brainstreaming. It's important you don't brainstream until we know you're all healed,' Dr Tavish says, smiling. 'I don't know what sort of image quality you might get, and there could be some . . . side effects. There's a possibility the titanium still lodged in your brain could affect what happens when you try to download images.'

'Titanium?'

'Yes, that's the type of metal that the splinters in your head are made from,' says Dr Tavish.

'Oh, OK,' I say, thinking for a second. 'Isn't that what units are made from?'

Dr Tavish looks up at me. 'Yes, it's the same, exactly the same grade,' he says, watching me carefully. Something about his look and the fractured memories from that day unearths an idea in my mind, a response, but I don't know what it is. I feel as though the fog is clearing, my brain sharpening and refining, but there's still so much drifting in and out of focus.

They tell me I will have monthly check-ups, and that if I see flashing lights, hear strange noises or feel dizzy, I have to immediately check myself into the medical centre. The Company picks me up in a helicopter to take me back to school. The moment I walk into the dormitory Shell throws herself at me.

'I thought you were never coming back!' she says. 'They wouldn't tell us anything. I thought you were dead and they just weren't telling us!'

'OK, OK, I'm all right,' I say.

'Millie, you got hit by a car!' says Shell. 'Don't you know how dangerous that is? Look at your head!'

'Oh, yeah,' I say. I still feel half a step behind everyone else; I don't remember a car at all. All that has come back to me is a crowd, and something metal passing by me, and a screen. 'If you think that's bad you should see the scarring on my face.'

I'm trying to speak lightly but my voice breaks.

'What did your parents say? Didn't they visit you in hospital?'

'Oh, no, not in the end,' I say. 'They were going to, but . . .

you know, they're busy. They've both got loads of meetings and stuff. I spoke to them on a video call, so they know I'm awake . . .'

Shell looks horrified as she takes in the size of the plaster on my left temple.

'But it'll heal, won't it? I mean, you're already pretty much back to normal?' she keeps saying.

I keep telling everyone I'm fine. I have to reassure them because of how bad I look. 'I'm fine,' I say when Lu and Riley come into the dormitory. 'I'm fine,' I say when I bump into Nick in the corridor.

That night, as we walk into the canteen for dinner, a glint of light bounces off a foodbot and I jump.

'What are you doing?' Shell says, several paces ahead of me.

'N-nothing,' I say, my voice hoarse.

But it carries on happening. Every time I see a unit – in the grounds, in our dormitory, serving food – I'm pinned down with a fear so instinctual, I can't even put it into words. I have no idea what I think they're going to do to me. And I don't know why I feel like this. I feel as if they know – they look up at me or turn round when I'm near, when before they just ignored me as much as I ignored them. Do they know that I've seen or experienced something I shouldn't have? Do they think I'm on to them?

I don't see Jake. I should message him, but I'm too scared to log on to the network yet. My head feels precariously taped together, rickety almost, and I can feel the stitches, which are lodged into my skull like steel girders. Walking to Mandarin a few days after I get back, I spot him across a crowded corridor.

'Jake,' I say, reaching out to touch his arm.

He looks up at me and, in seconds, my emotions rocket from mildly curious to absolute, all-consuming rage. My face flushes crimson and I have to clench my fists to keep from hitting him. This is all your fault, I think. You did this to me.

'Oh, hi,' he says. 'You all right, Millie?'

I can't speak. My teeth clench, making my skull throb, and my fingernails dig into my palms. My brain boils with hatred for him. I hate you I hate you I hate you.

'Millie? Millie?' He pulls his arm away from me. 'I've got to go, Mills,' he says, and walks off.

I can't understand it. I mean, I usually blame Jake when bad things happen to me, and I'm used to feeling frustrated with him, but this is totally different. I've never wanted to hurt him so much. And why? Cranshaw said Jake wasn't even there. The accident wasn't his fault. So why do I feel so strongly that it is?

The next time I see him, in the canteen, the same thing happens again. I'm holding a bowl of coconut-flavoured mudge and I have to physically resist the urge to tip it over his head.

'I need to talk to you,' I say through gritted teeth.

'What?' he says, mouth full.

'I—' I say, looking around to check no one's listening. 'I need to know what happened. In London. I can't remember.'

Jake looks at me, and slowly swallows. 'What makes you think I know?' he says. 'I wasn't with you.'

He's lying. I know, even though Cranshaw told me the same thing. I can't put my finger on how I know. 'I just—' I start to say, but he cuts across me.

'Maybe it's better that you don't remember, Mills,' he says. 'I mean, it might be traumatic for you—'

'This is traumatic for me,' I say. 'I'm so confused—'

'Yeah, but that's just because your head hurts,' he says. 'You'll feel better soon. We've actually talked about this a few times already, you know—'

'It's not just that, Jake,' I say, my teeth gritting again. 'I feel like . . . I feel . . .'

'What?' he says.

I feel like I hate you, I want to say.

'It's . . . the units,' I say, glancing around to check there isn't one nearby.

Jake's face goes very still. 'The units?'

'All I can remember from that day,' I say, and I feel right on the brink of crying all of a sudden, 'is something metal near me, and the sound of machinery. And now I can't stop thinking – I don't even know why – I feel like they're going to—'

Jake leaps up, grabs my arm and pulls me across the canteen – coconut mudge flying everywhere. He yanks me out into a deserted corridor, looks around and then leans close to me.

'Going to what?' he says, voice crisp. 'Hurt you? Attack you?'

'What?' I say. 'Why did you—'

'Do you think the units are going to hurt you?' he says, each word like a punch.

235

'Yes,' I say. 'I don't know why, but I know – I mean, who really knows what they're capable of?'

Jake looks down at me, his jaw clenched. Probably the exact same face I'm making at him right now.

'It wasn't the unit,' he says in a low voice. 'For the last time. I don't know what you've heard or what you remember, but It. Was. Not. The. Unit.'

'What?' I say. 'What wasn't?'

'Don't even go down that road, Millie,' he says, and I realise how angry he is. 'It just malfunctioned. It was an accident. These things happen, even in public places.'

'What unit? I don't understand, Jake!' The pain in my head beats in time with my heart.

'Do you know how many times we've had this conversation?' he says. 'Listen to me. Units don't hurt people. You can't start to think they do just because of one incident. The unit that exploded at the rally—'

His mouth snaps shut as though he's said something he shouldn't.

'Jake, what do you know? What rally?' I say. 'What happened that you aren't telling me?'

He looks slowly at me, then turns away. 'Nothing.'

236

Fifteen

Something's standing over me. I can't open my eyes but I know it's there. It glints through the darkness. I need to jump out of my bed and escape but I can't wake up. It's reaching out towards me but I can't move . . . it's going to kill me . . .

'Millie, wake up!'

'Argh!' I scream and launch myself up, grabbing whatever's shaking my shoulder so hard. It takes me a second to realise I'm face to face with Shell. My hand is locked round her wrist.

'What are you doing?' she says, squirming away. 'I was trying to wake you up!'

'Oh, sorry, sorry,' I say, blinking in the bright sunshine.

'We're going to be late for the debate exam; everyone else has already left. Hurry up and get dressed—' She looks at me closely. 'Are you . . . already dressed?'

I look down at my clothes. I'm still wearing the navy blue T-shirt and leggings from yesterday. I didn't put them back in the wardrobe so there won't be any clothes hanging in it. 'Er, yes,' I say. I disentangle my legs from the straps of my backpack – I've been sleeping on top of it, along with my tablet.

'You're not going to wear violet today? Honestly?' says Shell. '*You're* going to wear the same clothes two days in a row?'

'Yes,' I say again, getting up to splash water on my face. My ankle doesn't hurt – I must have only jolted it.

'Millie, there's mud all down the back of your legs!' Shell's eyes meet mine and she reels back. 'Did you *try to leave*? In the night? You—'

'Shell, shut up,' I say, grabbing her shoulders.

'*Millie!*' Shell's voice rises an octave. 'There's no way Dr Cranshaw won't find out. How did you even . . . how are you still here?'

'Look, Shell, calm down,' I say.

'No, I won't,' Shell says, wriggling out of my grasp. 'What were you thinking? You've actually—'

'We're going to be late for the exam and then we'll *both* be out of Oaktree,' I say in a low voice. 'We'll talk about this later, OK?'

Shell looks pained. 'I don't understand you any more,' she says, shaking her head. She's looking at me like I might sprout wings and fly out of the window at any moment.

'Let's just go,' I say, standing aside so Shell can open the door.

I keep hold of Shell's elbow as we go down the stairs, my eyes on the floor. Just the thought of seeing a unit makes my heart drop into my stomach. There's a pressure on my chest, stopping me from breathing properly, and the image of the units' blank expressions keeps playing in my head. I'm going to die. I'm going to die. I'm going to die.

We trudge across the grounds to the canteen, but as we approach it, it's obvious something's wrong. At this time it's usually packed, but people are leaving in droves, heading towards the courtyard.

'What's going on?' says Shell. 'Where's everyone going?'

'I don't know,' I say.

Riley appears beside me. 'Hi,' she says, making me jump.

'Oh, hi,' I say. 'Do you know what's going on? Is the canteen still serving food?'

'I don't know,' she says flatly. She blinks, closing her eyes for a few seconds too long. 'The debate exam's been cancelled.'

'What?' Shell and I say in unison.

'I just saw Welbeck,' says Riley. 'There's no reschedule date or anything.'

'But why?' I say, suddenly overcome by a sense of foreboding. 'The school never cancels exams. Did Welbeck not say why? Not even a hint?'

'No,' says Riley. She hasn't put iris drops in today; I always forget her eyes are naturally deep blue. 'I was waiting outside his office and he ran straight past me. Barely stopped to tell me. Cranshaw's sending an alert message round as we speak.'

'Have you seen Finn or Lu?' says Shell. 'Do they know already? We were last to leave the dormitory.'

Riley shakes her head. 'No, just you,' she says. 'They'll find out in a second though, I suppose.'

A group of second-years rush out of the canteen, one of them nearly bumping into Riley. He doesn't stop to apologise but hurries on past, towards the courtyard.

'What *is* everyone so desperate to see?' Shell says.

Riley shakes her head. 'I need to go and work. See you later,' she says, weaving her way back to the dorm.

'Should we . . .' I say, watching the stream of people heading away from us.

'Yeah,' says Shell.

We follow the others into the courtyard, and see what must be at least half the school gathered round the oak tree. The crowd isn't still though. The pupils near the tree are pushing forward, but almost immediately turning back, and there's already a steady stream of pupils moving towards us out of the crowd, their eyes unseeing.

We push our way through them. Conversations seem to die away whenever people spot Shell and me. I'm sure I'm not imagining it. No one's making eye contact, and people are turning their backs on us as soon as they spot us, as if they're talking about us. But we don't even know most of them.

'Is everyone being weird or is it just me?' says Shell as we push further forward.

'It's not just you,' I say, straining my neck to see what could be ahead.

I can see Welbeck, Llewellyn and Harrison right next to the oak tree. They're standing in a circle, their heads bowed, like they're looking at something on the tree's roots. As I crane my neck, I bump into a fifth-year girl with lilac hair. She spins round. 'Hey, watch where—' She breaks off when she sees us, drops her eyes and pushes past us as fast as she can.

Suddenly Harrison pops his head up at the front of the crowd. 'Move away! You all have somewhere else to be! This is not a spectator event! Please!'

There's a desperate edge to his voice, indicating not only that no one's going to listen to him, but that he doesn't really expect them to. He immediately turns back to the huddle of teachers.

'What is it? Can you see?' Shell says to me.

'I don't know,' I say.

A dark-haired boy from our year turns round and sees us. 'You – you need to—' he says, gesturing towards the oak tree.

'Huh?' I say, but he doesn't respond. He pushes past us, back towards the school.

Shell slips into the space he's just vacated, right at the

front of the crowd. '*Oh*,' I hear her say, as if all the breath's been knocked out of her.

'What? What?' I say, moving forward next to her.

The teachers are blocking the view. There's something on the ground covered in a white sheet.

'Oh,' I say, like an echo. 'Who . . . ?'

Shell turns to me, her face an odd shade of yellow. She grips my forearm.

'Lu's striped sleepsuit,' she says almost in a whisper. 'No one else has one like that.'

I don't know what she's talking about until I turn back, and see the foot poking out of the bottom of the sheet.

'No!' I say, pushing past Harrison and throwing myself forward into the circle of teachers. Shell's only a step behind me. I feel like my heart's trying to escape out of my mouth. *They killed Lu*. They had me cornered last night but I got away. So they got someone else instead. How can it be a coincidence that the girl who sleeps one bed over from me has been killed?

'What happened to her? What did they do?' I gasp.

'Get back—' Llewellyn starts to say, but Welbeck puts a hand on her arm and whispers in her ear. She looks at us.

'Millie, Shell,' Welbeck says. 'Let's not discuss this here, we need to—'

'No!' I say. 'What's happened to her?' My heart blocks my throat, and I can't seem to catch my breath.

242

'A terrible accident.' A voice comes from the other side of the oak tree. Cranshaw. She moves into the little clearing hovering over Lu's body, Florrie at her shoulder like a shadow. I automatically take a step back, bumping into Shell.

'She must have jumped from the tree during the night and broken her neck,' she says, looking down at the sheet. 'A terrible, terrible accident.'

'You liar!' I yell. There's a beat of silence as the teachers, Shell, and the pupils in the crowd pause, shocked, and then the noise rises like someone's pushed a button on a stereo. Cranshaw, lips tight and head held up high, looks at Shell and me. Welbeck darts forward, as if to shoo us away, but Cranshaw holds up her hand to stop him.

'What did you say, Millie?' she says.

I don't realise there are tears on my face until I try to speak, and they choke me.

'It's a lie, it's a lie,' I say, my breath catching wetly in my throat. 'They got her. They killed her. They finally did it.'

Cranshaw turns away dismissively, but Llewellyn asks, 'Who? What does she mean?'

'She knows,' I say at Cranshaw's back. Florrie faces my way.

Llewellyn doesn't know where to look. 'What?'

'The units got her!' I yell, not caring who hears me now. The crowd of pupils around me goes quiet again, and this time the sound doesn't pick back up. 'Can't you see, are you all blind? The units are rising up! They've been

243

attacking pupils for weeks, and now they've killed someone! And Cranshaw's just ignoring it!'

Cranshaw turns back, her face glowering. Florrie fixes
me with those blue eyes. My heart quivers but at the same
time it's a relief to finally get it all out. At least now everyone will know the truth. And they're listening. Finally
people are listening to me.

'It's the units!' I yell. 'They're the ones doing all these
things! They killed Lu and now Cranshaw's going to cover
it up! Admit it! They murdered Lu!'

Shell grabs my hand, I think for support, but then I
realise she's trying to tug me away, out of the circle. 'What
are you—' I start to say, but she's not looking at me. She's
looking at the faces in the crowd. I thought they'd fallen
silent because they were listening, but now I see they're
not. They're whispering to each other, staring at me with
pity.

'What?' I say, still angry. 'Aren't you listening?'

Jess pushes her way to the front, her jaw jutting forward in a grim smile. 'No one's listening, Millie,' she says.

I draw breath, about to let all the anger and frustration
from the last week engulf me, when I spot Jake's face in the
crowd. His jaw set, he looks murderously at me and slowly
shakes his head.

Suddenly the swell of anger and fury I had a second
ago crashes, and the tears well up and spill over, so I can
barely see. Shell tries to hold on to me but I shake her off,
pushing through the crowd, back to the dormitory. I shut

myself in my wardrobe again, sobbing until my eyes throb and my face feels numb.

Lu's gone. And it's all my fault. Lu's gone. And it's all my fault. The words thump round and round my head, sandwiched with flashes of Jake's furious face and Florrie's eyes boring into mine. What have I done? I should have just let them get me yesterday.

Somehow they must have messaged her, coaxing her out into the grounds after I escaped from them. It must have been Cranshaw doing Florrie's bidding. How else would they lure Lu outside in the middle of the night? I can picture it too easily. Lu curled up in bed in her sleepsuit, woken up when a message beeps through. She pads down to the courtyard, maybe using her tablet to light the way, reaching the oak tree . . . looking around, waiting for Cranshaw . . . then a dark shadow rising from behind the tree . . . I burst into tears all over again.

Is that what's going to happen to me? I sit up suddenly, my sobs subsiding into raspy little gasps. Am I just going to wait here until Florrie arrives for me? I wipe my wet cheeks with my palms, jittery and feverish with fear. I know they're after me. I know I'm next. And everyone already thinks I'm crazy. Why am I still running away?

I need to confront Cranshaw again in private. She won't say anything in front of other people, but if I get her alone and tell her I know everything – I know what the units have been doing, I know what Florrie's been doing, and I know *she* knows – and I have proof and I'm going to tell the Company, and if I can just get her to admit something or try to shut me up, then I can show everyone my brainstream. My teeth bite into my lip as I think of confronting her in her office with Florrie beside her – but she can't exactly say I fell out of a tree *in her office*. My hands won't stop shaking, but the rest of me is resolute. I unlock the wardrobe. I'm able to slip out of the dorms as someone enters. I march down into the grounds, not making eye contact with anyone or looking anywhere near the oak tree, where a little knot of pupils are still gathered, and barge straight through the front doors of the Main Building.

My vision tunnels as I walk down the corridor; everything seems hyper-real. Don't look at Florrie, whatever you do, I think. I lift my hand, still shaking, to knock on Cranshaw's office door, but before I can it opens and Jake barges into me.

'Wha-what?' I yelp.

He slams the door behind him and looks at me in surprise. Close up, he looks different – his skin has turned a mealy-grey colour and he's shiny with sweat, like he's about to throw up. I'm too nervous to feel sorry for him.

'Move. I need to talk to Cranshaw,' I say.

'No,' he says, blocking my arm from the door. 'You can't.'

'I don't care about getting in trouble any more,' I say, struggling against him.

'You're not just going to be in trouble!' he says, his voice hushed. 'Get away, *now*!'

I flinch. 'What?'

'Get away,' he hisses at me, his eyes wild. 'Go to the shuttle, go to Company headquarters and *tell them*—'

'I can't!' I say. 'My chip is blocked; I can't go anywhere!'

'Oh no,' Jake says, slumping back against the wall. 'Oh no, oh no.' He slides right down to the floor.

'What—' I say, trying to steel myself. 'What's going on?'

He looks up at me from the floor. 'You're right,' he croaks.

'I'm what?' I say.

'You're right about Florrie.'

Sixteen

Jake flops down on the grass, holding his head in his hands. 'Oh God,' he keeps saying. 'Oh God, oh God.'

He's dragged me out of the Main Building, to a meadow about as far away from the school buildings as possible.

'What's going on?' I say. 'What did you mean about Florrie?'

Jake looks out over the dandelions, his eyes glazed. 'Cranshaw's . . . gone rogue,' he says eventually, sounding like he's aged ten years.

'She's gone what?' I say. 'You mean . . . from the Company?'

'No, from AIR,' Jake says. 'Well. From the Company too, I suppose.'

'Tell me,' I say, sitting next to him.

'This is . . . big,' he says. 'You can't tell anyone else. It's more than just what's going on at school—'

'I know,' I say. 'Just tell me.'

'Do you remember that rumour years ago, that there's an unexploded bomb from World War Two under the school?'

'Er, yeah,' I say. 'Finn still thinks it's true.' I see Jake's eyes widen. '*Is* it true?'

'Not exactly,' he says. 'But it's based on the truth . . .' He takes a deep breath. 'When the Company first built the school, they were worried one of their rivals or some criminal looking to make money could ambush the school and take all of the pupils hostage. To save their children being used as blackmail against them and having to pay a huge ransom, and more importantly to save any Company secrets getting out . . .'

'Company secrets?' I say. 'What secrets?'

Jake shakes his head. 'I don't know. I don't think I *want* to know.'

'What?' I say. 'But we—'

'Let me *finish*,' he says. 'The Company decided it would be better if . . .' His eyes watch mine closely. 'If the head teacher was entrusted with an elimination device.'

'What's that?' I say, the dread in my stomach growing.

'It would immediately wipe out all life within a three-mile radius. If anyone attempted to take the school hostage, the head teacher could detonate it, leaving nothing to blackmail with.'

249

'But . . .' I say. 'But that would mean all of us, all the pupils, would be . . .'

Jake nods slowly, his face grim.

'But they . . .' I say. 'But they're our parents! The Company loves us—'

'Not as much as they love their bottom line,' says Jake. 'We make them vulnerable. They needed an out.'

He keeps talking but my head fills with white noise. I can't quite catch my breath. I watch his lips move, like a movie on mute.

All the times we've been told the Company loves us, that we should be loyal to them, that we should work hard to make the Company as productive as possible in the future, reel through my head. All lies.

I can't seem to support myself any more. My knees wobble and I sit down heavily on the grass.

'Millie?' Jake's saying. 'Millie?' It's like an echo in the distance.

'Really?' I say, angry tears prickling at my eyes. '*Really?*'

Jake nods, watching my face. 'Cranshaw says it's an absolute last resort. But . . . it is an option.'

I knew it really. I knew the school wasn't the safe haven we were told it was. I knew it since last night when I bumped against the wall. I just couldn't accept it.

'How did you—' I feel as breathless as I did in the library. 'How long have you known?'

'Cranshaw just told me,' Jake says. I notice that his

eyes are rimmed with red. 'But there's something else, OK? Something even worse.'

'What?' I say flatly. I can't even think. Can there be anything worse?

'She did something,' Jake says. 'Cranshaw. She told me earlier. She thought I would be on her side.'

'What?' I say. 'What has she done?'

'We were in her office,' he says. 'She said the government will be voting on unit freedom any day now, and she isn't sure what is going to happen afterwards, with the Company and AIR, and she asked me if I'd stand with her, whatever happens. I said yes.'

'And . . . ?' I say, feeling slightly hysterical.

Jake jerks forward, gripping my forearm. 'She's issued the Company with a threat. If they don't vote in favour of the Unit Rights Act as part of the Big Four Committee, she'll detonate the elimination device on the school.'

'Oh my God.' I can't think. I can't even let it in, except to say over and over, 'Oh my God, oh my God.' I just sit on the grass, the shock and the horror colliding, making me feel numb.

I clutch my head. 'This can't be true! How can she want unit rights that much?'

Jake grimaces. 'It is. She does.'

'But I don't understand!' I say. 'She would die too surely, if she detonated the device? And Florrie?'

'Well, yes,' says Jake. 'But she'd do it for the cause. She'd put unit rights above her own life.'

'And all of our lives,' I say. 'She's risking all of our lives on the decisions of three rival companies.'

'I know,' Jake says.

'So the Company just agreed? They just laid down and accepted it?'

'Well, only the board members know. Cranshaw said she would detonate the device if any of them tried to get close to the school. The moment any outsider's chip is sensed at the border or the shuttle station, she's going to blow everything up. Haven't you noticed how there hasn't been any senior Company presence on the school grounds at all?'

'I did,' I say. 'Was Cranshaw behind the missing pupils too?'

'I've only just realised it,' he says. 'When . . . when they found—'

'Lu,' I say, clutching my face.

'I didn't think anything of it when Nick disappeared,' Jake says slowly. 'But after I heard about Lu, when Cranshaw was telling me what else she'd done, I remembered that units can download brainstreams, if they've been programmed to attack. And with what you said, and what's been happening, my first thought was that it was—'

'Florrie,' I say. I was right. I've been right about her all along.

'What you were saying earlier . . .' says Jake. 'I thought you were crazy.' I automatically glare at him. 'But you're right. It must be Florrie. Cranshaw's programmed her to kidnap the pupils. The children of the Company's board members.'

'But why?' I say. 'If she's already got the whole school under threat—'

'Maybe the Company hasn't changed their vote,' he says. 'Maybe it wasn't enough. Maybe they don't think she'll do it. So she's got Florrie to attack their children. So they know she's serious—'

He suddenly stops mid sentence. 'What's that?' he whispers, cocking his head towards the edge of the meadow.

I try to listen but my heartbeat fills my ears. 'What?'

'Didn't you hear—'

Suddenly I hear it. The tiniest shift in the distance, an almost inaudible clank from behind a thorn bush.

Instantly cold brushes over my skin. I grip Jake's arm with both my hands, digging my fingernails in.

He looks at me, confused. 'What is it? It sounded like—'

'It's a *unit*,' I say. My jaw won't unclench. 'They're watching me!'

Jake's eyebrows knit together. 'Millie, that can't be right . . .'

I can't believe it. 'What have we just been talking about? You just said that Florrie—'

'No, it's not that,' he says. 'They wouldn't hang around outside when they're working – it can't be—'

He gets up and walks over to the thorn bush. 'Jake, don't!' I say, but he's pushed past it.

253

There's nothing there.

Jake looks back at me. 'What—'

'This is what I've been trying to tell everyone,' I say. 'They're watching me, all the time. Every time I turn round!'

He walks slowly back over to me, his face pinched with confusion. 'But that doesn't make any sense,' he says, sitting next to me again. 'They aren't that interested in humans . . .'

'Jake!' I say. 'After all you've just told me—'

'Unless—' he meets my eyes— 'Cranshaw's got them all doing her bidding. Watching you . . . because she knows you know something?'

'What can we do?' I say.

Jake takes a deep breath. 'There's only one thing we can do. We've got to break into Cranshaw's office and disable the device, then get out of here before she finds out,' he says.

'What?' I say. 'But that's so dangerous!'

'What else can we do?' says Jake. 'She'll blow us all up otherwise!'

'But won't that mean the Company will vote against unit rights without Cranshaw's threat hanging over them?' I say.

'So?' Jake looks at me again. 'You think I'm that desperate? You think I'd sacrifice the entire school for the cause? Do you think I'm as crazy as she is?'

'No, no,' I say. 'I can't think. This is all insane! What if Cranshaw catches you? What if the device goes off?'

'It won't. I know what to do with it,' Jake says.

I gape at him. 'This is not a game, Jake. This could kill us all. If you think you can just guess—'

'Why do you think Cranshaw told me about this in the first place, Millie?' he says. 'She told me exactly what to do. Where it is, how to disable it and how to set it off. She wanted me to take over in case she couldn't do it.'

'What?' I say. He doesn't meet my eyes. 'She . . . trusted you with something like that?'

'Who else could she trust?' he says. 'I'm the only one at school who knows.'

'I know, but—' Cranshaw made a thirteen-year-old boy second in command of her murder–suicide mission. More than anything else I've just heard, this confirms how completely deranged she must be.

'Dismantling the device won't be a problem,' Jake says. 'We just have to get away from here once it's done—'

'That won't be easy,' I say, but Jake cuts across me, his eyebrows raised.

'We can't just *stay*, Millie. She'll know it was me—'

'I know!' I say, furious. 'But there's no way out! There's a wall at the border! My chip won't work on the shuttle because I tried to run away from the Woodland River Centre—'

Jake's eyes widen. 'You tried to run away?'

'Twice,' I say. 'Last night I tried to cross the border but three units chased me. They had me cornered . . .' I shudder at the memory.

Jake looks horrified.

'I knew I was a target,' I say. 'But what can we do? We're trapped. Or at least, I'm trapped. I doubt they'll be watching if you go to Woodland River.'

Jake's eyes go distant for a few moments. He looks at me, then over at the school buildings, then at me again, his eyebrows drawn together.

'This is what we'll do,' he says, looking decisive. 'I'll beep you through the shuttle, then you go to Woodland River and on to London. Your chip will still work on the shuttle there, I'm sure. They wouldn't be able to disable it on every station. Just the school one. Then you get to Mum and Dad's house and stay there.'

'I can't go,' I say. 'I have to help you!'

'Millie, you're clearly a target,' he says. 'Florrie could— Do you really think you'll be any help if you're d—'

He stops talking abruptly, but the unsaid word hangs between us.

'I *can't* leave,' I say, jumping up. 'How can I, with what you've just told me? I have to help you bring Cranshaw down!' My heart's pumping, but for once it's not with fear.

'You can't stay, knowing any moment Florrie could attack you—'

'Look, I don't care what you say. I'm not leaving. I'm coming with you.'

Jake looks at me, then towards the school, then back at me. And a strange mixture of resignation – and could it be relief? – settles over his face.

'The Hendrick twins,' he says. 'On another whirlwind adventure.'

'Do you really think we can work together?' I say, thinking about the history lessons, London, our first ever day at Oaktree.

Jake looks at me for a second. 'No,' he says. 'But we have to try.'

Seventeen

The rest of the day seems never-ending. We were meant to spend it celebrating the end of the exams, preparing for the ball and anticipating a week of lazing around in the sun. Instead we sit in the common room in shock.

Shell sobs on to my shoulder for an hour saying over and over, 'The last thing I said to her was "Don't be too long in the bathroom"!' Finn doesn't cry but his face has turned a greyish-beige colour and he's not talking to anyone. When I ask him how he is he just shakes his head.

I can't cry either. Since my outburst this morning I feel like all my tears have been used up. My eyes sting and my skin feels dry, like all the liquid's been wrung out of me. I feel jittery and sick with anger every time I think of Cranshaw. I'm so desperate to make her pay.

The other two don't ask me about what happened this

morning. All Shell says about it is, 'It was just such a big shock. We all had a horrible shock.' I'm half expecting Cranshaw to haul me into her office and yell at me, or maybe even expel me. But she doesn't. We don't hear anything from the teachers all day, except a message to say that a memorial service will be held tomorrow. If the plan for tonight goes well, or very, very badly, I'll miss it. This is more of a relief than anything else. The thought of Cranshaw standing over Lu's coffin reading her eulogy makes my stomach feel sour.

It's a while before we realise someone's missing.

'Where's Riley?' says Shell, lifting her tear-stained face from my shoulder. 'Is she still in the library? Does she even . . . *know*?'

'Oh,' says Finn, his voice hoarse. 'I heard . . . Riley checked herself into the medical centre.'

'What?' Shell and I say in unison.

'Well, you saw her,' Finn says grimly. 'She's completely exhausted. She hasn't slept in four days, and she's been mainlining Rush. She's probably in some lovely dreamless doctor-administered sleep right now.' There's an edge to his voice. I think we'd all like to have that option tonight.

Shell's twisting a tiny flower bouquet in her hands, wrapping the ribbons trailing from the base round her fingers.

'What's that?' I say.

'Oh,' she says, looking down as if seeing it for the first time. 'I was going to wear it tonight.'

'Oh,' I say. 'Well, maybe another time . . .'

'What?' Shell looks at me. 'I can't wear it, or my dress. Ever. It'll always remind me of . . . today. We'll have to get rid of them.'

I realise she's right. Whatever happens now, this summer at Oaktree, maybe even our whole time at the school, will be tainted by the events of today. My memories of Lu have already begun to warp under the weight of what's happened. I can't think of her for even a second without a sharp pain in my side. Will it ever go away? Will I ever be able to think of her happily again?

We don't eat dinner. We go to bed at eight. Shell and I sit on our beds, looking at the two empty ones. For the first time in a long time I wish I could be a seven-year-old again, sleeping in a dormitory with all the other girls from my year. Tonight the dormitory feels so big.

'They're dismantling the ball tent,' says Shell, looking out of the window. 'It would all be starting about now.'

'It would have been amazing, wouldn't it?' I say flatly. I couldn't care less.

We sit in silence. Out of the window we can see the pupils from the ball committee taking the tent down. They have to pull every single light out of the structure before they can take the beams down. As the last few lights from the very top of the tent are put away, Jake messages me. There's nothing in the body of text so Cranshaw can't intercept it. The subject just says *Hi*.

By this time Shell is lying on her bed, flicking through documents on her tablet too fast to actually read anything. She's not crying any more, but her eyes are swollen and unfocused, staring blankly into the middle distance. I feel terrible that I'm about to leave her. I don't even let myself think that it might be the last time I ever see her. I tell myself that she'll understand when she finds out tomorrow. Whatever happens.

'Oh, Shell,' I say. I try to keep my voice casual, but it squeaks oddly. 'Could you beep me out quickly? I think I left my tablet downstairs in the common room.'

Shell looks at me, confused. 'Isn't that it on your bedside table?' she says, pointing.

'Oh – oh yes,' I say. Idiot. I should have made sure it was hidden.

'You're not trying to sneak out again are you?' Shell says, her eyebrows knitted together. 'For crying out loud, Millie! This is insane!'

'I'm not!' I say, holding up my hands to pacify her. 'I just mislaid it for a second—'

'Is it not enough that you accused Cranshaw and Florrie of *murder* today?' Shell's face is bright red. Her whole body has tensed up. 'Why are you trying to run away again? Are you ever going to grow up and stop imagining things?'

I flinch, as if she's hit me. 'Bit harsh, Shell,' I say quietly.

'I'm so tired of this!' She slumps back, limp like a doll, the last of her energy used up.

'Shell,' I say. 'I'm not trying to run away. I just forgot where I put my tablet.'

Shell looks at me, and I can tell she doesn't really believe me. 'You can't leave me alone, Millie,' she says. 'I can't be alone. Not tonight.'

'It's OK,' I say, moving over to her bed and putting my arm round her. 'I'm not going anywhere.'

I'm mentally cringing at my own words. What am I going to do now? I can't message Jake in case Cranshaw sees it. But I can't get out of this room unless Shell beeps me out.

Shell attaches a sensor to her forehead and starts downloading a brainstream into her tablet. Lu's face wobbles on to the screen and I have to turn away; the sight of her makes the pain in my side intensify to the point of nausea.

'Shell, don't look at that. It'll just make you sad,' I say, moving back to my own bed.

'I just want to see this bit,' she says, focused on the screen.

'What?' I say.

'There!' she says. 'The last thing I said to her. "Don't be too long in the bathroom". Why did I *say* that?'

She replays it over and over until I want to put my hands over my ears and scream to block her out. I open my wardrobe on the pretext of getting my sleepsuit out when really I just want to look at something that isn't Shell's fixated face.

My ball dress is hanging in the wardrobe. This morning I couldn't have told you what colour it was. But now that I actually see it again, it's quite pretty – layers of grey tulle with beaded embellishment on the skirt. I stroke the fabric for a second, thinking about Lu's vintage dress. Will her parents ever know what really happened to her? The look on Cranshaw's face this morning pops into my head again. She looked so smug, her mouth turned down at the corners, mock-sad. And she knew all along what Florrie had done. She was so blatant. Suddenly I'm overwhelmed with anger. It's churning in my stomach, mingling with the grief of losing Lu. I have to help Jake bring her down. I have to know she's been defeated. And if it means letting Shell down this evening, then so be it.

I glance at her; she's still engrossed in her own brainstream. I pull the dress out of the wardrobe and smuggle it into the bathroom. I let the silky fabric run through my fingers once – and then dump it in the loo. It swirls round in the bowl a few times and then the automatic flush swallows it up completely. I wait two seconds . . . and then there's a squeak and a grinding sound from the inner machinery. The error message flashes up above the bowl, blinking over and over again.

'She-ell,' I say, walking back into the dormitory. 'You'll never guess what. The loo's on the blink again.'

Shell eyes me suspiciously.

'So . . . could you just beep me out so I can use the downstairs one?' I say. 'I really need to *go*.'

Shell turns back to her tablet. 'The loo's fine, Millie,' she says flatly. 'You don't need to go anywhere.'

'Check for yourself then,' I say, eyes widening in what I hope is an innocent look.

Shell looks at me again, considering it, then pulls the sensor off her head and launches herself off her bed. She opens the bathroom door and stops.

'See?' I say, as the error message blinks at her.

'It really is broken,' she says.

'Yes, so, would you mind?' I say, dancing a little from foot to foot.

Shell isn't stupid. She knows something's going on. She looks at me, her eyes worried. 'Will you come straight back?' she says, moving towards the door. 'You have to come straight back.'

She beeps me out, but before I can leave, she grabs my wrist. 'Seriously Millie. I can't stay here alone,' she says.

'I know,' I say, feeling like the worst person in the world. 'Don't worry, I'll be back in two seconds.'

She just nods as I slip out of the door. My insides are heavy with guilt and I hope everything turns out how it should, so Shell can see I did the right thing. It hits me that if the plan doesn't work, I'll never see her again. And she'll never know why I ran away. I steel myself. The plan *has* to work.

I'm expecting to have to hang around by the front door, waiting in the corridor until someone comes through, but luckily there's a big crowd of fifteen-year-old girls coming in as I reach the bottom step. The last one holds the door open for me and I slip through, out into the night.

Jake's waiting for me, hidden in the shadows of a little clump of birch trees near the library. His face looks set with tension.

'Any time today, Millie,' he says, but his voice is too weak with relief to sound sarcastic.

'Shell wouldn't . . .' I start.

'It's OK,' he says. 'I wasn't worried or anything.' He smiles weakly. Despite his bravery earlier I can tell he really wasn't looking forward to dealing with the device on his own. We retreat back into the trees, hiding behind a clump of bushes.

'We just have to wait for Cranshaw to leave her office for her rooms,' he whispers in my ear. 'It should be soon. She'll walk right past us on her way to the teachers' house.'

'OK, then what?' I say.

'Then we break into her office,' he says. 'Easy. The device is in the safe.'

'Are you sure Florrie won't be in there?' I say.

'Yes,' says Jake. 'Florrie stays outside Cranshaw's room at night. She's paranoid about security.'

'Why is Cranshaw's office protected by a code? Why not an IndexChip scanner?'

'It's so the Company executives can access the head teacher's office, if they need to,' says Jake. 'Otherwise she could just set it to block any chip but hers. I mean, we always think of Cranshaw as being the one in control. But, until recently, the Company was always there, breathing down her neck.'

I can't bear to feel sympathy for Cranshaw, even for a second.

'So, what happens after we get into the office and break into the safe? How do we disable the device?'

'It has four separate segments,' says Jake. 'Each needs to be disabled with a different code. They're all explosive on their own so we have to be careful. Using the wrong code could set the whole thing off.'

'OK,' I say slowly. There are so many things that can go wrong.

'It should be fine, as long as we take our time,' says Jake. 'I'm worried Cranshaw will have some kind of alarm set up on the room or the safe. If something does go off, we'll just have to run for it. Head for the shuttle station.'

'What do you think she'll do if she catches us?' I say.

'I don't know. But if she sees me . . .' He trails off. 'Well, she'll know I'm not on her side any more.'

'Do you think she'll have an alarm on her office?'

Jake sighs. 'I don't know – she's not expecting anyone to try to disable the bomb. No one knows about it except the Company, and they can't get on to the school grounds. And she doesn't expect me to . . .' He looks at me. 'She thinks I'm like her, that I'd do anything for the freedom of units.'

'Jake . . .' I say. I grip his arm.

'But I'm not,' he says. 'I'm not like her.'

We sit in silence. The closest I've ever seen Cranshaw to angry was in her office last week. Even then it only simmered under the surface. She's always been so composed; I can't imagine her shouting and screaming. But then again, no one's ever broken into her office before.

Messages from Shell blink on to my RetinaChip. *Where are you? You said you'd come back. I can't believe you're doing this.* I'm about to reply when Jake leans forward.

'There,' he says.

Cranshaw and Florrie have come out of the Main Building. For some reason, I'd expected her to be sneaking around, but she's as upright as normal. She walks confidently and slowly across the grounds, talking quietly with Florrie. There's not a trace of guilt in her demeanour. I have to squeeze my eyes shut and bite down hard on my lip to keep from running towards her, thumping her on her stupid bony head. The sight of Lu's body under the sheet pops into my mind and I clench my fists.

Cranshaw and Florrie travel past us. Florrie lifts her head for a second, when they're a few metres away, and we both tense up, but then they're gone, round past the library and up to the teachers' house. I make a movement to stand up, but Jake stops me.

'Just a second,' he whispers.

A beam of light spreads over the grass as the door to the house opens, and then disappears.

'She's in.' He stands. 'Let's go.'

Jake takes my hand and we run, stumbling in the dark,

across the lawn and through the courtyard to the Main Building's doors. The pupils never use them, so they don't have a chip scanner, but they aren't locked. One of the other teachers must still be in there. Jake opens one a crack and lets me slip through ahead of him. As we walk through the hall to Cranshaw's office, every sound I make seems to be amplified a hundred times. Our footsteps seem deafening in the silence. I'm afraid to breathe too loudly. My ears are straining for a telltale metallic clink, even though I've just seen Florrie leave with Cranshaw.

We reach the office door and Jake taps in the code at the side of the door. I'm braced for the sound of an alarm but, miracle of miracles, nothing happens. I let out the long breath I didn't realise I was holding and we slip inside.

It's pitch-black inside. Jake flicks the light switch, and in the split second between the sound and my eyes adjusting to the light I expect it to reveal Florrie in the middle of the room, waiting for us. But no – it's empty. I put my hand over my chest, willing my heart rate to slow.

Jake's already on the other side of the room, moving the back panel of one of the bookshelves aside. There's a safe door behind it.

'How did you know?' I say.

'I've seen her use it,' he says. 'She keeps confidential documents in here.'

I'm shocked at Cranshaw's stupidity until I remember Jake had already been trusted with her biggest secret. I suppose she never imagined her little protégé would end up siding with the Company against her. Jake carefully types in a code, and the safe door clicks unlocked. He looks back at me, grinning with relief as he opens the door.

I see before he does. My stomach drops like a cannon-ball. 'It's empty!'

'What?' he says, wheeling round. He grabs the sides of the safe, disbelieving, and practically sticks his head inside it. But there's nothing there. It's been completely cleaned out.

'What . . . what do we do now?' I say, fighting the urge to throw up.

'I don't know, I don't know!' says Jake, frantic. 'She must have moved it! She must be trying to protect it from the Company. She knew they wouldn't play by the rules.'

'Do you think she has it with her? In her rooms in the teachers' house?' I say, panic making my head swim.

Jake shakes his head. 'No, she doesn't trust the other teachers. It must be in here somewhere. We just need to find where she's put it . . .'

He tears through the bookshelves, knocking books to the floor. 'Check the drawers in the desk!' he says.

I run to the desk and pull the drawers out, emptying their contents on the floor. 'I don't know what I'm looking for,' I say.

'It's really small and sort of a disc-shape,' says Jake, sweeping a shelf full of framed pictures to the floor. 'It's got four segments.'

I pull out the last drawer, which is crammed with

paper books; Cranshaw's clearly been hoarding. I rifle through the pages but there's nothing there. The device could be in a million places. We could be looking forever.

'Maybe we should go,' I say, as Jake pulls more books off the bottom shelf and leans right down to check the back panel. 'While we still can.'

'No, no, it has to be here.' He jumps up and starts on another bookcase. There's no mistaking the desperation in his voice.

'Jake . . . I really think we should go,' I say. He doesn't say anything; he just carries on throwing books on the floor. I open my mouth to say something else when a glint of metal on the desk catches my eye. It's the little unit statue Cranshaw knocked my hand away from when I sat in her office last week. I pick it up, my mind whirring. There's a hinge down the back of it. I hold it in both hands and feel for the join down the front with my fingernails. It's not at all visible and I can only just feel it. I wrench the statue open and a little metal disc rolls out on to the desk.

For a moment I freeze, anticipating an apocalyptic explosion, but then I snap into sense.

'Jake! Jake! I've found it!' I shriek. Jake stops pulling books off the shelf. He rushes over and stares at the device on the desk.

'Millie,' he says, and his face crumples as though he's about to cry. 'I'll never say this again, but you are actually a genius.'

'Can we disable it here?' I say, looking at the device.

It's so tiny. It's barely the circumference of a satsuma, but it's flat and quite thick, like a wheel of cheese. The four segments are locked rigidly together. There's a touchscreen where the four corners meet in the middle. It's flashing up, asking for a password.

'Yes, quickly,' he says, leaning over and typing it in. 'Now it'll ask for each segment's code, but we only get one chance and there's a time limit. If we get it wrong, the segment explodes, taking all the others with it.'

A blank dialogue box and a number keyboard are flashing up at me. I quickly hand the device over to Jake.

'How much time have we got for each segment?' I say, as he types the numbers in.

'It depends, the device owner sets it.' He finishes the code and the screen goes blank. We both tense up, waiting for the impact, but it suddenly flashes to life again. It's filled with icons. Jake goes to CONTROL PANEL, SETTINGS, and then DISABLE. A little hourglass hovers on the screen for a minute, and then the dialogue box is back. One of the segments lights up, glowing bright white.

'Well, that was easy,' I say. My heart's thumping in my throat.

'Just three more to go,' says Jake. He starts typing in the next segment's code – and the door slams behind us.

All of my senses are suddenly tuned to red alert. We turn to see Florrie standing in the doorway.

I have a moment when everything stops and I look inwards at myself, standing there, blinking at Florrie

271

stupidly, and I think, I knew this would happen. I knew it all along. And now, after everything, we're going to die.

Jake moves before I do. In one motion he flips the device over his shoulder to me – I only just catch it on the tips of my fingers – and runs directly at Florrie, both of them smashing ear-splittingly loudly into the door. Clutching the device to my chest, I dive under the desk and try to focus on the little screen. Jake has already unlocked the second segment. Fingers shaking, I go to CONTROL PANEL, then SETTINGS, and disable it.

I hear a metallic scrape and a yelp like a dog being kicked. I nearly stick my head over the desk when Jake suddenly runs at me again, holding the side of his face. 'What did you—' I start to say, but he wrenches me up and pulls me towards the sash window.

'No time,' he says, opening it and pushing me out. We land in the bushes outside and, scrabbling past them, run across the courtyard, not pausing to breathe.

The device screen is flashing again. 'Quick,' I say, grabbing Jake's arm. 'You have to do the next one.'

'We can't stop,' he gasps. There's a raw graze all along his cheek. 'She'll be after us in a second.'

'We have to!' I shriek. At that moment we reach the oak tree. 'Now!' I say, pulling him behind it. I thrust the device to him and he types in the code and disables it. The third segment lights up.

'We're so close now,' I say, as he hands the device back to me. 'Do the last one.'

'No, we can't. We have to move,' gasps Jake. 'Florrie will find us. I only surprised her – she just wasn't expecting it to be me. She'll be back on her feet at any second.' He grabs my wrist and pulls me forward.

'Please, Jake, do the last one; it doesn't matter if she catches us!' I say.

'We can do it in a second,' he says.

'But—' Before I can finish something slams into Jake at such force he's knocked to the floor, his hand wrenched from mine.

Florrie. She crushes Jake into the grass, her forearm across the back of his neck. She meets my eyes.

I scream, stumbling away from her, clutching the device to my chest, and walk straight into Cranshaw.

'Millie,' she says pleasantly. I jump away from her, my stomach lodged somewhere in my windpipe.

'Now, what are you two doing out of bed so late?' she says, her eyes barely flickering at the sight of Florrie leaning on Jake's throat. 'Like brother, like sister, I can see.'

'We . . . er . . .' I say. I can't seem to catch my breath.

Jake makes a choking, gurgling noise, and Florrie shifts slightly, crushing him further. I can only just see him out of the corner of my eye. Cranshaw moves closer, closing in on me.

'I think it's time you went to back to your dormitory, Millie, and handed that over to me,' she says.

I step back from her. 'No,' I say.

'You won't get very far at this school with an attitude

like that, dear,' says Cranshaw. She glowers at me, betraying the anger her voice is masking.

'It-it's not what you think,' I say wildly. My brain is blank. I take another half-step back, purely on instinct. Cranshaw immediately fills the space I've left.

'I know exactly what that is,' she says, teeth gritted. 'I know you broke into my office, and I know you found the device. I knew the very second you opened my ornament.'

I swallow, though my mouth is totally dry.

The device is flashing at me again.

Cranshaw sees it too. 'Just give it to me!' She lunges towards me, her fingers scrabbling against my forearm, but I jerk away, nearly losing my balance, wheeling away from her. She stumbles and falls to the ground. Florrie immediately sits up, releasing Jake. Before Cranshaw or I can move, Jake yells, 'Two-three-eight-nine-nine-four!'

The code. I know what it is. Cranshaw knows what it is. Florrie knows what it is. The unit smashes Jake's face into the ground again.

Cranshaw's eyes lock with mine. 'This isn't a game, children!'

She launches up from the ground in one movement but I'm already gone, running flat out across the courtyard. I have no idea where I'm going. Cranshaw's a step behind me. The device bleeps loudly. I try to focus on the screen but I trip on a furrow just as Cranshaw grabs at my hair and we both tumble over. She tries to take the device from me but I pull it back, jumping up.

'You don't know what you're doing! You don't what will happen!' she screams, trying to swipe at my ankles from the ground.

'I do,' I say, kicking her away. 'I know exactly what will happen to you!'

'No!' she says, her eyes flashing. 'Don't do it!'

'You killed my friend!' I yell at her. 'You deserve everything you get!'

I focus on the screen. My hands are shaking but I know I haven't got much time. Two-three-eight-eight-nine-five. The screen bleeps, but it doesn't show the home page. It goes completely black, and a tiny message flashes at the corner of the screen. INCORRECT CODE. INCORRECT CODE. INCORRECT CODE.

'Oh no,' I say.

I look up, confused, searching for Jake in the darkness. But before I can think another thought, I'm blasted through the air, weightless, arms flailing, white noise filling my ears, until I slam into something hard, my skull and bones and organs shuddering with the impact. I've smashed against the oak tree – I must have flown across the courtyard. I automatically touch my head, to make sure it's in one piece. I can't see Jake. I can't see Cranshaw. How am I still conscious? I look down at my hand for the rest of the device, but what I see makes no sense.

Nausea rolls up my throat; I can't believe my own eyes. I try to focus, but the image wobbles in my mind. I look up at the sky instead, at the stars, but my vision smudges and skips. And then everything goes black.

Eighteen

The room around me spins steadily, shapes and colours blurring into one another. I feel . . . vague. My head thumps sickeningly and pain shoots up and down my right arm from my shoulder downward, but stops, as starkly as crossing a boundary, at my elbow. My forearm and hand are completely numb. I can't feel anything when I flex my fingers.

Where am I? What happened? I remember the rally, the crowd pushing in, the explosion, the stage falling towards me. But no, that was ages ago . . .

I'm in a room in the medical centre. There's a small window with the blind drawn, but hardly any light is coming through – it must be around dawn. Why am I in here? And then it all comes rushing back – Cranshaw, the device, Florrie.

There's something else niggling at my brain, jumping up and down, begging me to remember it, but I can't. It's something important. I try to sit up but my forearm, bandaged from the elbow, is attached to something with sensors. The machine next to my bed whirrs gently, and a tiny screen shows a thin green line slowly moving up and down.

'Millie.'

I jump, making the machine beep in indignation. I hadn't realised there was someone else in the room.

It's Dr Tavish. 'I'm sorry. I scared you.'

'No, it's fine,' I say, as my heart flutters in my chest.

Dr Tavish moves out from the corner to sit at the chair next to my bed. He takes a tiny appliance, no bigger than his thumb, from his pocket, switches it on and places it on the bedside table. A green light on it blinks. He speaks into it. 'TAV201198 interview, 13 June 2099.'

He turns to face me, adjusting his thick glasses. 'Millie, I have to tell you some delicate information now and it is very important you listen closely. When you completely understand what I've told you, you need to sign this form.' He holds up a tablet, which displays a document. 'This conversation is being recorded, as you can see, for the official record.'

'Oh, OK,' I say. My brain's feeling fuzzy. I wish I could remember what this niggling thought was.

'Don't worry, your hand will be fine,' Dr Tavish says. 'You will be fitted with a new IndexChip shortly. This may take some time but it's very important we do this now and that you understand everything.'

'Could we do it a bit later?' I say. 'My brain's still feeling a bit fuzzy.'

'I'm sorry, but it has to be done now,' Dr Tavish says, glancing towards the door. Is it just my frustration with my brain or does he seem on edge somehow?

'First, we need to establish you're of a sound mind after bumping your head again,' he says. 'Can you tell me what day it is?'

'Er . . .' There's early-morning light coming in from behind the window. But I don't know how long I've been out for. 'Saturday?'

'Yes,' says Dr Tavish. 'Now, do you remember why you're in here, Millie?'

'It was Cranshaw . . . She had a device . . . we had to disable it . . .' Suddenly the image of Florrie crushing Jake into the ground flashes in my mind. I sit up straight, nearly yanking the sensors out of my arm. 'Wait – what happened to Jake? Florrie—'

'Calm down, Millie,' says Dr Tavish, rushing to soothe the machine. 'Jake is fine.'

'Really?' I don't know if I believe him. 'What happened? I remember the device going off—'

'Your Company representatives arrived on the scene shortly after you detonated the segment,' says Dr Tavish. 'I'm afraid your head teacher, Dr Euphemia Cranshaw, was killed in the blast. The school year has ended early and the pupils are currently being sent home.'

'Oh.' I have no idea what to say. Cranshaw's dead.

'Jake was saved because Dr Cranshaw's companionbot—'

'Florrie,' I interrupt.

Dr Tavish glances at me. 'Yes, Florrie. The unit was covering Jake and he avoided the worst of the blast. He's fine.'

There's something wrong with what he's telling me but I can't quite work it out. I can't kick my brain into gear.

'How did the Company know?' I say. 'I thought Cranshaw had cut them off from all communication . . .'

'Apparently the Company were tracking the status of the device and immediately swooped when they saw it had been partially disabled. However, my organisation had its own, er, tracking implement on the school grounds, and we had already arrived to remove that.'

'Your organisation?' My head's pounding. 'Humans First?'

He nods. 'You weren't quite correct on all the details of your head teacher's offences against the Company,' Dr Tavish says. 'But you did come very close.'

'What?' I say. He's moving too fast for me. How does he know what we thought Cranshaw had done? Then I realise Jake must have told him.

'Dr Cranshaw did blackmail the Company over the

Unit Rights Act,' he says. 'Like you said, the board members have been unable to make contact with anyone at the school. She had been threatening to detonate the device.'

'Yeah, that's why we tried to disable it.' I can remember typing the code in; the device screen flashing INCORRECT CODE . . . although after that it's a blur.

'But Cranshaw was not the one behind the disappearances and the attacks on the pupils.'

'Wha— Yes she was,' I say. 'Unless – was it Florrie? Working alone?'

'No, no,' says Dr Tavish, smiling sadly. His expression is so at odds with what we're talking about I feel slightly alarmed. What is it I'm not getting?

'Forgive me, Millie, I haven't been . . . entirely honest with you,' he says. 'I'm not a normal doctor. I don't work in a hospital.'

'Yeah, you told me: you're a head specialist.'

'No, no, that isn't entirely true, I'm afraid,' he says. 'I'm not a doctor in the traditional sense at all. I don't work with *humans*.'

'Oh,' I say. But you've been working on my head all this time, I think. 'Then . . .'

'I work with units,' he says, smiling tightly. 'I'm an engineer.'

That doesn't make sense though.

'But I thought . . . aren't Humans First against units?' I say, my voice coming out a bit strangled. 'I thought they didn't want anything to do with them?'

280

'That is a very simple way to look at Humans First, yes,' Dr Tavish says. 'But it's not that straightforward. There's a section of scientists and engineers who keep their activities underground. We're just as opposed to unit rights as the members who simply don't trust units.'

'But why?' I say. 'Engineers make the units. I thought you liked them?'

'We do, but, you see, units are machines. And if units are given equal rights to humans that ends all experimentation,' says Dr Tavish. He's not smiling any more. His jaw is tense and his words are clipped. 'Every unit created will be filed in the system – we won't be able to test, to break units down for parts just because we can see a better use of it. The Unit Rights Act could grind technology to a halt.'

'Oh,' I say, not really sure how to respond.

'Humans First recently became focused on your head teacher,' he says. 'Her act of blackmail tipped the Big Four Committee's vote in favour of the act.'

'What? How do you know that?' I say. 'No one knows what's decided except the Committee members.'

'When you have the technology we have, Millie, you know everything. We knew exactly what Cranshaw had done, had been doing for some time. It certainly seemed to faze your Company – they weren't expecting to be black-mailed from inside the school. But this left us at a distinct disadvantage. You see, in the past Humans First became famous for derailing the vote on the act with rather underhand tactics, but this was far more serious than anything we'd done. And it guaranteed your Company's vote.'

'No, it didn't, because she still felt the need to attack the pupils,' I say. 'And what do you mean by "underhand tactics"? I know there was some explosion, some anti-unit politician who got killed, but surely—'

'That couldn't have been Humans First, because their leader died? Wrong. Do you know how easy it is to rig a unit to explode? And no one from AIR could ever do it. They don't think it's morally right to tamper with units.'

'What? I thought it malfunctioned.'

'Take my word for it, Millie. Units never malfunction. Not if I've built them anyway.' He laughs under his breath, but there's a grim edge to it.

My mouth turns dry. I glance at the window. Definitely locked – I can see the metal bars across the bottom and top. The door. There's a type pad next to it. I'd need the code to open it. I'm trapped – again. I've escaped from one jail into another.

Dr Tavish continues. 'We decided something radical had to be done, to meet Cranshaw head on. And then AIR launched the campaign featuring your brother.'

My mind skips. *No.*

'What have you done to him?' I sit up, pulling all the sensors out of my arm in one movement. The pain that hits my wrist is excruciating.

I scream, barely aware of anything in the room around me. The very core of my bone burns. Dr Tavish is beside me, injecting me with a needle filled with a pale-green liquid. I don't even care what it is, as long as the pain goes away.

'For pity's sake, Millie, you need to have your wits about you right now,' he says, reattaching the sensors. The pain immediately subsides.

But I can't calm down yet. My heart's battering against my chest.

'Where's Jake?' I say.

I don't know if it's the pain or the fear that has suddenly made me wake up, but I don't feel at all groggy any more.

'As I told you before, he's fine,' says Dr Tavish, glancing at the door again. 'Listen to me, don't pull those sensors out again.'

'Why should I listen to you? You're insane!' I say. 'You're working with a terrorist organisation!'

'No more terrorist than your own head teacher, Millie, and your twin brother,' says Dr Tavish.

'That's not fair. Jake didn't know anything about what Cranshaw was doing,' I say.

'Oh? Is that what he told you?' Dr Tavish says.

I open my mouth but no words come out.

'We needed a stunt to go up against Cranshaw and AIR. We decided the best way to embarrass AIR would be if Jake Hendrick met his end in a tragic accident with a unit. A malfunctioning unit.'

'The unit at the rally!' I say, horrified. 'The one that got me! That was meant for Jake?'

Dr Tavish rolls his eyes. 'Please, Millie, would that make the required statement we needed? Something AIR could easily write off as an accident? Which they did, of course.'

'I thought you said there were no malfunctioning units? If it wasn't you—'

'I'm not saying it wasn't us,' he says. 'I'm just saying that wasn't the big finish.'

'It wasn't? What . . . what did you do?' I say, trying to breathe evenly. Now the pain's subsided, I'm beginning to worry about what he injected me with. My heart's racing.

'We monitored Jake's network presence, keeping track of who he messaged and who appeared in his brainstreams—'

'But how? There's no way to get into it if you're not part of the Company.'

'I told you, *we have access to everything*.' He glares at me, his eyes intense.

'But even if you did,' I say, my voice wavering, 'you can't just hack into someone's account, there isn't the technology—'

'Millie, we make the technology,' says Dr Tavish. 'Please don't interrupt me again.'

'I don't understand what all this is about!' I say. 'Where am I? Where's Jake? If he's fine like you say he is, let me see him.'

'Jake has gone home to your parents' house,' says Dr Tavish, 'where your Company will decide what happens to him. Now, are you going to listen?'

I'm tempted to yank the sensors out of my arm again and make a break for the door, but the memory of the pain stops me. I meet Dr Tavish's eye. 'Yes.' I'm defeated.

'We discovered Jake had a twin sister,' he says, and looks at me closely. 'We decided to target her.'

'Me?' I say. 'Humans First targeted me . . . ?' My brain whirls. 'Is that why I kept getting those messages?'

But Dr Tavish isn't listening. 'We constructed a unit replica of Millie Hendrick. At the rally we planted a device that killed the girl, then we placed the replica at the scene. It was found and taken to the hospital and then back to the school in Millie's place.'

'Huh? What? When did this happen?' I say. 'No one told me about this.'

'Millie, do you understand what I'm saying to you?'

'Er . . . not really,' I say. 'Was that before I got back from the hospital?' I'm so confused.

'*You* are the replica unit,' Dr Tavish says. 'We downloaded Millie's thoughts and memories into your brain and made you identical to her in every way. We put a device in you that we could detonate remotely. And no one suspected, not for a minute.'

'Wait, what?' I say. 'But *I'm* Millie . . . I don't get it.'

'You're not,' he says. 'The human Millie died at the rally.'

I just stare at him, trying to understand. I glance down at my arm, stuck with the sensors, and finally, in a blinding moment of clarity, I remember that niggling memory from last night.

The device had gone off. I'd been thrown back against the oak tree, cracking my head. I couldn't understand how I was still conscious. I looked down at the device in my hand, but it had exploded into a million pieces. The explosion should have blown my hand apart. But . . .

The skin had been torn off, hanging in shreds from my fingers, but instead of blood and flesh and bone, I saw metal. In place of my hand was a gleaming titanium skeleton, tendons and bones and muscle, still perfect, unaffected by the explosion. And then I passed out.

'But . . . but . . .' I say, my voice strangled. 'But I have a pulse. And I feel and I think and—'

'All constructed,' says Dr Tavish.

My breathing is coming too fast. Every time I exhale there's a squeaking, scraping sound from my throat. Am I crying? I don't even know.

'I thought this bit would be difficult,' Dr Tavish says. 'We did too good a job.'

He paces the room, talking fast. 'The plan was that the night before the Unit Rights Act went to Parliament, we would detonate you while you were near Jake, blowing you both to smithereens. Then we could point out the dangers of letting units get too close, that a killerbot could fool AIR's poster boy into believing it was his own sister. *Then* we could convince the public that unit freedom could be dangerous. The act would be thrown out, hopefully forever.'

He smiles ruefully. 'But then you and Jake had that

fight. You'd been created to think with your constructed emotions, and we couldn't control your every action. You don't know how many times we regretted doing that.' He grimaces. 'But it was necessary, otherwise pupils and teachers would have begun to suspect. We had to let these new emotions of yours play themselves out and lead you where you wanted to go. But we had a trick up our sleeves. A Plan B.'

I clutch my head, wondering if this is all a horrible dream. Or a hallucination.

'We could shut your brain down while you were asleep and remotely log on to control your body. This proved extremely . . . useful in the last few months.'

'Sleepwalking,' I say. 'Shell said she saw me sleep-walking.'

'Yes, she did,' Dr Tavish says. 'They kept pushing the date of the act's hearing back and back and back, and we worried we'd never get to stage our grand finish. But we could still use you. We had to wait until you were asleep, but then we could log on remotely and have you carry out certain actions for us.'

'Like what?'

'Like messaging pupils whose parents work for the Company, persuading them to meet you after everyone else was asleep . . .'

'The attacks,' I say, my stomach freezing. 'That was you?'

'It was *you*,' Dr Tavish says. 'There was a chance you

might not get near enough to Jake in time, so we needed to put Plan B into action. A unit programmed to kill, infiltrating a high-tier Company school and attacking pupils would hit home with certain members of the public even more than Jake's death. Even if it wouldn't quite have the political message we had hoped for.'

My stomach jabs with pain as I remember. 'Oh God, Lu,' I say, gripping my face with my fingers. What have I *done*?

'Yes,' says Dr Tavish almost proudly. 'We made sure you crushed their IndexChips, so there wouldn't be a record of them leaving their dorms. I don't know what happened with your friend Lu exactly, but that was a particularly . . . frenzied attack.'

I close my eyes, wishing he was dead. Wishing I was dead.

'You took their brainstreams as well,' he says. 'That was a particular stroke of genius on the part of one of our younger scientists. They're all stored in your brain, somewhere. Don't worry – you won't be able to access them without the password. They make for pretty grim watching. But even if you wanted to see them, you don't have clearance for that part of your mind.'

I just goggle at him, my fingernails digging into my face.

'Plan B did work out rather well for us in the end,' Dr Tavish says. 'Cranshaw didn't know what was going on. She thought it was a trick by the Company. That's why she tried so hard to keep it a secret. She let far too much slip though in the beginning. That's what an honesty policy does for you. She really shouldn't have told you all about that first girl. She regretted that.'

'What happened to Daisy?' I say. 'Did they ever find her?'

'I don't know,' says Dr Tavish idly. 'It was the first time we'd used you remotely, and she managed to get away from you. She ran off into the woods. Her IndexChip was disabled, so there was no way of tracking her. She must have scaled the wall and died out in the wilderness somewhere. We were terrified the whole plan had been ruined, but luckily it all turned out fine.'

I can't take this much longer. I want to pull my brain out of my head so I don't have to listen. Then I think of something.

'Was it you,' I choke, 'who was sending me those messages?'

'You were very worried about them, weren't you?' says Dr Tavish. 'Unfortunately your brain hasn't been completely perfected. That's why I had to give you all those check-ups, performing manual updates on your brain. Luckily the head-injury story covered most of your irrationality. Every time we logged on to you and controlled you remotely, a ghost message would be left behind. We had no way of getting rid of it, but it was hardly likely you would figure out the truth.'

'And the Old Section?' I say. 'You locked me in there?'

'We thought it would really unnerve Cranshaw if a pupil died right next to her precious books, so we used you to hack into the system and set the air dispensers to turn off two hours early. Then you end up being the pupil trapped in there when the air cuts off.' He rolls his eyes, as if the irony tickles him. 'You were never in any danger, of course, but a few moments more and people might have started to wonder why you didn't pass out.'

I clutch my throat. 'But I felt—'

'It just goes to show how well we constructed you,' he says. 'Even you believed it.'

I push my fingers into my eyes. This can't be real. This can't be real. I look at the sensors on my arm, wondering if the pain can really be that bad. I need to get away from him.

'My memories . . .' I whisper. 'My whole life . . .'

'All downloaded from Millie Hendrick's brainstream before November last year,' says Dr Tavish. 'Didn't you wonder how you survived the explosion last night? A human would have been blasted into a million pieces.'

'I can't listen to this any more,' I say, choking on the words. 'Please let me go. Please.'

'Don't worry, Millie, almost done,' Dr Tavish says. 'Aren't you wondering why I'm telling you all this?'

I shake my head, my eyes still covered.

'Well, as a unit that's completed your mission, even though it wasn't successful, you would normally be destroyed right now, without ever knowing why.'

This gets my attention. I lift my head up in surprise, expecting to see him there with a deprogramming gadget poised next to my throat, but he's only holding the tablet.

'Luckily for you, the government passed the Unit Rights Act in secret last night,' he says, his face grim again. 'Every unit in the world, created for whatever purpose, now has a right to live and a place on the system. In your case, we have to explain to you your origins, as you've been under the impression you're . . . something else.'

'They passed it?' I say.

'Yes. About the time you were rummaging through Cranshaw's office last night. The government didn't want to risk any terrorist attacks from AIR or Humans First affecting the vote, so they kept it secret. I need you to sign this form to confirm you understand what you've been told.'

I take the tablet, pressing my index finger into the space at the bottom. 'Does that mean I'm free? I'm not . . . owned by Humans First?'

'Free?' Dr Tavish laughs. 'Oh no, not at all.'

'But the act was passed . . .'

'Yes, but unfortunately for you, our little stunt worked as it was supposed to; it was just too late to stop the act. News of Humans First's killerbot infiltrating Oaktree has been reported on every news site in the world. The police are on their way to arrest you for the murder of your friend and the attacks on the other pupils. You're infamous.'

'What?' I say, clutching my head again. This doesn't

make sense. 'But units can't go to prison; they're not responsible for their actions.'

'Oh, Millie,' says Dr Tavish. 'You're independent now. And all the evidence is contained right in there.' He taps my forehead.

'But . . . you did it! I had no choice, you were controlling me!'

'It doesn't matter,' says Dr Tavish. 'There's no way you can prove it wasn't you. Humans First gets off with a small fine for building you in the first place, but only because you were unregistered. All your actions are your own.'

'What if I show people this, in a brainstream?' I say. 'Show them everything you just told me—'

'Millie,' he says. 'You can't show them. Your brainstreams have been turned off since last night. You don't have a human brain. You don't even have a chip, and you won't until the prison guards fit a new one—'

'What? Why are you doing this to me?' I shriek.

'We created you,' Dr Tavish shrugs. 'Just be glad you're alive.'

To my surprise, I laugh at him. I'm responsible for the murder of one of my best friends. I'm about to go to jail for the rest of my life. And I'm not human. I'm a soulless metallic abomination. I have never wished so fervently not to be 'alive'.

I blink back tears but even as I'm doing it I know they're not really tears. My heart thumps hard and my elbow tingles painfully and my stomach squeezes with anguish – but none of it is real. It's an illusion created by my brain, to make me believe I'm something I'm not.

Dr Tavish switches off the recording device.

'Millie,' he says in a low voice. 'The police will be here in less than an hour.'

'Yeah, I get it. I understand why. You can go now,' I say.

'Let me say something first.' He glances quickly at the door. 'You don't understand what a feat of technology you are. You're the future of engineering. There's no way I could have a conversation like this with any other unit on earth. Do you know how amazing that makes you?'

I shrug, barely listening to him. He's praising his own achievements. It's nothing to do with me. I'm just the annoying emotional centre that stops them having full control over their 'feat'.

'I can't bear to see you rot in a jail until you power down,' he says. 'It's not right. You weren't created for that.'

I snort. 'I was created to blow up at an opportune moment,' I say.

'No, no, you were created to take the place of a human and you did it perfectly.' There's no mistaking the admiration in his voice. 'You passed medical tests without the nurses even blinking. No one suspected, not even senior members of AIR. Not even friends you'd known since birth. Not even your own brother!'

'What?' I say. 'What are you—'

'I tested you,' he says. 'I told you explicitly never to

293

look at your brainstreams and you still went ahead with it, even though you knew how traumatic reliving that day in London would be. Do you know how many units I've created can feel that level of emotion, experience complex thought processes? *None.*'

'But what does that mean?' I squeak.

He stands up, moving towards the window. 'I can't let the police take you,' he says, flicking the blind up. 'The school's borders have been opened to let the pupils leave.'

I sit up, suddenly interested. 'What do you—'

'I have to leave now,' he says, unlocking the window and opening it a crack. 'But I hope you take into account what I've said.'

He comes up to me, injecting me again with the pale-green liquid. Then he turns off the machine and removes the sensors from my arm. There's no pain this time. He stands up, nods at me once and then leaves the room, locking the door behind him.

I get out of bed – I'm only dressed in a thin hospital gown, but it hardly matters any more – and climb out of the window, landing in the grass below. This is it. I have to leave everything I've ever known behind.

I sidle along the wall of the medical centre, my breath coming in short bursts, and peer round the corner. There's no one around; a low black cloud hangs over the school buildings, and the smell of burning is shoving its way right up into my nostrils.

I run across the grass to the Left Building, ducking

behind it. From here I can see into the main courtyard and for a second I think I should run across and hide behind the oak tree, but when I lean round I can't see it. There's a huge crater, still belching out smoke, and a metal barrier barely a metre away from me. But no oak tree. It's gone.

I slammed into it last night, in the explosion. Did I . . . have I destroyed the oak tree?

Despair rises but I shove it down. I have to keep on going. I run along the Left Building, keeping low, round the library and towards Hawthorn house. The school grounds are almost eerily quiet. I crawl round the edges of the building. It seems utterly deserted. I spot a discarded tablet in the grass, playing a news story. Someone just left it behind? How fast were they hustled out of here?

The screen is showing a shot of the school grounds. The smoking crater, a shot of Cranshaw with RIP on it, the Company's chief executive making a statement from head-quarters in London. I watch, my mouth going dry, as Jake appears, sitting up in a hospital bed, his cheek bruised, his head bandaged. A reporter asks him over and over again for a comment. 'What?' he keeps saying. '*What?*'

I chuck the tablet aside. No time for that now. I peek round the corner of Hawthorn house, and jolt when I see a figure standing outside the front doors. It's Shell. She's not going anywhere, just waiting. She's dressed all in black – is that today's colour?

I start towards her, wondering how she knows. Then she whips round and sees me.

'Millie!' she says, eyes wide. 'Why are you out here? You didn't come back last night! I thought you'd gone!'

'I . . . Haven't you seen the news?' I say.

'I haven't had time to check it yet,' she says. 'Why?' And she logs on to her RetinaChip.

'No, Shell, don't!' I say. 'Don't look!'

'What?' she says, focusing on me again. 'Why?'

'What's happening?' I say, trying to distract her. 'Are you going home?'

'I'm just waiting for Finn; we're going to catch the last shuttle,' she says. 'Everyone else has gone. Welbeck's already come over to shout at us once; he'll probably be back soon. Why are you—' She seems to take me in for the first time. 'What . . . what's wrong with your arm?'

'I—' I start to say. 'You're . . . you're going to hear a lot of things.'

'What?'

'You're going to hear a lot of things about me,' I say. 'But it wasn't me. Well, it was me, but it wasn't *me*.'

Shell's eyes are flicking between mine. 'Huh?'

'I've got to go, Shell,' I say.

'But . . . Finn'll be down in a second—'

'I can't wait,' I say, backing away.

She shakes her head at me, and I realise this is the last time I'll see her, looking at me in confusion as I turn away from her. I rip my eyes away, focusing on the line of trees in the distance.

Now I'm on my own.

Acknowledgements

I owe a huge debt of gratitude to my agent, Claire Wilson, and her assistant Lexie Hamblin, as well as my editors at Quercus, Sarah Lambert, Rachel Faulkner and Niamh Mulvey. I have to thank my parents for providing a constant stream of books during my childhood. And James, for reading all those first drafts.

MILLIE
RETURNS

March 2016

www.quercusbooks.co.uk
@quercuskids